POOR DEVILS

By David Ely

TROT

SECONDS

THE TOUR

TIME OUT

POOR DEVILS

POOR DEVILS

DAVID ELY

BOSTON

HOUGHTON MIFFLIN COMPANY

1970

PART I

"Do you know what treason is, Bell?"

"No," Bell said.

He was sitting on a wooden chair, facing a light. He couldn't tell how many men were in the room. The light in his eyes made everything dim; besides, they'd taken his glasses.

"Treason is an act of betrayal." The interrogator was speaking in deep, earnest tones. "A traitor is one who knowingly endangers the safety of society. I emphasize the word knowingly. That's very important."

Bell saw cigarettes glowing. Some of the men were gathered in a corner, whispering among themselves.

"What," he said, "you're calling me a traitor?"

"I didn't mean to imply that," the voice responded. "There's some kind of treason involved, Bell. I don't know whether it's treason in the narrow, legal sense — it isn't my job to figure that out — but if you could establish to our satisfaction that you didn't know the real meaning of your actions, you see, that would make quite a difference." The interrogator's voice conveyed a sincere anxiety for Bell's welfare. No doubt he'd been chosen for that reason.

"See what I mean, Bell? You'd be the victim of others. The question is, are you willing to acknowledge this? If you tell us everything you know, openly and honestly, it would go a long way toward relieving you of this shadow."

Bell said, "I've never betrayed anybody."

"But you've been betrayed, Bell."

"You think so?"

"I'm convinced of it. There's nothing in your personality or background that would lead you into antisocial activity. You've always met your obligations in a forthright way — nothing to hide, nothing to be ashamed of — with no evidence of any twisted negative thinking." The voice was slightly oratorical, as if the interrogator had at one time attempted the ministry or radio broadcasting. "We feel that basically, Bell, you're as decent an American as any man in this room."

Bell began to chuckle.

"What's funny?" the interrogator asked.

Bell laughed outright. He couldn't help it. The other men stirred restlessly, evidently watching him. He'd proved a rough customer. It had taken three of them to handle him.

"We don't have much time, Bell," the interrogator said, rather sharply. "We want you to tell us everything you know — "

"You're wrong." Bell controlled his laughter long enough to say that.

"Wrong about what?"

"Wrong ab-b-bout — " He had to stop for breath. The interrogator's head appeared beside the glowing lamp, but the man's features still weren't clear.

"Go on, Bell. Tell us."

Bell glanced about the room — shadows everywhere. Something was wrong. They'd tricked him somehow; his perceptions were becoming confused. What, a quick little needle jab in that scuffle he'd had? Something like that.

"Speak up, Bell."

The figures of the men might be stains on the walls. Squinting in the direction of the interrogator, Bell now saw only the fierce light of the lamp. The voice itself seemed to come out of it.

"Come on, Bell."

"What'd you do to me?"

"I can't quite hear you, Bell."

"Oh, hell," Bell mumbled. It didn't matter. But there was something he wanted to say. It was swimming up in his mind, but hadn't quite arrived. He waited for it.

"We're listening, Bell."

"Okay." He almost had it.

"Go on."

"We've lost," said Bell.

"What's that?"

"We've lost."

"Lost? Lost what?"

"We've lost our importance."

"What are you saying?"

"We're unimportant men. Didn't you know that? We're unimportant. That's what the betrayal is."

Then he bowed his head to avoid the light, and offered no resistance to whatever it was they'd managed to do to him, letting it flood through his arms, legs, everywhere. The last words he heard, muttered not far from his ear, were "son-of-a-bitch traitor" — and before he sank, relieved, into the oblivion of the drug, he nodded his head, or tried to, and if he'd been able, he would have expressed his full agreement.

Bᴇʟʟ's ᴛʀᴏᴜʙʟᴇs ʜᴀᴅ begun with his involvement in what he later thought of as the Lundquist problem — and that started soon after he met Mrs. Lundquist.

He first saw her at a cocktail party. It was just an ordinary affair, but Bell was ill at ease. This was the first time he'd gone out since his wife had left him, and he was afraid that people who hadn't heard what happened would ask him where Norma was. But no one asked. Everybody knew about it, evidently. So be it, he thought. He drank two martinis. Things began to seem more cheerful.

He and Professor Pico were entertaining a small circle with whoppers about their war experiences — e.g., when the Japanese surrender papers had blown overboard, how Lieutenant Commander Bell had dived (in dress whites, still at attention and saluting) into Tokyo Bay to catch them before they fluttered into the water, and how Captain Pico, using three thousand fart-inflated condoms, had made the first recorded balloon escape from a German PW camp. Then a man in the next room spilled a tray of drinks on the rug. Everyone went for a look, and in the interval a little red-haired lady tapped Bell's elbow.

"You couldn't have been in World War II," she said. "You would have been much too young."

"I lied about my age," Bell said. Slightly tipsy, he was unable to distinguish her features clearly.

"No, really."

"Then it must have been some other war, madam." He bent down a bit, squinting at her. She seemed to be a pretty little thing, but in her forties, if he had to guess. "One of the wars to end the wars between the wars to end all wars — "

But someone stepped between them, someone else brushed his arm, making him lurch to keep his drink from slopping over, and by the time he had worked his way over to Pico to ask whose wife she was, she had gone, and he soon forgot her.

Two weeks later she appeared unannounced at his office. He was lunching on a chicken sandwich his father had made for him that morning, and was reading a magazine, his stockinged feet propped up on his desk.

"I'm sorry to barge in on you like this, Professor Bell."

Bell's mouth was full of chicken, skin included. He dropped the magazine. What embarrassed him the most were his feet, which smelled.

"Please, not at all, um." He managed to get his feet off the desk without knocking over the telephone. "Won't you sit?" he mumbled, chewing fiercely.

"Thank you." She was smart and sleek in a tailored suit; a pocket Venus, rouged and powdered, her hair as red as Bell's flushed ears. "We haven't been introduced," she said with a tight little smile that showed age wrinkles at her eyes. "I'm Rose Lundquist."

Bell was on the verge of removing a piece of skin from his mouth but swallowed it instead, deferentially. Lundquist was the only scholar of real eminence at the University, a mountain among molehills. "I haven't had the honor of actually meeting your — " he said, hesitating when it occurred to him that she might conceivably be the old sociologist's daughter. To cover his confusion, he reached back with one long arm to raise the window and banish foot smells. The draft began thumbing riotously through the pages of the magazine, which had fallen into an exposed position on the floor.

"My husband," she said. "I came to see you about him, actually. Professor Glass suggested it. He said you could be relied on absolutely."

"Um," said Bell, still obsessed with his feet.

"I have what may seem to be a rather strange request, Professor Bell." She shivered. Bell obediently closed the window, but not before the draft had managed to slam the door, which she'd left ajar. It was opened immediately by his neighbor, Pico — ex-football lineman, 250 pounds — who stopped short in the doorway at the sight of Bell closeted with this mature redhead, said "wow," and shut it again.

"A rather strange request," Mrs. Lundquist repeated, in some bewilderment, having had a sidelong glimpse of the giant on the threshold. "But first, you must understand that I am depending on your discretion."

"Yes, yes," said Bell. He'd tied his shoes; it made him feel more secure.

"Professor Glass mentioned your name immediately. He had no hesitation. And so I came directly from his office to yours. It's a matter of some urgency to me." She was treading water, so to speak, giving him a quick study before letting him know what she wanted. Bell tightened his necktie.

Then she leaned forward and said quietly, "I want you to locate my husband for me."

Bell stared at her, noticing how freckled she was beneath her powder. "Locate him?" he said. "I'm sorry but I don't quite — "

"I want you to *find* him, Mr. Bell."

Bell was confused. "You mean he isn't here?"

"He's in the field. Somewhere. Another project — but it's been six months this time."

She gestured vaguely at the window. Bell stole a glance that way over his shoulder as though he might see Professor Lundquist wandering there among the dull square buildings. Clouds were fattening in the sky. It would snow, and he'd left his galoshes home.

"You haven't heard from him?" he asked.

"Not a word. Nothing. Oh, that in itself isn't strange. He never writes, not even a postcard, and he refuses to telephone. It's a matter of principle with him, Professor Bell, to isolate himself in his work. But I'm worried now." Bell was getting worried, too. This little lady really wanted him to do something. "You see," she continued, "it's his age — he's sixty-four and as strong as a mule, but suppose he had a stroke? I might never know." She spoke in a throaty whisper. "He carries no identification whatsoever."

"Fingerprints," Bell said. He was trying to be helpful, but Mrs. Lundquist sucked in her breath, and he added hastily, "Have you considered any official action?"

"The police? Oh, no. I couldn't do that. Professor Glass agreed with me completely on that point. Anything of the sort is out of the question. You aren't acquainted with my husband, Mr. Bell. He would regard such inquiries as the grossest interference with his privacy. You may know his reputation. He's not a man to be trifled with."

"Yes, ma'am." Bell knew, all right. Professor Lundquist was seldom seen but well remembered. Once he'd descended from the lecture platform to eject forcibly, with his own hands, a student who'd offended him by yawning. There were quite a few such stories. Bell regarded his visitor with apprehension. *Why me?* he wanted to ask. But he wasn't sure of his ground — had old Glass really committed him? He'd have to find out later.

"Maybe a private investigator would do a better job," he suggested, with little hope.

She was ready for that. "Oh, no. They're so sordid. Besides, they're just like the police. It would come to the same thing. There has to be a plausible professional reason for getting in touch with Carl, you see. Professor Glass fully agreed with this. It would be fairly easy for you, Mr. Bell. Professor Glass said you're writing something that includes a study of the welfare and poverty programs —"

"Yes."

" — and naturally you'd want Carl to read it in manuscript."

"Well, that's true. I'd thought of asking him."

"It's very apt, you see."

"But, Mrs. Lundquist, wouldn't it seem unusual for me to chase after your husband with this chapter? The normal thing to do would be to wait for his return and then approach him about it, wouldn't it?"

"You don't know Carl. He respects force and brashness. It's the only way to handle him. You see, if you search him out with your manuscript and insist on obtaining his opinion, he'll find it quite natural. Oh, he might refuse to do it. I can't promise he wouldn't. But he certainly wouldn't doubt your motives, precisely because it's the kind of thing he'd do himself."

She was hemming him in. Every word stitched up escape routes. "But this must be kept private," she continued. "Strictly between ourselves."

"Surely in your husband's own department — "

"No, no, no." She rejected this almost indignantly. "I'd never breathe a word among Carl's so-called colleagues, let alone seek their help. Nothing would please them better than an opportunity to embarrass him. The story would be everywhere. Carl would hear of it — he'd be furious. He'd never forgive me. No, I was forced to go to the only man here with whom Carl is on speaking terms — Professor Glass, who of course is rather elderly and can't himself be expected — "

"Still you have no specific reason to be worried," Bell broke in.

"About Carl? I have my intuition. And — circumstances. I mean his age, chiefly." Her eyes, the color of hot mustard, spread a spicy gaze on Bell; she was ready to gobble all six feet three of him, from those steaming feet to his bony skull where thinning hair was packed in place by dandruff. Bell squirmed. A voice within announced his doom: *Bell, you're screwed.*

She said, "You've simply got to help me, Professor Bell."

She'd stormed him, for sure. He took off his glasses, as though to demonstrate his helplessness. She became misty, younger, more attractive; he put the glasses on again. "I certainly would like to help you, Mrs. Lundquist. But of course I don't quite know what's involved in the way of time, you see. I have a pretty full teaching load, for one thing."

"I've discussed all that with Professor Glass. It could definitely be worked out. And we do have a point of departure — Carl's papers, in his study at the house. Of course, there are some practical problems to decide. . . ."

He gestured feebly with surrendering hands. It was futile.

"Do you know our house? It's rather far out." She snapped open her purse, withdrew her gloves, and began putting them on.

"Well, you see really — "

She took no for yes. Now she was giving him directions. Turn left, turn right, five miles past Burger Heaven. He was to come out that very night to look at Lundquist's papers and make plans.

"Actually I doubt whether — "

"I'm terribly sorry. I forgot all about your family obligations."

"No, my wife — " Pico was sneezing. Bell heard him through the wall. Had Pico been listening, one mittlike ear pressed against that plywood film? Bell felt a sudden wildness in his chest. The half-eaten sandwich lay in front of him, oozing grease on his graduate seminar notes. The students soon would be waiting to munch on his thoughts. "My wife — " He moaned internally, as memory cramped him.

"In fact, I don't know where *she* is." He was trying to joke —
a poor subject to choose — but he wanted to make his status
clear. "I'll make a deal with you, Mrs. Lundquist. I'll find
your husband if you find my wife." She looked at him
blankly. "I mean we're separated," he concluded lamely.

"Well, then, you're free to come," Mrs. Lundquist said,
cheerfully, rising to her feet. "Don't bother, please," she cried
out as he began struggling up, and before he got unwedged
from the desk she had clattered delicately out into the hall.

PROFESSOR GLASS, the history department chairman, was
no help at all. Mrs. Lundquist had alarmed him greatly. To
get rid of her, he'd offered Bell. But he was too old to bother
with apologies.

"Carl Lundquist is a prickly fellow," he said to Bell, "but
he's distinguished in his field, and we owe him every consid-
eration, however eccentric we may judge his working habits
to be — and they *are* eccentric, damned eccentric. Whatever
the present case may be, we must defer to Mrs. Lundquist's
wishes. I don't know her, but I do know Carl. Privacy —
that's obviously called for. Carl's been in some pretty un-
savory situations before, and the less said the better." He
gave Bell a glance almost of reproach, as though Bell some-

how were responsible. "All this is unofficial, you understand. The department is in no way concerned. Nor is the University."

"Why do you think she wants him found?"

"She didn't say. I didn't ask. I have no wish to know. Perhaps she really thinks he's dead. It would be a grievous loss, but again, that's primarily her affair, not mine."

"Well, somehow it seems to have become mine, too," Bell complained, but Professor Glass cut him off with a wave of his paper-white hands.

"Do it for me, young Bell. I don't want that woman coming back. She's frightful. You know how I detest these aggressive ladies." Professor Glass was an authority on colonial America, a period when females were properly subjugated; he spent as much time there as possible. "Perhaps she needs to be aggressive, living with Carl — there's a temper for you, Carl's. Once I took him to Francesco's and he threw the pasta on the floor because they served it tepid. My heart nearly stopped." He pursed his lips fretfully. "But Carl is a man of consequence. I don't imagine there's another scholar in the country who knows more about poverty than he does — and it's the coming thing, poverty. Lord knows why. Everyone seems to be rushing into it. But about Mrs. Lundquist's little request, Bell, just do the best you can — and kindly, kindly don't trouble to keep me informed. I admire Carl from a distance, but — well, perhaps you see my point."

"Sure do," said Bell, dejected.

SNOW WAS FALLING when Bell left at dusk for home. Professor Pico had invited him to stop for a drink but he'd said no. Pico's wife had been insulted by Bell's failure to confide why his marriage collapsed. She'd tried several roles — sister, aunt, mother — with no luck, for he kept mum; she took revenge in sugary sweetness to Pico in his presence, tickling Pico's bull neck and wagging her hams in Pico's slab face, to remind Bell of marital joys, of poor Norma (who, however, had no hams to speak of and wouldn't have wagged them if she had).

Norma had left him six weeks ago. It seemed like yesterday; their affairs were that tangled. The old Ford he drove was legally hers; she'd gone home to Detroit by train. He kept finding lipsticks wedged behind the seat cushions and Tampaxes in the glove compartment; grocery lists fluttered up from the floorboards every time he drove, gourmet rosters of lip-smacking goodness — TV dinners, hot dogs, peanut butter, canned soups. Norma had taken his love and given back heartburn. The Ford, too, which she'd fed on cheap oil and bargain gasoline, still was belching.

Bell drove slowly through the campus. A sharp breeze bit leaves from tree branches; snow-dusted, they danced like white moths in his headlights. The lecture halls were dark now; the night-blooming dormitories were blossoming with lamps. He passed the library, where he and Norma once had played hide-and-seek in the stacks, and the gym, where a dozen years before he'd ruined his arches as basketball captain. Beyond was the town proper (pop. 27,000), with its fleshpots — e.g., movie theaters, drugstores, Roseman's Delicatessen, and the Gadfly Bookmart, where left-wing instructors and radical students met each Thursday afternoon at four over coffee and doughnuts — and its quiet residential streets, on one of which was located the two-story frame Victorian house where dwelt a dynasty of Bells, three generations deep: Bell himself, age thirty-three; his father, sixty-two, and Grandpa Bell, nearly ninety.

It was one of those square prairie towns of the northern Midwest. When the night train to Minneapolis blew a distant whistle, young men like Bell sat up in bed in a panic lest their lives prove wasted. The prairie was too vast, the northern sky too tremendous. Each winter some Swedish farmer would massacre his family out of the anguish produced by such intolerable vacancies of space. Suicides were frequent, drunkenness endemic, mental breakdown commonplace. This was the American steppe: the endless fields were choked with wheat and wildflowers in summer, and burdened in winter by heavy snows piling down from Canada. The drifts reached rooftops sometimes.

But this present snow was just a late-September sneeze. Bell knew it couldn't excuse him from driving out to the Lundquist house. He was pledged anyway, not so much by the cowardice of Professor Glass or the coercive powers of Mrs. Lundquist as by his own manic honor: once a thing began, he had to seize it lest it seize him. Norma's leaving had really shaken him. He'd taken to staring in mirrors and listening to the dull chiming of his heart. She'd brought him nothing; what had she carried away? His convictions were intact. Nothing was missing. He still believed in the innate goodness of man — his own goodness, too — and yet he was plagued by contrary reflections. He was crumbling, just a little. It now occurred to him more frequently that in five years he'd be bald.

He entered his house and went back to the kitchen, where his father, aproned and with plump hairy forearms revealed by rolled-up sleeves, was fixing Grandpa's supper on a tray for Mrs. Watt, the nurse, to take upstairs.

"Evening, son. Hear from Norma today?"

His father always shook that question in his face, and Bell, whose weekly letters to Detroit came back unopened, whose long-distance telephone calls were declined, usually answered with a simple no. This time he decided to say nothing at all.

"She'll be back," the elder Bell remarked in a pious voice, sticking his forefinger into Grandpa's oatmeal to check its warmth. He gave Bell a sidelong glance. "That girl loves you, son. I know that for a fact!" Bell could not hide a wince; his father inhaled noisily, a snuffle of satisfaction.

The old man went to the back stairs and shouted up, "*Mrs. Watt, it's ready.*" Returning, he licked his finger, and tested the oatmeal again. "Yes, sir, boy," he said, his bald dome gleaming beneath the filthy overhead bulb, "any day now you'll be getting a letter. Maybe a telegram!" He was fat, and seemed to waddle even standing still. Mrs. Watt could be heard descending. Bell senior waited until she was within earshot and then resoundingly declared, "Suppose Norma's pregnant! You never know! Just think of it — me, a grand-father!"

He broke off in a show of confusion as Mrs. Watt entered the kitchen. "What am I saying?" He laughed as if in embar-rassment and rushed over to the tray, where the viscous oat-meal in its bowl had not yet flattened out the finger dents. "Here it is, Mrs. Watt — piping hot for dear old Dad!" Mrs. Watt, a good-natured widow in her fifties, whose fathomless stupidity Bell often envied, smirked and sighed and took the tray upstairs.

Bell's father bustled about the kitchen getting out a skillet, greasing it, patting hamburger meat into shape. "Every man gets three chances in this life, you know. First as a son, then as a father, and finally as a grandfather." He turned the gas flame up to scorch the meat. "I admit I've swung twice and missed — but I'm still at bat, aren't I?" He smeared mayon-naise on the hamburger buns before Bell could intervene with mustard, his preference. "Yes, sir! And I think I could hit a homer this time! I'd belt it out of the park, you can bet, if only I could hold a little creature on my lap — "

"I'll go set the table," said Bell.

His father, a short man in a tall family, had devoted his life to covert resentment, as though Grandpa had deliberately scanted him at the moment of conception, dealing out a sec-ond-rate squad of sperm. He had in one respect been callously treated. Grandpa (like Bell, a historian) had been complet-ing his doctoral dissertation on the early career of Aaron Burr, and it was in Burr's honor that he impulsively christened his newborn son. Aaron Burr Bell grew up pudgy and near-sighted. He learned to mask his despair in clownishness and to savor vengeance. When his turn came at Bell's birth, he couldn't resist: he named him Aaron for himself and Hamilton for Burr's rival, whose memory Grandpa loathed.

Aaron Hamilton Bell. Bell's father referred to him as Hamilton in Grandpa's presence, and otherwise as Ham. (Bell's mother had called him Jimmy, a family name, but when she died — he was ten then — the Jimmy died with her.) Boyhood nicknames hadn't stuck. For years most people, Norma included, had addressed him simply as Bell.

But it was as Hamilton and Burr that he and his father dueled across the dining-room table each evening — and at other times in the yard, the kitchen, up and down the stairs, in the attic, in Grandpa's room where the old scholar's senile requirements were precisely fulfilled by the offerings of the television set — fat little Burr firing soft bullets of spiteful joy, and lean lank Hamilton riddled time and again, dying nightly, rising gloomily so he could fall once more.

"Maybe she's keeping it a secret, Ham!"

Bell took a bite of hamburger, a quarter inch of blackened crust enclosing raw soggy meat.

"She always was a quiet little thing — she wants to surprise us, that's all!" Bell's father wore his apron to the table, but ate fastidiously, masticating each tiny mouthful into paste. "Motherhood — it has a tremendous effect on women. Take a girl like Norma, son. You might call her shy and on the reserved side — far from earthy, in any case, and certainly not a demonstrative person — why, I remember she'd hardly say a word for days on end, just sort of drift about the house with a book in one hand and a dustrag in the other. I called her the Moon Goddess, remember?" Bell's father delicately patted a spot of mayonnaise from his upper lip. "But once life begins stirring in the womb — ah! Then it's a different story, Ham. That brings these little girls out — opens 'em up like sunflowers. . . ."

The house grumbled in the wind. It was insulated in patches; some rooms were snug, others drafty. The dining room was dark and chilly. It still smelled sour because of an ill-natured cat, months dead, which had urinated daily in the fireplace. Through loose windowpanes the snow filtered in and melted on the sill.

". . . maybe that's why Norma left, boy. She may have recognized the first signs — a little queasiness in the mornings, a missed period — and at such a time a young girl wants to be with her mother!"

Bell crammed half his second hamburger into his mouth.

"You need more mayonnaise on that," his father shouted, rising swiftly and darting into the kitchen before Bell could make a protest. "No, no," Bell elder's voice came back at him, "of course I'll get it — it's my job, isn't it?" He rushed back with the jar. "With Norma gone, boy, who's going to take care of you, I'd like to know?" He set the jar down out of Bell's reach and ran into the kitchen again and up the back stairs to fetch Grandpa's tray. Bell could hear him roaring over the television racket, in amiable argument with Mrs. Watt, who proposed to bring it down herself.

"Maybe I ought to get a job — nobody needs me!" old Bell cried from the kitchen a few moments later. He appeared bearing a sad store pie, still in its plastic jacket. "But who'd hire a worthless old fool like me? Can't cook or clerk or even grease a car — never learned a darned thing in school — " He slapped the pie down on the table. "Forks! Forgot 'em!" He scurried back to the kitchen. Bell's silence on the Norma subject had excited him. He was determined to make Bell speak. "Think the University could find a custodial position for me, Ham? Maybe to rake a few leaves?" The old man puffed down into place at the table and began clumsily hacking the pie. "Or would that embarrass you, eh?" He gazed at Bell with hungry, glittering eyes.

Bell surrendered. "That wouldn't be a good idea, Dad. Better not think about that."

"It would be demeaning to you, I suppose. Yes, I don't blame you, son. To look out of your office window and see your old tramp of a dad out there with a rake and a burlap bag! And some of the real old-timers there who remember Father — what would they say?"

"It isn't that, Dad — "

"Your mother had faith in me, son. It was my tragedy she died so young."

"We don't need the money."

"I could hold a job back then, Ham. I hadn't gone to pieces. Here, eat your pie."

"You never went to — "

"Remember the pie Norma made once, son?" Bell's father burst into a whinnying giggle. "Bride's pie! That's what you get for marrying one of your students! That crust was like leather. What kind of a mother does she have, I wonder, to teach her to bake like that?"

"Let's drop that subject, Dad."

Bell's father squirmed in his chair. "I sympathize with you, Ham. But sometimes it's better to talk. It hurts me, too.

You're not the only one. Gee, but I miss that little girl!" He wagged his moon face; the light glinted on his spectacles. "Remember her singing with the radio? What a sweet little voice!"

"I'm going out this evening, Dad."

"What?" Bell's father let his fork fall to the plate. "Going out?" He leaned forward, goggling. "So soon? And suppose Norma calls here, what am I supposed to tell her? That you're out on a date?"

"It isn't a date. There won't be any call anyway."

"Secrets — secrets!" Bell's father drummed his fingers on the table. Bell wolfed the pie. "And what do you think Norma's up to, back there in Detroit? Didn't she have a boyfriend there, Ham? Don't you think it's time you went there to find out. the score?"

Bell wiped his mouth on the paper napkin, which his father had thriftily saved from breakfast, and got up. The old man pursued him from the room. "Did it ever occur to you that I might remarry someday, Ham? *Me.* Is it out of the question to suppose that someone might not be too repelled to wish to share my loneliness?" In the front hall Bell wrapped his scarf around his neck and stuffed the ends inside his suit jacket. The old mirror was cracked; the wallpaper was peeling. "Mrs. Watt is not immune to my attractions, Ham." Aaron Burr Bell was fairly dancing around his son, tugging at Bell's overcoat in a pretense of helping him put it on. "Not what you'd call a brilliant intellect — but good enough for me, don't you think?" Down the stairs blew a draft of audience laughter from the TV set. Bell could hear Grandpa neighing, too; Mrs. Watt, a bit slow, gave a hee-haw solo after-

ward. "But of course I'd need your permission, Ham!" Old
Bell was whispering stertorously. There were scabs on his
skull where he'd scratched himself. "I mean literally— from
a financial standpoint! You'd be supporting her, too, Ham!
What do you think? Would you like us to come hand in hand
to you to seek your blessing?"

Bell disengaged himself. "Don't be ridiculous, Dad," he
said. He put his hat on.

"Ridiculous! Is that what I am, son — ridiculous?" Old
Bell squeezed around his son, fumbling for the doorknob,
managing to block Bell's way. "Yes — that's what we'll do.
A pair of miserable old idiots, she and I — we'll come crawling to you, son — crawling!"

Bell had to pry his way out. "Goodnight, Dad. I may be
late."

The snow blew past him inside, sprinkling his father's spectacles. The old man snatched them off and peered greedily
out. "You didn't say where you were going," he shouted.
Bell slammed the car door. "I'll wait up for you, Ham!" old
Bell yelled, and stood there in the open doorway, aproned, his
bald dome gathering snow, a jack-o'-lantern grin across his
face, a terrific image of domestic bliss for Bell to glimpse as he
drove off.

Bᴇʟʟ ʜᴀᴅ a passion for finishing things. A psychologist friend told him it was a condition called "closure," mild seizures of which were beneficial to man. True, Bell caught trains and planes with plenty of time to spare, invariably arrived at classrooms before his students did, never left the house half-shaved or unzipped (Pico, a sloppy opposite, sometimes made scandalous public appearances); on the other hand, he was reluctant to start anything new. Once begun, he feared he might drive himself to destruction rather than give up. For that reason, he'd never vowed to give up smoking; for him, it would have been final. Instead, he decided to cut down to seven cigarettes a day (he numbered them in ink each morning). Seven a day; no more — and no less, either. Once a sore throat had made him omit his ration — he figured he'd catch up later — but he woke before midnight in a psychic fever and sat up hollow-eyed and gagging to chain-smoke all seven.

This was the zealot who'd pledged his troth to Norma Elizabeth Hirlinger, an anemic senior with pale green eyes and an ethereal manner, a Botticelli in blue jeans. He'd first noticed her obliquely: she'd been the only one in his Constitutional History class who could spell. He encountered her often at the library — a dreamy virgin, delicately wandering among the open stacks. He took her sometimes to Roseman's for blintzes, to the Gadfly for coffee. Her field was English (she'd read all of Dickens, twice), but when Bell spoke of the great historians whose names Grandpa had trumpeted to him in the days when his own dreams were shaped, she didn't seem lost. She'd heard of von Ranke (if not Namier), and she'd even read Turner. Bell was grateful. He'd found a literate girl!

They'd been married in Detroit. It was a Lutheran ceremony, punctuated throughout by the typhoon sneezes of best-man Pico, who had a cold. At the reception Bell's father got drunk (or so pretended) and treated the guests to a teary discourse on his career as a professional failure, toad, clown, fatso, nonentity, etc., a performance interrupted only by the arrival of a telegram from Mrs. Watt: Grandpa was sinking. So much for Bell's honeymoon. They'd climbed into Norma's Ford and headed home, Bell doing most of the driving, his father beside him, a human radio steadily broadcasting, and the slender bride in back braking in alarm each time great Pico, her neighbor, honked his nasal horn. On arrival at the house, Bell's father slipped on the icy steps — it was March — twisting an ankle, so that the marriage parody was properly concluded: Pico carried old Aaron across the threshold while Bell and Norma followed with the suitcases. Upstairs, Grandpa was preparing to meet his Maker by watching the Groucho Marx program. The doctor's prognosis was grave: the old viewer might never survive the summer reruns.

Bell and Norma should have moved out at once. But first there was the new invalid with his ankle sprain for daughter-in-law to nurse, and then in April, Norma had to sub for Widow Watt, sidelined in the hospital to have a pound of guts removed. After that it was too late. Norma retreated into the works of Jane Austen — she read *Emma* alone five times — as Grandpa had escaped into arteriosclerosis and TV. She became listless, Bell desperate. He actually paid a month's rent on an apartment, but she kept postponing the work of moving until August 11, when she left for the Motor City on the noon train.

Why? Bell was tormented by this question. Unlike her Janeite heroines, Norma was silent and apathetic; she couldn't say, or wouldn't. Bell wept, Norma yawned. He fell to his knees, she napped. He blamed his father in part — who could live in proximity to that nosy old jabberbox without losing all interest in life? Miss Austen, too, was at fault. Her heroes — like Bell, tall, polite, sometimes high-spirited and generally brainy — never attempted to straddle the ladies. Norma's defloration required weeks. Bell felt brutish in the face of her indifference; he suffered bouts of shame, of impotence, of irritation, perplexity, despair — and even as he floundered like a seal atop his ice-floe maiden, he suspected that his wily progenitor was skulking alimp in the hall, prepared to celebrate their climactic cries with snorts and wheezes beyond the door. But there were no cries. Bell had a cardboard bride, it seemed. She didn't return his passion; she just blotted it.

Still, he had sworn to love, to honor, to cherish. On August 12 he had driven to Detroit; Chez Hirlinger was vacant. A neighbor said they'd just left for parts unknown, perhaps to an aunt's in Ypsilanti or a cousin's in Kalamazoo. For three days he drove back and forth across southern Michigan, checking phone books for Hirlingers and calling any he found, without luck. He returned to the University. Later, when it became clear that Norma was incommunicado, impervious to letters and calls, he began to suspect that she didn't intend to come back at all, not ever, and he'd lie awake at night not so much lovelorn as vexed by an unredeemable pledge.

Mrs. Lundquist answered the door. She looked older and tougher in black-rimmed spectacles and a corduroy suit. Greeting Bell as though he were the plumber, she led him through the hall to the living room, where two chairs were posted before a hearth that was empty of fire, of logs, even of andirons. Between the chairs was a footstool on which several file folders had been placed.

She didn't waste time. "Do sit down, Professor Bell." Bell sat. "Here's my proposition," she said. "I pay all expenses, naturally. Plus fifty dollars a day as compensation for your time." Even in the corduroy, which made her look dumpy, she had a *grande dame* manner. "Professor Glass assured me he'd make it easy for you to find a few free days here and there, Of course, I have no idea how long this will take."

"Hum," said Bell, wishing he hadn't come. The room was underfurnished, and its lighting was grim.

"In any case, my part in this must be mentioned to no one — particularly not to Carl."

"Assuming I locate him."

"Assuming he's still alive, Professor Bell."

That was a stopper. Bell sat pondering her motives. If Lundquist were dead, she might want proof. Would she ask him to bring back a finger, or would a dental plate be enough?

"He's always lived a hazardous life," she added, and then went on to describe her husband's habits, history, and condition when last home, while Bell took mental notes. On the mantel he saw a photograph of the absentee. Professor Lundquist somewhat resembled a berserk polar bear: mad black eyes, an aggressive snout extruded above close-cropped white whiskers, thin dark lips drawn into a sour smile.

"That's what he's working on now," Mrs. Lundquist said at length, indicating the folders on the footstool. "At least I think it is — or was. Take a look at it, Professor Bell. I'll go make some coffee."

Alone, Bell stretched himself, made a quick check of the bookshelves — Lundquist's own works were placed between Shakespeare and the Bible — and tested the mirror, where he saw a gaunt frame in a dull blue suit topped by a long dour face. That was Bell. It wasn't a heartening sight.

He picked up the folders and read through them. The project they described was titled Nomad. It seemed ordinary enough. A group of universities in the mid-Atlantic states planned to establish a joint program of ecological and human studies on marginal farmlands. Poor soil, poor people. The area involved stretched from Connecticut to Georgia, a narrow belt between the Appalachians and the richer lands east. The people were itinerant farm workers who traveled from north to south and back again, following the crops and the seasons. With funds to be provided by a philanthropy called the Thomas Jefferson Foundation, the universities proposed to buy six small farms along the migrant route; these would be the project centers.

Had anything actually been done? Bell could find no evidence — but none of the memoranda and correspondence was dated more recently than two years ago. He supposed that Lundquist had taken the later material with him when he'd gone. The old boy had left his mark, though. He'd scribbled testy notes on various items in the remaining files, and had decorated others with obscene drawings.

Bell sat thumbing papers. He could visualize Project Nomad well enough — a string of hillbilly farms staffed by sober scholars counting birds, taking soil samples, and tape-recording the case histories of agricultural vagabonds — but somehow he couldn't picture Lundquist there.

Lundquist was a soloist. In his time — some forty years — the old fellow had tramped his way through much of the North American continent, always alone, without assistants, without colleagues, and disdainful of the conventional academic trappings of statistics, questionnaires, and charts. He'd always set out equipped with hardly more than a pencil. In the late 1920s, he'd done southern sharecroppers; in the thirties, Bowery bums and Mexican wetbacks; in the forties, Negroes in Chicago and Port-au-Prince, followed in the fifties and sixties by Eskimos, Seminoles, Cajuns, and Puerto Ricans. He always worked incognito and cut off from the outside world until he at length emerged to write his books, which betrayed no taint of sentimental attachment to the unfortunates among whom he'd lived: he dealt with them as shortly as he did with everyone else.

No, Lundquist wasn't an organization man. He had a prima donna style. He signed his letters in the grand manner — last name only — and when he disapproved of something, his scorn was scorching. Bell guessed that the poor had to accept him — they couldn't kick him out — but he doubted that a group of scholars would for long. Lundquist was an eccentric, an oddity, a Thoreau with a foul temper. Perhaps he'd earned the right to be cranky. Forty years of sociology had left scars. According to his wife, the Eskimos had cost him a pair of frostbitten fingertips, he'd parted with an earlobe in Chicago and three teeth in San Antonio, and had acquired, in various other places, a game leg and hernia, and on top of this had undergone cures for piles, lice, and the crabs. And this battered old pilgrim had set off again in mid-March — his last trip? — lugging a green-splotched tin suitcase containing one change of underwear, a fifth of whiskey, a spare truss and an enema bag, and wearing on his ursine form the same rust-colored suit he'd owned for years.

Mrs. Lundquist came in with the coffee.

"Finished?"

Bell nodded.

"Well, I don't have much to add," she said, pouring the coffee. "In the past few weeks I made several phone calls to this Thomas Jefferson Foundation in Washington, without any satisfaction. I finally got switched to a man named Grosch — he's identified in the correspondence as Project Coordinator, whatever that may mean — and after a great deal of hemming and hawing, he told me that Carl had been working on the migrant project but that he'd quit. He said he had no idea where Carl had gone or where he might be now, and then he mumbled something about having an appointment and cut the conversation short. I decided there wasn't much point in my trying again."

"Well, do you want me to call him?"

"No, no. You'd better go there, to Washington. The foundation is the logical starting point. Tell them it's about the book you're writing. But don't say a word about me. It might get back to Carl. I'd like that absolutely understood between us."

"Sure," Bell said.

"Then, if you don't get any information from this man Grosch, you can begin on the universities. If there is a migrant project — I mean if it's still going on — then someone is bound to know something of Carl."

"Guess so," Bell said. He had the impression that she was holding something in reserve, for she seemed to be carefully gauging his reaction to what she'd said so far.

"If you do find him, let me know at once. If I'm not here, I'll be in St. Paul. I own a lingerie shop there, with an apartment above. I'll give you the numbers."

Bell nodded. Fifty bucks a day. He could use it.

"But be sure you remember not to — "

"Won't mention your name," Bell said. "All right. I'll go."

"When?"

"Soon — this week, I guess — whenever I can work things out at the department." He decided it oughtn't to take long. Mrs. Lundquist had flubbed her call to Grosch somehow. Lundquist was too well known to be lost.

"I hope this doesn't upset your domestic arrangements."

"I don't have any," he said. He had finished his coffee, but now she refilled his cup.

"Oh, that's right. You said your wife left you."

"Yes." He regretted having mentioned it. Mrs. Lundquist was inspecting him with female curiosity, like Pico's wife. But she was more direct.

"Why?"

Bell was nettled. "Actually she didn't see fit to explain that, Mrs. Lundquist."

"Do you mean she simply walked out?"

"Simply that."

"But wherever did she go?"

"She went home to Mother, Mrs. Lundquist." He supposed that his wry tone would warn her off the subject. It didn't.

"Really? She must be rather young."

Bell didn't respond. He took out a cigarette and rolled it fretfully between thumb and finger.

"Even so," Mrs. Lundquist continued, "one would think she'd say why."

"Apparently she didn't want to live with me any more."

"That seems obvious."

Was she goading him? He felt justified in making a retort: "Excuse me, but your husband doesn't seem to spend much time at home, either."

This amused her. "He never has. But, you see, Carl and I compensate."

Bell busied himself lighting the cigarette. He'd rolled a hole in it, though. It lasted for two puffs.

"Professor Bell, I think I may have shocked you. Apparently you believe in fidelity."

"As a matter of fact, I do." Bell's annoyance was mixed with uneasiness now. He gave her a quick glance through the smoldering ruin he still held in his fingers. She didn't seem to be ridiculing him; she wasn't tempting him, either. She sat there plump and owlish with her spectacles — a solid little lady, all of a piece and unbreakable. She'd have to be. Lundquist would have bounced her all over the house.

"Your wife feels the same way?"

"So I recall." Bell sullenly stubbed out the cigarette.

"Well, that's rather sterile, isn't it? I mean, you here and she there, both of you being faithful?"

Now he glared at her.

"Are you offended?" She wasn't in the least perturbed. "You'd better stay away from Carl if a little thing like this upsets you."

"It doesn't."

"I hope not. Remember, he likes people brash."

"You must please him greatly, then."

"I try." Mrs. Lundquist made a social smile, as though they were exchanging conventionally pleasant remarks. Bell was impressed. If this was her idea of polite conversation, what sort of disputes did she have with that curmudgeon spouse of hers?

"So, you believe in fidelity," she said. "What else do you believe in?"

"You're poking fun at me, I suppose."

"Not in the slightest. Are you ashamed of your beliefs?"

"Perhaps I'd better get my hat, Mrs. Lundquist."

"If you wish. Do finish that coffee, though." She poured some more. "I must say your skin is a bit thin, Professor Bell. I'm not trying to be impertinent. My husband and I are in the habit of talking about the things that really interest us. People react to that very oddly. Either they get angry or they're ashamed — unless they're drunk at a party."

"Some subjects are private, you know."

"You were the one who told me about your wife."

"I just happened to mention it."

"You're not accustomed to direct questions, evidently. They seem to trouble you."

Bell finished his coffee. "Maybe it's because as a teacher I'm the one who usually asks the questions."

"The questions are based on what you've taught. So, do you believe what you teach?"

"Of course I do. But it isn't a matter of belief. I teach facts."

"American history?"

"Yes. There happen to be a few facts available on that subject."

"But what do they add up to?"

"I'm not a preacher, Mrs. Lundquist. I don't get paid to draw moral lessons." She was watching him with composure; he sensed he was under some sort of inspection. He was provoked, and felt obliged to respond aggressively. "I try to trace the origins of our society and the main lines of development through the various periods."

"Development into what?"

"Into what we have now."

"Which is — ?"

"Which is a highly complex social mechanism, dominated by government, capable of maneuvering greater amounts of power and energy than any other organized group of human beings ever, anywhere."

"Well, is it good or not?"

"Good? That's an impossible question. You can't characterize a whole society as being good or not." Her quizzing bothered him more than it should have — was it because he suspected that she saw him as a man deeply wounded in his pride, a rejected husband now driven to prove himself in his career? "This country is a combination of practical materialism and the idealism of Lincoln and Walt Whitman and the Roosevelts — and a lot of other things, too, good and bad. We're capable of the gross misuse of power — take the case of the extermination of the Indians, and Negro slavery, but on the other side — " Sweat broke beneath his arms. He gripped his bony knees with his fingers. "Oh, it's fashionable to sneer at it, I suppose. But what else have we got? We've accomplished something, anyway. I mean we've brought an incredible prosperity and security to seventy percent of the people, and — well, I realize that your husband is chiefly concerned with the other thirty percent, but you've got to remember that that's just part of the story."

He felt gulled, outraged. Norma had found him a flop as a husband, but she'd done nothing to help, so he'd had the whole burden of marriage alone — not just their own marriage, he'd sometimes thought, but the very institution of marriage, everybody's marriage, marriages in the millions. And now in the same way this woman, prodding him to defend himself professionally, seemed to be forcing him to justify the entire bloody system! It was too much. Still, he'd bitten and must chew.

"Think of those immigrants coming into New York harbor without a nickel in their pockets," he went on, in gloomy earnestness, "and then their children going to law school and sitting in the Congress. American history is pretty real for those people."

He eyed her closely, alert for signs of mockery. She seemed impassive. Behind her on the wall he saw a print of Washington crossing the Delaware. "They struggled to get here, the immigrants — and a lot of people have been struggling, too, to make this country a reasonably decent and safe place to live in and bring up k-k-kids in." Something was wrong with that print, though. He got up to inspect it. Someone had altered it with ink and crayon. General Washington's face wasn't a mask of stern dignity. It was cross-eyed and grinning red-lipped, like Dracula. "Tell me, did your husband do this?"

She nodded.

"Well, excuse me," said Bell, returning roundabout to his chair and eyeing other wall decorations, "but we're being frank with each other. Doesn't that strike you as being a rather childish sort of thing?"

"Men are very childish," she agreed.

Bell found another piece of impudence. It was a photo of the Statue of Liberty, rouged like a whore. "I mean to say, it's easy to thumb noses." He wondered what would be in Lundquist's study — a U.S. relief map modeled in moose pies? "The real question is, if we didn't have these institutions, what would we have?" He was stalking about rubbing his hands together, peering suspiciously at books, pictures, fixtures. "I don't conceive of my job as being an apologist for American society — far from it — and I certainly don't consider myself old-fashioned or conservative in my approach to personal questions." She was just sitting there, observing him. "Well, you know," he went on, furious with himself for failing to be more coherent, "we don't have an aristocracy riding us, do we? We aren't under the rule of priests, either. If you want to move somewhere else, you can do it, without asking anybody's permission. You have to pay your taxes — but that's about all, apart from military service. Why shouldn't I point these things out to the kids I teach? They're the ones who'll be taking the institutions over — and it would be awfully easy, and if you'll pardon me, awfully cheap, too, to try to influence them in the opposite direction. Does that sound pompous? I don't think so." He tried to fix his face in the gravity that Washington had had before Lundquist perverted him.

Mrs. Lundquist smiled up at him, but without derision. "And what do you know about these institutions, Bell?"

"I've studied them. It's been part of my lifework."

"But have you ever known what it really means to have them on top of you?"

"Of course not. How could I?" He was still fuming, and anxious to leave. "I'm not in the poverty class, as it happens. Neither is your husband. My skin is white, too. Not my fault! But that doesn't disqualify me as a history teacher. And it doesn't prevent me from doing what little I can to — " He made an impatient gesture. "To, um, see that our institutions are used properly. To right social wrongs, dammit. Up here, though, we're out of the mainstream. I realize that. Do you know that there are fewer than a thousand Negroes in this entire state?" She gazed stolidly at him but said nothing. Bell cracked his knuckles. "My grandfather was a Populist back in the days when that really meant something," he went on.

"Of course, there isn't a hell of a lot to do nowadays. Not up here. I worked two summers in the Indian free school project, but —"

He broke off, wearily. She removed her glasses. "My God," she said. "How old are you, Bell? Thirty-five? I'm sorry about your wife. But don't you ever want to kick over the traces? You don't want to end up like that old gasbag Glass, do you?"

"Mrs. Lundquist, I don't know what gives you the right to say these things. You're needling me."

"You're needling yourself, Bell. I guess that's all to the good. Just don't take it so personally. You're such a tense young man. But you aren't smug. *I* was smug, before I met Carl. He really bowled me over, he did." She laughed suddenly, a merry shout that made Bell start. "Impulsive isn't the word for it, Bell, but it'll have to do. He was fifty then, and as lively as a kid. Goat, I mean." She glanced at Lundquist's photograph, as though daring it to deny what she'd said. "That's why people have always avoided him. He's so obviously a man who follows his passions that they're afraid of him. He's a violent man."

"Well, you can't blame them, can you?" Bell, still standing, had taken up a defensive position behind his chair. His legs felt weak. He was tired.

"They *ought* to be pushed and shoved. Some of them. There are a few worth the trouble." She gave herself a little shake, a sign of impatience. When she continued, her voice seemed lower, as though she were trying to repeat Lundquist's words in Lundquist's voice. "People accept the rules and conventions of life against what their blood tells them. That's what I mean about being institutionalized." She had the knack of sitting energetically, in dynamic composure. "How can you possibly judge anything unless you can stand outside of it and take a good, long, hard look?" She fitted her glasses back on her nose and stared at Bell. "I don't suppose you've ever been outside. Have you?"

"I don't know what you mean." But he did, and she knew it.

"You haven't," she said, decisively. "Well, Carl has *lived* outside. That's where he is now, I imagine. Somewhere. Do you think you can find him if he is?" Bell licked his lips and frowned at the floor. "Maybe what you need, Mr. Bell," she went on, "is to be pushed and shoved, too, to point you in the right direction."

Bell's discomfort had mounted. He was twice oppressed, by her and by the ghostly presence of Lundquist that seemed to be expressed through her. Had she been reenacting with him some earlier scene in which old Carl had savaged some greenhorn teacher? He felt less mocked than challenged, but was unsure who was doing it. He glanced suspiciously at the doors, the windows. Outside, the dreary snow came salting down. Perhaps the poverty king himself was roiling through the frosty evergreens, clawing a homeward path. Thoughts rose like wraiths in his mind — thoughts of Norma, his drop-out bride, and of his father's lockjaw glittering grin —

"To be violated," she said.

He had been, in a way. She hadn't made a move, but he felt pummeled by her aggressive concentration. What was it she wanted? To outrage him?

"I'll find your husband," he said, harshly. His huge hands wrung a sob from the chair back. "I said I would and I will."

She seemed ready to spring at him or burst out laughing or both. He was furious. "I'll find him, all right," he went on, loudly, "but you have no business making these, these — allusions about my p-p-private —"

He stopped. She seemed to be pleased, somehow, even impersonally triumphant.

His hat and coat were laid on a chair in the hall. He grabbed them up. "I'll let you know when I've found him," he called back at her.

"Poor Bell," he thought he heard her say. She followed him, but not hastily. He was outside by the time she reached the door. Then he remembered he didn't have the foundation's address or telephone number, nothing, and so he tramped back in and sat down with the folders, still wearing his coat and hat, and took rapid notes for several minutes. "You don't need to do this," she said. "I could get someone else."

He quelled her this time with a look.

"Well, okay," she said, standing aside, and he strode out again into that empty, endless northern night to where Norma's Ford was waiting, snow-patched, like an old piebald bitch.

Bᴇʟʟ ɢᴏᴛ ʙʀɪsᴋʟʏ out of bed in his Washington hotel room. The night flight from Chicago had cleared him of gloom. He'd been hurtled over clouds. His chest still hummed with sensations of power. In the shower he took the full force of the cold spray and sang old Wobbly songs. He was a hairy fellow; his wet legs were plastered black with hair, and every year it grew more thickly up his chest and back, as if rushing to reach his skull and beat the imminent baldness there. He dried himself, flexing muscles before the mirror. Last week he'd wrestled Pico to a draw in the faculty gym (his ribs still ached where Pico'd crunched him). He might be no beauty, but he was man enough to fetch that crusty old Swede and drop him at Rose Lundquist's feet like a bone — and to haul Norma back from Detroit. Maybe. He eyed the phone. He could call, yes — but would she listen?

His appointment with Dr. Grosch at the Thomas Jefferson Foundation was for ten o'clock. He went there by taxi, passing the federal buildings he'd seen twice before (first time as a boy, taken on a trip by Grandpa after his mother's death, then ten years ago as a soldier with an hour between trains): Monument, distant Capitol, White House, and the imperial Department blocks like concrete clouds frozen in mid-billow and shaven smooth. He gawked through the windows of the cab. Quite a sight for a midwestern boy, accustomed to grain silos.

Then:

"Love them niggers," came the voice of the taxi driver softly but distinctly from the front.

Bell stared at the back of the man's neck. It was pale, plump, and hairless.

"Oh, Lord, yes," intoned the driver, "we all sure do love them dirty niggers." It appeared to be a sort of song.

Bell glanced down. His shoes, he saw, were in a pond of cigarette butts with crusted Kleenex wads as lily pads. He noticed, too, that the cab windows were grimy. Through them now he saw official Washington not as white but as gray, and shadowed by slums.

"Um, sweet Jesus, love them nig-nig-nigras." The driver's eyes met Bell's in the rear-vision mirror. "Them big black dirty —"

"Knock that off," said Bell, leaning forward, suddenly furious.

"Say, mister. That's the cabdrivers' anthem."

"I don't care what it is." Bell raised one hand like a gavel, clenched.

"Okay, mister. Most people don't mind it, though."

The driver seemed indifferent. He began to whistle instead. Bell sat silently burping. He could taste his breakfast bacon again. *Most people.*

"Stop right here," he said. "I'm getting out."

"Yassah, boss."

"Damn you to hell," said Bell. He dropped a dollar over the seat, and when the cab stopped he was out in a flash, walking with his hat in his hand so the air could cool his head.

He had several blocks to go. On each side of the avenue were stone mansions built in an era of robust dignity; if the earth shook open, Bell thought, these structures wouldn't crack and crumble, they'd drop into fissures all of a piece, bearing with them undisturbed their occupants, the staffs of tax-exempt organizations, who would continue writing memos and filing correspondence all the way down. He glanced up. The sky had darkened. It might storm later. The avenue trembled from traffic. He lengthened his stride.

The Foundation was modestly located in a small building around a corner on a side street. Bell entered, his hair blown awry by the wind. The receptionist directed him through a carpeted passageway decorated with early American prints (rural scenes of pioneer husbandmen plowing, felling trees, fowling, fishing) that led to several offices at the rear, including one marked *Dr. A. J. Grosch*.

Dr. Grosch was a thickset, muscular old party with a lumpy dome either bald or shaven, and he wore old-fashioned pince-nez eyeglasses attached to his vest by a ribbon. His office was sparely furnished. There wasn't much room.

"Please sit down, Professor Bell. Watch your head. We're under the stairs, you know. That's why the ceiling slopes so." Dr. Grosch spoke between his teeth, which were clamped on the stem of a pipe. His heavy torso was encased in tweed. "Well, sir. You phoned about some information on migratory labor."

"Right," said Bell.

"You say you're doing a book."

Bell nodded.

"Migratory labor," Dr. Grosch repeated, in a vague and thoughtful way.

Bell prompted him. "The Nomad project."

Dr. Grosch removed his pipe from his mouth, studied its bowl reflectively, laid it in an ashtray on his desk, and then picked it up and put it between his teeth again, as though its presence there were necessary for speech.

"Eh, what-was-that-you-said?"

"Nomad."

Dr. Grosch repeated the word several times, frowning and gently shaking his head. "Sounds like a guided missile, doesn't it?" he said finally.

"I understood that's what the migrant project was called," Bell said.

"Well, sir, we haven't called it that in a couple of years, I guess. Nomad — I'd almost forgotten. Wherever did you hear that?"

"It doesn't matter."

Dr. Grosch leaned back in his chair and began polishing his pince-nez with a handkerchief. He darted a glance at Bell.

"What university did you say you're with?"

Bell told him.

Dr. Grosch noted it down. "And would you mind spelling out your full name for me?"

Bell did so.

Dr. Grosch wrote this down, too. "Now, Professor Bell, you understand that we foundation folks are not running the migrant studies. That's strictly the business of the participating universities. They've established a special nonprofit corporation which owns and operates the farms, hires its staff, and so forth. Our interest is twofold: to provide a portion of the funds required, and to assist in matters of coordination and cooperation. There are many little projects here and there in the country from which we try to glean useful data — " He broke off with a frown, as though he'd allowed himself to stray from his subject. "Well," he continued, "when the scholars reach the point of publishing, we'll doubtless help. But that's some time in the future. Nothing's been published, nothing at all." He exhaled, sending pipe ash flying. "There wasn't even a public announcement made at the time we began." He clapped his pince-nez on his nose and eyed Bell closely. "We should have made one. We were going to, but somehow we never got around to it. Too much to do, I suppose. But of course the word does get around, doesn't it? Would you mind telling me how you came to hear of this little program?"

"A friend mentioned it," Bell said. He hadn't expected to be questioned on this point.

"A colleague, I imagine."

"Um, yes." He wasn't supposed to bring Mrs. Lundquist's name into it, but Dr. Grosch had his pencil out again and was gazing inquiringly at him, so he said, "A friend named Pico." Dr. Grosch's eyebrows remained at question level. Bell dutifully spelled out Pico's full name and title.

"Excellent," said Dr. Grosch. "We certainly appreciate your interest and Professor Pico's, too. You'll be on our mailing list, I can assure you. You're both historians, which is — well, I won't say it's strange, because it isn't, but I mean one would think that you'd have heard about us from someone in agriculture. Or sociology."

Bell said nothing. Dr. Grosch's teeth seemed very large. He wondered if they were false.

"You've got some very fine men in sociology," said Dr. Grosch.

"That's true." Bell waited for Dr. Grosch to utter Lundquist's name; Dr. Grosch, it seemed, was waiting for Bell to do so.

"Excellent," said Dr. Grosch, at last, once more polishing

his pince-nez. He seemed disappointed. "Our purpose here," he went on, as though in answer to a question, "is to work for the ideals of Thomas Jefferson, with special reference to agriculture." He stole a glance at his wristwatch. "Now, I don't mean we want to turn America into a nation of small farmers!" He smiled broadly, his eyes focused on Bell's forehead. "We can't fly in the face of economic realities. But we try to promote, in our small way, the spirit of Jefferson's views on democracy as founded on a stable rural society." His face became grave, but again he looked at his watch. "Well, Professor Bell, don't let me ramble on. You must have a dozen other things to do. I mean, surely you wouldn't have come all the way to Washington just for this." Bell made no reply, and Dr. Grosch went on quickly, "As for data on the migrant project, we'll do the best we can for you. We don't have a public information program, you know, but I'll tell you what I'll do. Where are you staying? At a hotel?" He wrote down the name of Bell's hotel. "I'll have a man scrape something together and run it over this afternoon for you. Let's say around two o'clock. And is Professor Pico with you on this trip?"

"No."

"Back at the University, then. We'll mail him something."

"That would be kind of you."

"Nothing of the sort," said Dr. Grosch, rising with Bell to shake hands. "Anybody who's interested in what we're doing certainly deserves our prompt attention." He squinted cagily at Bell. "Now, are we clear and square for the present? Nothing else you had in mind?"

Bell decided to hold Lundquist's name in reserve. "Nothing, Dr. Grosch." At the door, he hesitated. "Sometime later I might want to visit the project. Would that be possible?"

"Lord, yes. Nothing easier." Dr. Grosch followed him out and walked with him toward the front. "Actually, they're not set up for visitors, but I'm sure if you get in touch with the data center people they'll be able to arrange a little trip to one of the farms. It would have to be off-season, probably. When the migrants are coming through the boys have their hands full, you know." They parted at the front door. "Remember — two o'clock at your hotel!"

Bell began to walk back. No more taxis for him. His route took him along the edge of the slums, that different world, the Outside where Lundquist lived his chameleon life. But was it really so different?

He walked past pawnshops and gun stores, past bars and cheap cafés and rooming houses. He'd seen it all before. Those thickets of chipped brick and scabby frame, smelling of piss and garbage, crawling with cats and rats — yes, it was familiar, quite familiar. In fact, it was so familiar that he paused, slightly puzzled. The darkening sky was sucking colors away, leaving a black-white pattern, and made Bell wonder if he weren't wandering through a documentary slum, with only TV memories in his mind. Had he seen the reality before — or had it just been a film on the ever glowing screen?

He began scanning faces. Most were black or brown, some white, but it seemed to make little difference. He was having some difficulty with them. He found it hard to distinguish individual features. Those faces all looked a little blank to him — without depth or substance, as though he were viewing them from some easy chair in the living room of his mind, seeing them as two-dimensional abstractions. He scraped his shoe against the rough cement. That was real. So was that cruddy mitten lying there. So were the people shuffling by. And yet he had a sensation of foreignness, of having lost some functional power.

He stopped to wipe his glasses. He'd better make an effort to improve his perception. Lundquist himself might stroll by and go unrecognized.

But the sky was growing even darker. No one could see well on such a day. He kept trying, proceeding more slowly. No, there was nothing wrong with his sight. Those two men across the street, lounging against a car, had well-defined faces — and then he realized that one was a policeman, the other a cabdriver.

Enough, Bell decided. No point in wandering aimlessly about at the mercy of psychological quirks. He'd better return to the hotel and eat a proper lunch and maybe take a nap. He headed toward a gap between ragged buildings where the far-off Washington Monument shone like a slender silver keep. The wind sprang up, whistling — a vicious old slum wind that mocked him, that sang in his ears, tried to spin his hat around, threw ash in his eyes to blind him further, and went hawking last week's newspapers out of the gutters and against his ankle to chase him on his way. He turned his coat collar up, lowered his head a bit, and walked faster. When a taxi came cruising by, he had to jam his hands in his pockets to keep from hailing it.

He ate lunch at the hotel restaurant; then, back in his room, he flung his coat on the bed, his hat on the chair, and seized the phone. He'd never tried to reach Norma until evening, after the rates changed. Now, at noon, he'd surely find her steamfitter dad at work and maybe her mantis mom out shopping. But when the hotel operator got the call through, it was Mrs. Hirlinger who answered: "Who is it?" Bell disguised his voice with a handkerchief and a southern accent, and, to pique Norma's curiosity, chose his *nom de phone* from the cast of *Pride and Prejudice.*

"It's Fitzwilliam Darcy, ma'am, for Miss Norma, if you please."

There was a minute of confab in the background. He had to guess at it. Mom would be squinting through her steel-rimmed specs. Did Norma-baby know any fella named Darcy? Did any Darcy know her? Norma was no ninny; she'd know who this Darcy would be. If she took the call, that might mean she'd been home long enough. But was there an extension on which Mom would listen?

"Hello?" It was Norma.

Bell was caught by surprise. He made a glugging sound.

"Yes? Hello?"

"Listen, Norma, it's me." Would she hang up? He listened for a few seconds. There was an interstate silence — no disconnection, nor could he hear Mom's iron breath bugging the line.

"Yes?"

"I've got to see you, Norma. I've got to talk to you. It's been terrible, these last few weeks!"

"Oh," she said.

"I haven't been able to eat or sleep!"

"Um."

He guessed then that Mom was in the kitchen where the

phone was, listening to Norma's responses. He tried to keep his voice low. "You've got to see me, Norma. It isn't fair to treat me like this. Why wouldn't you answer my letters? Why wouldn't you take my calls?"

"Well, I don't know."

Even now, they weren't really conversing. It was a one-way connection, like the marriage. "I c-c-can't force you to come back. I couldn't do that. I wouldn't want to. But don't I have a right to know why you've been doing this?"

"I guess so."

In the mirror, Bell saw himself wild-eyed and ludicrous. He sank to his knees beside the bed to avoid the dismal sight. "Listen, Norma. I'm coming to Detroit. Sometime. I don't know just when. Things can't go on like this!" He was breathing hard. With his free hand, he kneaded the bed-clothes. "You've got to see me! I've got the right to demand that!" He imagined himself as a human bomb, blowing himself to bits in Norma's sight. But how far should he stand from the door? He didn't want to splatter her. "You've got to!" But his enthusiasm was fading. How could he manage it — ring the doorbell to summon her, than walk back a safe distance before lighting his fuse? With his luck, she'd be at the movies; he'd explode just for good old Mom.

All she said was, "Gee."

"Norma, I don't want to alarm you, but this business of being cut off from you, it's driving me out of my mind." He wondered if he wasn't taking the wrong tack. Wasn't he capable of Darcyesque dignity? "You've got to promise to see me, that's all I ask." It seemed that he could either roar or whimper, neither of which Darcy did. "It isn't much,

Norma." His agitated fingers finally pulled down the bed-spread and pillows; trying to shield the phone, he got tangled in them. "Promise me!"

"Well, maybe."

He was crouched on the floor, trying to free himself. His elbow jarred the bed table, toppling a flimsy lamp. He watched it slide down the wall. "Norma, Norma. I've tried so many times to think why you left me." (And there were so many reasons. She couldn't cook; she might simply have gotten hungry and gone home to eat.) "Can't we c-c-communicate?" Pity for them both made him teary. The Gideon Bible had thumped down with the lamp. Bell laid one hand on it. "Norma, are you there?"

"Um, yes."

"Norma, a marital relationship may be impossible for us, I realize that, but a human relationship — two people, Norma, not necessarily man and wife but just two persons wanting to clarify — " His nose was running. He wiped it on his sleeve. Was marriage clarification? He'd chosen badly, that was all. So had she.

But then she said, "Okay."

Okay. From his laconic princess, this was a cry of affirmation. Was it possible she wanted him to come? Tenderness clamped his throat. He envisioned her nibbling her nicotined fingernails and wriggling ensandaled toes there in her awful mother's kitchen — Norma, his Norma, his reluctant mistress, one delicate blue-veined hand thrusting the telephone receiver up beneath her long black hair.

"Thank you, Norma."

It was over. The line was dead. Bell sat bemused amid

bedclothes, Bible, lamp. The joy he felt, was it honest love for Norma, or just the vibration of his closure complex, newly tuned by hope?

He went to the window. A storm was wheeling in with lightning spokes. It might scrub clean those gray walls, those black streets. He touched the phone again, still warm from his hand — and when it rang, he snatched it up eagerly.

It was a man named Muller, in the lobby. Dr. Grosch had sent him. Could he come up? Bell just had time to wash his face and pull his tie straight before the man arrived.

Muller was a hard-faced youngish man with a hearty smile and a fast handshake. He gave Bell an envelope containing one sheet of paper. "It isn't much, Dr. Bell," he said. Bell took a look. It wasn't — just a list of the member universities, names of top staff personnel, an office address in Roanoke, and some quotations from a memo he'd seen in Lundquist's files describing the scope of the studies: birds & beasts, flowers, soil, migrants & insects. His eyes caught a phrase, *environmental control.* He glanced up. Muller had eased himself into the chair near the window. Thunder was rattling the panes.

"Well, thanks anyway," Bell said. "This will help." He was still thinking about Norma. Maybe he could go back by way of Detroit.

"There was another matter you mentioned to Dr. Grosch this morning."

"Was there?"

Muller was sitting at his ease, cross-legged, the smile still spread on his face. There was gray in Muller's hair; it gleamed like metal when the lightning flashed.

"The word was Nomad, I believe," said Muller.

"Right."

"Well." Muller's smile was a masterpiece. It conveyed a sincere, friendly impatience. "Maybe if you told me a little more about it, Dr. Bell, then I could try to help."

"Help with what?" Bell was vexed. Nomad obviously had some special meaning for Dr. Grosch, and for this aging halfback, but it had none for him. "I don't know anything more about it than I told Dr. Grosch this morning."

Muller's smile was diminishing. "Well, I thought if you could give me a few details, you see, then perhaps I could dig around in the files and give you further information."

"I don't have any details, Mr. Muller."

"I see."

Bell could tell the fellow thought he was lying. It annoyed him.

Muller sat for a few moments gazing at Bell in a penetrating manner, which Bell began to find offensive. "Well, I guess that does it, then, Dr. Bell," he said at last, getting to his feet. Bell silently accompanied him to the door. "Say," Muller added, "I may know an old friend of yours — Colonel Pickett. He was a captain then, I guess."

"Yup." But Bell wasn't giving an inch. And this time he got the jump on Muller with the handshake. "So long, Mr. Muller." He squeezed hard, let go fast, and eased the door shut.

He stood alone, cracking his knuckles. The rain was sweating down the panes. He'd pressed somebody's button, all right. Muller's last words had been clear enough. Captain Pickett had been Sergeant Bell's instructor in the aerial photo intelligence school some ten years back — not a distinguished photo-analyst (once he'd mistaken cows for tanks), although an eminent teller of smutty stories, and now, it seemed, a colonel — but of course Muller had just been letting him know that they'd made a check on him. "We know all about you, buddy." That was the message. So, damn them anyway, he thought. Did they know about Norma, too, and about old Aaron's false teeth? That Grandpa sang along with the Sunshine Lady every Saturday at 9:45 A.M.? That Bell himself was supposed to lecture next Monday morning to forty-six sophomores on the Rise of Executive Power?

He grabbed his hat and went for a walk in the rain. If they'd checked on him, they might have checked on Pico, too. But who were "they"? He stared resentfully at the gray silhouettes of federal buildings, lashed by rain gusts. Did the government have the right to show Muller his service record? Maybe so, but it nettled him. So did the thought of Dr. Grosch, who'd sent Muller prying in the files. He'd uttered one little word — *Nomad* — and they began acting as though he'd gotten loose from a zoo. "Nomad," he said aloud into the rain. Two men hurrying by in raincoats gave him a look. "Nomad," Bell said, louder. Then he stepped into a drugstore, went back to the telephone booths, and put in a long-distance call to Mrs. Lundquist. But she wasn't home; no one answered.

He returned to the hotel. As he crossed the lobby the chief porter arose from ambush behind a bank of potted ferns to hand him a note. Dr. Grosch again. Bell was invited to meet him for a drink at a nearby men's bar at five o'clock. At the bottom of the note, underlined, was the word *urgent*. Bell put the note in his pocket and took the elevator up to his floor. In his room he sat thumbing through the notes and chapter drafts of his manuscript, which he'd brought along on the chance he would find Lundquist right away and have to produce the pages on poverty. There was a section in some other chapter that dealt with federal record-keeping. He found it. Yes, he'd written quite clearly about that. Federal services were necessarily based on federal records. The government could hardly serve you if it didn't know you existed. If you were a bird, it tagged you; if you were a man, it punched a hole in a computer card — and if that made it easier for Muller to go nosing about in the past, it wasn't the fault of the system. But what voluminous records there were! What tireless services! And which came first? Did the services require the keeping of records, or in some cases might it not be the other way around? Ah, he hadn't covered that point. He got up to shave — his jaws turned blue with beard by late afternoon — and to change his shirt. It was nearly five.

The bar selected by Dr. Grosch was dark and quiet. Its Muzak was muted to a whisper. The motif was blood sport: severed heads of elk and moose hung on the walls like retired topers. Dr. Grosch was waiting at the bar, a glass in his hand. He led Bell through the gloom to a table where Bell, warily, ordered beer.

"Your man Muller brought me the information on the project," Bell said. His eyes were still adjusting to the dimness. Dr. Grosch was like a Cheshire cat; only his magnificent teeth, reflecting light from the bar, were visible.

"Yes, yes. Muller."

"He seemed to have checked up on me, too," Bell added.

"He's thoroughgoing, all right."

"I mean he evidently got hold of my military service record."

"Did he? I wouldn't doubt it. Muller's a regular bulldog for facts."

"But I don't see what business he had doing that."

"I was a bit old for combat," Dr. Grosch said, ignoring Bell's complaint. "They enlisted my brains, however. I'm a mathematician," he confided, pulling his pince-nez up from his vest and fitting it carefully on his nose. "Each in his own way, as he's able. Serve your country and your country will be glad to serve you in return." He drew in his breath decisively. "All right, Professor Bell. Tell me. Where is Carl Lundquist?"

"Damned if I know," said Bell, startled.

Dr. Grosch regarded him quizzically through the pince-nez.

"I was going to ask you the same question," Bell added. The waiter brought the beer and another glass of whiskey for Dr. Grosch.

"You say you don't know where he is?"

"I don't have the slightest idea."

Dr. Grosch removed the swizzle stick from his glass and tapped on the table with it. "Come, Professor Bell. A little fencing is all very well, but let's put our cards on the table. We've got to know what Carl has in mind." He pulled a pipe from his pocket and began filling it, eyeing Bell suspiciously. "Carl may not want to disclose his whereabouts. That's his privilege, I suppose. We'll deal with you, if that's the way he wants it. Just tell me his terms."

"I don't know his terms. I don't know what you're talking about."

"Surely Carl told you I was the man to see. What did he expect? The Joint Chiefs of Staff?"

"I tell you I haven't seen Professor Lundquist."

"All right," said Dr. Grosch shortly. "What's your story, then?"

"Actually, I came here to find him. I suppose I should have told you that right away."

"Find him? Why?"

"I need his advice on something I'm writing about poverty and welfare."

Dr. Grosch stared at him morosely. "You say you came here — to Washington — for that?"

"Are you suggesting I'm not telling the truth?"

"We're not getting anywhere," complained Dr. Grosch. He finished his whiskey with one long last swallow and signaled to the waiter for another. "Look here, do you expect me to believe that an associate professor would travel hundreds of miles for advice from a man who isn't even here?"

"Where is he, then?"

"I don't know. Our assumption is that you do." Dr. Grosch lighted his pipe, sending up great gouts of smoke. "Very well. I'm willing to grant that you may not literally have seen him, even that you may not know his exact location — but you must have been in touch with him. Why else would you have come here to see us, eh? Why would you be dropping hints about Nomad? Oh, yes," he continued, with a touch of sarcasm, "you said your friend Pico told you about Nomad, but it may interest you to know that Pico denies having any knowledge of it whatsoever — "

"You mean you talked to Pico today?"

"We had to. Obviously. Yes, we sent a man to see him — and of course it was another dead end." Dr. Grosch's voice had thickened. He was squinting. The drink in his hand was his third, at least. "I was sixty-four years old last week, Professor Bell. That's no age for a man to be sitting around in bars. I ought to be home in my armchair with my feet propped up, reading my mathematical journals. I'm not cut out for these intrigues."

"There aren't any intrigues." Bell was at a loss to know how to deal with Dr. Grosch's misunderstanding. Was the old fellow shamming, in order to draw him off guard?

"No intrigues? Then why did you call from that drugstore today? A man with nothing to hide would have made that call from his room, but no, you had to make a special trip — you didn't buy anything at the drugstore, so it's obvious the phone call was your only purpose in going there — and, well, you see it all adds up, you know, and yet now here you're pretending — I must use that word, like it or not, Professor Bell — pretending to know nothing about anything."

"You had me followed, then."

"Of course we did! You knew we would! Bell, you're a damned devious fellow!" A curious change was coming over Dr. Grosch. Where he'd been brisk and canny, now he seemed suddenly to age in his chair, becoming querulous and mistrustful. Bell supposed it was the liquor. "When I was a young man, we were taught to be plain-spoken." Dr. Grosch wagged his gristly head. His pince-nez sat askew. Behind it, his eyes blinked resentfully. "I suppose things are different now. New times, new fashions. Secrecy, guile, craftiness — the whole bag of tricks. And I'm the one caught in the middle! Come now, Bell, do kindly tell me how to get in touch with Carl Lundquist."

"I wish I could, but I can't."

Dr. Grosch uttered a groan. "Bell, I have never encountered such artfulness in another human being!"

"Your assumptions are wrong, that's all."

Dr. Grosch gave him a discouraged look. "Muller warned me you'd be a slippery customer, Bell. On the other hand, Muller thinks everybody's slippery — and do you know why? Because Muller himself is pretty slippery, blast his soul." He groaned again. "I never thought mathematics would lead to this!"

It was becoming clear to Bell that Dr. Grosch was rapidly sliding into inebriation. "Better not finish that drink, Dr. Grosch," he said. "I think you've had enough."

Dr. Grosch defiantly took a large gulp.

"All right," Bell said. "Tell me about Nomad, then."

"Ask your friend Lundquist. He knows."

Bell remembered the phrase in the foundation material. "Environmental control — what does that mean?"

"It means exactly what it says."

"I don't understand it."

"I'm disappointed in you, Aaron Bell. You say you're a historian. You study the works of man, don't you? Well, then. What have men been striving for down through the ages? Environmental control, that's what." He drained his glass and gazed muzzily at Bell. His pince-nez had fallen off. "Oh, I wish I could tell you about Nomad, Bell. It's not a big project, I admit, and we're a bit tight for funds — you saw that cramped little office of mine, didn't you? — but there are people in very high places who are counting on us to come up with something of real value. Right now, we're experimental. Pure research. Well, almost pure. *But.*" He brought his fist down heavily, barely missing his glass. "To me, Nomad's a jewel. A thing, you see, of beauty — of the kind of beauty that only mathematics can produce. But you're not a mathematician, are you? Neither is Muller, confound him."

"Listen, Dr. Grosch," Bell said decisively, "I'm going to take you home." He signaled for the waiter. Dr. Grosch tried to order another drink, but Bell forestalled him and paid the bill. He had some difficulty maneuvering Dr. Grosch outside to the street. In the taxi Dr. Grosch argued in favor of going to another bar and refused to disclose his home address, so that Bell had to overpower him, wrestle his wallet out of his pocket, and looked up the address on his driver's license. Dr. Grosch proved to be quite strong, but once Bell had conquered him he became docile and slumped in the corner of the rear seat with his hat tilted over his eyes. Washington was jammed with rush-hour traffic; it was a dark, wet, windy evening made noxious by exhaust fumes from automobiles.

"Don't tell Muller I got drunk," said Dr. Grosch from his corner, in a piteous voice.

"Why shouldn't I?" Bell adopted a bullying manner; brusquely he set Dr. Grosch's hat straight on his head.

"In decency, I ask you not to, dammit." There were tears in Dr. Grosch's eyes. "Muller's out to get me, you know. He wants me kicked out. Not that I'd care much. I've got no business in this end of the project. I ought to be down with the computers where I belong."

"Down where?"

"At Roanoke. Oh, they've got such fine equipment there. The best that money can buy. Everything new." Then he stared at Bell with alarm. "Damnation — you're probably one of Muller's men!"

"Don't be a fool."

"How tall are you?"

"Six feet three."

"Really? Then you're too tall. They don't like their Mullers to be too tall. Makes them conspicuous. That's your trouble, Bell. You're conspicuously tall." After that, Dr. Grosch lapsed into silence until they arrived at his address, a large apartment building on one of the avenues. Bell hauled his host out of the taxi and paid the driver.

"Nomad is our last best hope, Bell," Dr. Grosch declared as Bell propelled him into the building. The elevator required a key. Bell had to frisk Dr. Grosch to find it. "It boils down to this," Dr. Grosch told him as they rose aloft. "Either we do it the Nomad way — the orderly, logical way — or we turn everything over to Muller, and he'll start shooting. He's armed, you know." The elevator stopped. Bell led Dr. Grosch into the hall. "Carl disagreed, damn him." Dr. Grosch weaved and wobbled; his face was a sickly off-white. "He left me alone to face Muller — and he knew I couldn't do it all by myself!"

Bell had difficulty entering the apartment, having to fit

the right key to the door lock and at the same time prevent Dr. Grosch from collapsing. "Rats leave sinking ships," Dr. Grosch whispered. "Carl's a rat." Bell opened the door and hauled Dr. Grosch inside. The old man feebly resumed his earlier struggles, and Bell had to waltz him across the tiny living room, around a corner into a kitchenette, back through the living room, testing interior doors one-handed en route. He pulled open two closets, found a bedroom, a miniature study crammed with books, and finally a bathroom, into which he danced his partner and forced him into a position of prayer before the toilet. He plucked off Dr. Grosch's hat and returned to the living room to retrieve the keys and shut the outside door.

It was a one-man apartment. Bell guessed that Dr. Grosch was a widower: a series of framed photographs showed Grosch in flower and in decay — a flaxen-haired youth taking strides toward the bier, losing hair at every stage, and gaining jowls — in company with a lady, likewise aging into plumpness and spectacles, but the most recent one had Grosch alone, looking doleful. Bell went to the kitchenette and put coffee on to boil, then took a look at the victim of drink, who was retching into the toilet bowl.

"I'll never forget your kindness, Professor Bell," Dr. Grosch said later. Bell had cleaned him up, helped him change into pajamas and robe, and brought him some coffee. "When I was in the Defense Department, I never touched a drop. Then Carl came along and I got myself into this foundation job and it's been downhill ever since. Because of Carl, you see. I hate to blame my troubles on others, but he's such a damned forceful fellow, you know — or do you?"

"I don't, except by reputation."

"Yes, yes, so you told me," Dr. Grosch said. "Well, I'm willing to believe you, Bell, but Muller won't. He never believes anyone." He glanced about the room uneasily. Then, without a word, he got out of the armchair and beckoned Bell to follow him into the bathroom, where he turned the shower on full and sat down on the toilet, having closed the lid. He began whispering, but the rush of hot water prevented Bell from hearing until he squatted down and put one ear close to Dr. Grosch.

"This may seem odd, Bell, but I'm convinced Muller's bugged my apartment, and I read somewhere that this is the only way to beat it."

"I thought Muller was your assistant."

"No, no. Obviously not. I'm not supposed to tell you exactly what he is, but you can guess. We call him a liaison man, but his real job is to keep tabs on yours truly, although he swears he doesn't." Steam was puffing from the shower stall. Bell's glasses misted over. He put them in his pocket. "I used to be a contented man, Bell," Dr. Grosch whispered. "But then I got mixed up with Carl Lundquist and all these Mullers, and quite frankly I'm in a state. Do you know what it does to a man to be shadowed and spied on night and day for God knows how long? Muller does it to protect me — I don't mean physically — and it seems to be a matter of policy in the case of top project people, no matter how insignificant they may be. I told him I didn't need it, I didn't want it, I was damned indeed if I was going to allow it — and he said okay they wouldn't do it, but I know they've gone right on doing it anyhow. It gives me the creeps! At first I was flattered. It was a mark of importance — me, Arthur Grosch, an object of such care and concern. But it's like a succubus. You can't get rid of it. It opens your mail and listens to your telephone, and by thunder, Bell, if you feel once in a while like having a frisk with some little lady of the evening — and I confess I'm no saint — then you're always wondering who's sneaking around with one of those thingamabobs for peeking through walls to watch you in the very act!" Wreathed in steam, Dr. Grosch sat there in his bathrobe barefooted and bald, like an old satyr doing penance. "It's not easy for a man my age to achieve the virile state under ideal circumstances, Bell, and I can tell you that the thought of Muller snooping from the next apartment has cost me much joy lately. And money, too, for the lovely creatures quite justly require payment whether or no. It's not their fault."

Bell's suit jacket was beginning to wrinkle, and his trousers were losing their press. The tropical atmosphere seemed to benefit Dr. Grosch, however; he was at an intermediate stage, no longer drunk but not yet sober.

"If I didn't believe in what I'm doing, I wouldn't put up with it another minute," he continued. "I'd quit this miserable place. I'd retire to some village in the mountains and teach little children in the schoolhouse, Bell, and raise flowers outside my cottage. I'd buy a dog — you can't keep a dog in the city, you know. That's what I've always wanted — a dog, a cottage, clean mountain air, curly heads in a simple classroom, tiny voices piping out their sums." He paused to blow his nose on a strip of toilet paper and dab delicately at his eyes.

"But you do believe in what you're doing," Bell said.

"Passionately. Totally. I couldn't have withstood Lundquist without strong conviction. How we argued — here,
right in this very apartment, and in various bars around town
— and how we drank!" Dr. Grosch used a towel to mop his
dripping dome, then wrapped it around his head, turban-style.
"Carl claimed I'd betrayed him, and it's true I wasn't completely candid with him at the outset, but I was under certain restrictions, and we needed him to set the migrant project up — and we still need him. *I* need him. He's a rock of
strength, young man. If only you could find him and persuade him to return to us!" Now Dr. Grosch was almost totally obscured by steam. Bell despaired of his suit. He'd
have to get it pressed overnight at the hotel. "But you won't
find him — Muller will. Carl made some foolish threats
before he left. He swore he'd wreck the project — as if he
could. Even Carl couldn't do that, you know. But of course
Muller was listening somewhere, and now they're trying to
find Carl, too."

"Why?"

"To get him back on Nomad, I suppose. But Carl
wouldn't, not for Muller. You'd have better luck."

"I could hardly do more than mention the subject, Dr.
Grosch. I have no idea what Nomad is."

"That's the devil of it. You're not cleared."

"I was cleared once for army intelligence, and Muller himself checked me out today, didn't he?"

"I suppose so. I don't know about these things. It's a lot
of foolishness anyway. My own opinion is that we ought to
shout Nomad to the skies," said Dr. Grosch, still whispering.

"It isn't the migrant project?"

"Not exactly, no. It's based on it, though. The migrant project is intended to yield information on the response of human factors — "

"What?"

"People, if you prefer. We are interested in the precise measurement and evaluation of mass human data. It's a by-product of the migrant project, you see. The sociologists conduct their own studies and make the results available to us in the forms we request, without being actually aware of the existence of Nomad, which is a sort of shadow project, you might say."

"What do you do with this data?"

"We write poems with it, Professor Bell. Mathematical poems." Dr. Grosch pawed away steam clouds in order to glimpse Bell, who was perched uncomfortably on the laundry hamper. "Have you ever heard of games theory? Ah, you've heard of it, but you don't know what it is. Well, it's a mathematical system for analyzing decision-making problems where the choices are enormously complex."

"It's been used by the military."

"True. It's used also in industry. Modern executives in the big outfits — military and civilian — are turning to it more and more. It reduces error to a minimum. If you can program a computer properly, then the computer will be able to compare all the possible consequences of all the myriad options available to you, and indicate the optimum course of action. It's called games theory because essentially it's the comparison of odds. For instance, which horse will win the Derby? Program your computer with all relevant facts about the competing horses and you'll learn the winner in the twinkling of an eye."

"Unless the jockey falls off."

"True, but the computer will also give you the odds on such an unlikely event. Computers are infallible only where the facts are unchanging — in the game of chess, for example. When you move into areas involving people, then naturally there's an element of risk and chance, all of which games theory takes into account. It's a mathematical mechanism for analyzing problems, as I say. Now, what's so exciting in Nomad is that we're attempting to move much further into the human area with games theory. In a way, it's a marriage of science and art — by which I mean mathematics and sociology — to reveal the patterns of certain types of human behavior in order to influence that behavior. In fact, one may be so bold as to say our object is to achieve a degree of control over that behavior."

"Over the migrants?"

"No, no. Not the migrants. The migrants are somewhat like guinea pigs. They're handy to work with, that's all."

"Who, then?"

"Now we're getting into ticklish matters, Professor Bell. Think of the world situation. All these masses of hungry people, unable to control themselves — spawning at a fearful rate, and lacking the capacity to deal rationally with their problems. Already there are people starving, and guerrillas are popping up all over, and God knows what will happen. Well, in such a situation, where people can't control themselves, then someone else must control them. That's reasonable, isn't it? The question is how you do it. Do you do it Muller's way with spies and then with guns and bombs? That's unthinkable — but it's bound to happen unless there's some alternative. Nomad is intended to provide that alternative."

"I don't see it."

"Instead of using sheer force, we have the option of maneuvering events by mathematical analysis — ech, it's impossible to explain it without charts and things, especially to someone without a mathematical background. But it's stirring up great interest these days, and well it should. Let me make a gross oversimplification for you. Picture a giant computer. Into this computer we feed all of the relevant information about a specific mass problem — birth control in New Guinea, if you like — and the computer produces an analysis of the almost limitless possibilities for corrective action. Properly programmed and accurately informed, the computer would select the optimum program, taking into account all political and economic and ethnic considerations. It would probably recommend a mixed program — that is, economic rewards for childless persons plus education in the use of contraceptives plus I don't know what, but the point is that we seek to avoid violent solutions. Muller would do nothing but polish his weapons and wait for the starving New Guineans to make a hopeless attempt to seize our food, and then he'd massacre them. You must understand that I don't mean Muller individually; I use him as a symbol for all that I abhor." Dr. Grosch blinked at Bell, regarding him earnestly. "We're idealists, you and I," the old man continued. "Thank God we're not alone. Nomad's experimental, it's true. We've got a long way to go. But it isn't just this one project, you see. It's actually more a system of data collection and analysis. You might say there are dozens of Nomads, because we draw what we need from many sources — from the hundreds of scholars who are busy digging out the facts of mass behavioral psychology and letting us use them. Of course, very few have ever heard of Nomad. Security is very touchy about that, Bell."

"Why?"

"Um, there's a possibility of negative reactions. Academic people are often immature politically. There are always a few hotheads. They might organize some sort of anti-Nomad boycott. It's happened before with other projects. Publicity just wouldn't help us right now, I suppose. We're better off doing our work quietly, without fanfare. The scholars who don't know about Nomad are helping all the same, God bless them. You, too, Bell."

"What do you mean, me?"

"As a scholar, as a historian, as a researcher of facts, as a teacher of youth — you're serving Nomad in your own way. We thank you."

"I'm not a sociologist. I'm not a psychologist or a mathematician."

"Ah, but you're part of the system we draw on, young man. You teach, you write, you whatever. It all helps. We've got men all over combing the professional literature for usable data. Perhaps something you wrote in your dissertation has already found its way onto one of our magnetic tapes down at Roanoke, who knows?" Dr. Grosch fluttered his eyelids wearily. "All contributions large and small are welcome. How could Carl possibly think he could stop it, eh? The migrant project is a special study of direct application — yes, but the indirect programs, taken altogether, are quite as important to us." He yawned enormously. "Wittingly or not, Bell, you're on our team. You've committed acts of loyalty, one might say. That's good, isn't it? I mean, you do love your country."

"Does my country love me?"

"Of course it does. It loves you, Bell, just as it loves Arthur Grosch — and Carl, too, no matter what he says. We all serve Nomad. We all serve America. All the documents, all the records, all the universities. The whole system, Bell. The whole society. The whole *literate* society, I should say. It's pumping up the blood that Nomad needs."

"Needs for what?" Bell's question went unanswered. Dr. Grosch was smiling faintly; his eyes were closed. Bell felt suddenly annoyed. *"Needs for what?"* He almost shouted it.

"Jefferson would approve if he were alive," Dr. Grosch mumbled sleepily. "Freedom and democracy — these things have changed in form but surely not in substance. Man himself hasn't changed, has he? I sincerely doubt it. We remain true to our heritage. I really believe that, Bell." He sneezed and shivered. "I'm whipped, to tell the truth. I've got to change pajamas — these are sopping — and crawl into bed. Would you be kind enough to open the door?"

Bell helped Dr. Grosch to bed. The old mathematician lay lumpily beneath the covers. His teeth reposed in a tumbler of water on the night table. "Remember this, Bell," he began, but lapsed into unintelligible mumbling, wracked by yawns. With his fallen chops, he looked as old as Grandpa.

". . . heritage," was the last word Bell caught. Dr. Grosch was asleep.

Bell snapped off the light and left the apartment. It was still raining outside. The city gave off a peculiar acid odor. Too many cars, Bell thought. Too many people sourly breathing. No wonder the public buildings were stained. How aged they seemed.

Rain blew in his face. It was acid, too, and stung him as he walked. He thought of Nomads as numerous as raindrops, of countless Grosches, too, and beyond them legions of Bells unwary and unknowing, all working toward environmental control.

The rain was bitter, but he kept walking. Every man he saw made him think of Muller, and as taxis passed, he imagined drivers and passengers singing together while cruising dry through the wet night.

How would Dr. Grosch program that?

"SOME OLD HALFBACK came looking for you when you were gone," said Pico.

"Halfback?"

"Yeah. I knew the guy. Name of Jerry Moss. He played at S. D. State."

They were in Pico's living room, drinking beer. Bell had come by taxi on his way from the airport.

"What did he want?"

"Damned if I know. He said he was just passing through town." Pico drank from a quart bottle and smoked a cigar. He lay emperor-style on a divan which his bulk had tortured into a permanent sag. "He's got a job with some foundation or other now. Moss, he played right half. I hit him once — he still remembered." Pico gurgled up a laugh from his ever rumbling guts. He was balding and blond, his once-fair skin a splotchy spread of reddish hues. He still could crush apples one-handed, but his beef was on a slow slide into fat.

"Thomas Jefferson Foundation."

"Yeah, that was it."

"Well, did he seem surprised I wasn't here?"

"Hell, I don't know. He talked to me about some damned thing or other, I forget just what, like I ought to know about it, but whatever it was I didn't. This Moss, I think he was a little fouled up, but you know once I hit them they're never just right afterward."

"Did he say he's coming back?"

"Didn't say, Bell."

"What did he look like?"

"Oh, hell, all these old halfbacks look alike." Pico gazed at Bell for a moment with his pale blue eyes between pig-pink lids. "You sound funny."

Bell shrugged.

"What's the matter?" Pico asked.

"I don't like halfbacks."

Pico gave a five-second belch. It rolled through the house

like thunder. In the kitchen, Mrs. Pico looked up from the stove, and in the playroom the two little Picos paused in mid-fight.

"Stay for supper," Pico said.

"Can't."

"Let's go bowling. Or maybe see a flick. There's a new pinball machine at the Legion Hall." Pico removed a sock and began picking his toes. "Stone the Seminary. Rape a coed. How long has it been since you raped a coed?"

"I married one."

"Sorry," said Pico. "Um, listen. Let's borrow Morgan's tape recorder and make a smutty tape. We could read the dirty parts of Limber Fast-Foot into it."

"Nope," said Bell. "Not in the mood. Got to go home." Limber Fast-Foot was a character from Pico's mock dissertation, "The Sports History of America." His thesis was that Americans are culturally obsessed not by religion or art or philosophy but by sports, and that therefore American history can be explained solely through the interpretation of sporting events. Lacking facts for early periods, Pico invented them. Limber Fast-Foot was a twelfth-century Apache track star about whom were built ribald legends.

"Do you know anything about games theory?" Bell asked.

"Games what?"

"Theory."

"Sounds like math. I seem to recall. It's military stuff. Nuclear strategy. Ask Dr. Slough, he'd know."

"Maybe we ought to know, too."

"Why the hell why?"

"I don't know." Bell sat cracking his knuckles. Without

moving from the divan, Pico opened his second quart. He lay poetically entranced, revolving lazy thoughts of Limber Fast-Foot and Sudden Goose, the Navajo high jumper. Through the kitchen doorway Bell got a glimpse of Harriet Pico scratching her tremendous butt with a spatula handle.

"Life is beer," said Pico. "Life is sport." He spoke basso through another lengthy belch. "Life is ever ready tail." He began picking the toes of his other foot. "I'll give you an address in St. Paul, Bell. You can get your hat blocked six ways there for fifty bucks. It opens up the sinuses, old buddy. You need it." In the kitchen, Harriet was frying steaks. Her breasts were meat sacks, her legs tattooed with exploded veins. The whole house smelled of flesh. "Tell 'em Peter Pico sent you," Pico said. He guzzled beer. Some trickled down his chins. "Peter Pico pumped a peck of pickled prosties, a peck of pickled prosties Peter Pico pumped."

"I'm off," said Bell. At the door he got his coat, hat, suitcase. His house was only a two-block walk away. "Well, we've had some good times," he said to Pico, who'd padded barefoot after him.

"What does that mean? You going somewhere?"

"No, no. I didn't mean that." In height, they were the same. Bell looked like the bone frame that had escaped from Pico's mass. "Don't you ever want to leave, though?"

"St. Paul's far enough for me."

"I didn't mean that, either. Sometimes I wonder if we've learned enough to teach."

"Old buddy, you must have had some little trip. We'll get up a party. Lots of folks. Booze to midnight, ice-skating at the pond, a few fast games of grabass among jolly faculty wives. Borrow Morgan's tape recorder. Borrow Mrs. Morgan. Record her climax cries — "

"Jesus, stop it."

"You're too tight, Bell."

"Is this all it amounts to?"

"It's a life," Pico said. "We're not hungry."

"No, I think you're wrong. We're hungry."

"I'm not, kid. Not Pico." But Pico seemed irritated. "Listen, Bell. We teach. That's our job. So we're surrounded by specimens of immaturity, right? And some of it rubs off on us. So what? You think it's better somewhere else?"

"Can't say."

"Well, dammit, if you want to do serious work here, you can. Nothing stops you."

"What stopped you?"

"I never began, Bell."

"Yes, you did. The Plains Indians. We used to talk about it. But now it's turned into Fast-Foot."

"Look." Pico was uncomfortable. He cracked his knuckles, but his fingers were so thick that the sounds were muffled. "I did just enough for tenure. You know that."

"You had something original."

"Well, it went nowhere. Who cared about those old redskins? Nobody. Even the specialists didn't give a damn about what I wrote or what I found, they were just worried about some new guy trying to break into their club. I mean, the subject didn't matter, right? Fast-Foot may be a joke, but it's an honest joke."

"You quit easy."

"I got wise fast, you mean."

"Okay," said Bell. "Life is beer, then." He went outside. Wind was skimming snow dust over the cleared road. On the sidewalk, old footprints had iced over within the crusty snow. The sky was an enormous black panel studded with millions of blinkers, computing the destinies of galaxies. He walked fast, gulping freezing air, his eyes watering so that he couldn't have seen any halfbacks if they'd been there, nor, if he had looked back, would he have seen Pico's house as anything but a bright carnal blur.

He stopped when he reached his house. There was the Ford in front where he'd left it, but the snow was thick on its hood, which meant his father had neglected to warm it up. Now it might be dead; gray icicles bled from its tail pipe. He glanced up. The house seemed to sag more than ever. The winter wind strummed the crazy gables and ragged eaves. On top, the TV antenna whipped about in its ice jacket as though possessed of Grandpa's soul straining to leak out into that cold sky.

Someone moved at a downstairs window. A curtain twitched. Bell mounted the steps, expecting his father to greet him, but he had to fumble his way inside unaided and grope for the switch to the front-hall lights. There was a stirring and snorting in the living room as Bell snapped that light on, too, and saw old Aaron springing back on the couch in an attitude of affrighted amazement at having been caught embracing the Widow Watt.

"Ham — it's you! We didn't hear you come in! You're early — !" Bell's father had leaped to his feet and was sidling about flapping his hands, as though in a fever of embarrassment. The widow sat blinking good-naturedly in the light.

"Mrs. Watt and I were just having a little chat!" The old comedian came waddling at Bell and tried to seize his suitcase. "I'll take it up for you, boy!" Bell managed to retain possession of the suitcase as he wrestled off his coat in the hall. "Guess you're pretty shocked, aren't you, Ham?" His father was whispering, scanning Bell's face with his bright little eyes. "This sort of foolishness at my age. Guess you're thinking of your sainted mother — and I don't blame you, son — but what's the harm in two lonely old people sharing broken dreams — ?"

"I'll stop in to see Grandpa." Bell started up the stairs with his suitcase. The treads croaked and the banisters chattered.

His father was disappointed. He'd gone to some trouble to stage Bell's entrance properly, and demanded more reaction than just this. "You're deeply offended, I can tell. Disgust is written all over your face. I suppose you're imagining all sorts of shameful things — "

Bell left him below with giant strides up into the dusty gloom.

One final shout: "We'll make you a nice cup of hot chocolate, Ham!"

Grandpa, hard of hearing, kept the TV volume high. It sounded from the back of the second floor like Armageddon: Beethoven cowboy music, gunfire, shouts and screams. The TV remained on always, even when Grandpa slept, even during those few awful hours when no programs were available, and the channel pattern stayed on, bright and eager. The old man feared that if the set went off, he'd fade out finally, too; he demanded that a second set be kept ready in a closet nearby, like an extra heart.

"Hi, Grandpa, it's me, I'm back."

Bell had to roar. Grandpa was hunched on his pillowed bed, holding the remote-control channel changer in one hand which, slightly palsied, often stuttered programs back and forth, mixing gangsters, cartoons, sports, news, and monster movies that were old when Bell was young.

"How do you feel, Grandpa?"

The professor emeritus was all bones and wrinkles, but his eyes were sharp. Bell sometimes wondered if he weren't playing some terrific joke on them all. The old geezer had surveyed life and man for nearly nine decades and decided finally that TV was better. Grandpa lived in that box — he rode those Indian ponies, he zapped cops in old Chicago, he frugged and sang on velvet stages — and everything outside was dull and gray.

"Want some water, Grandpa?"

Once Grandpa had ridden real horses. He'd been an imperious, black-haired rascal, given to bursts of enthusiasm and anger. The day he retired he'd gone hunting and killed a moose. Then what? He'd drifted down that same dream river the old adventurer Burr had traveled toward a vision of easy empire — and Grandpa had found it glowing at his fingertips. Lucky Grandpa. Burr had lived too soon.

"I went to Washington, Grandpa. Remember when you took me there?"

Grandpa had dispensed with conversation. The TV did all the talking. Even Bell, on his perfunctory visits, found his attention wandering toward the set, as though the real Grandpa were there inside, producing an endless lecture, vividly illustrated, with lightning costume changes and impersonations.

"It's still the way it was then."

But he knew it wasn't. He'd seen a different Washington with his own changed eyes. He'd been a boy before, viewing a myth. But now he'd seen an ancient city. The force of events had hustled it through centuries. It seemed exhausted. And if here Grandpa had aged into self-parody — the history teacher congealed before mock history, an endless succession of meaningless events — what senile jokes were snickering through those antiquated federal halls?

"Grandpa, let me fix your covers."

But Grandpa didn't want his covers fixed. He was soaking up Americana, and didn't want to miss a minute of it. What a lot of zapping there was. Burr zapped Hamilton, North zapped South, Sergeant York zapped Kaiser Bill, and now and then there were comic turns and songs that would put lumps in your throat, and quiz programs — "Who killed Kennedy?" — and then more zapping.

"Nice to see you, Grandpa."

Yes, it was wonderful. The old soul had been gathered to a many-channeled heaven. But those shadows dancing on that screen, weren't they as valid in their way as those other shadows men created as they groped through life's fog, shaping evanescent forms with blind fingers? Bell, watching the Old West myth on the TV screen, thought of the child Bell who'd viewed the folk dream of capital Washington on the screen of schoolbook myths. Yes, maybe Grandpa knew well enough. He'd taught history all his life: a superspectacular, with zaps and gags and songs. Was it real, was it true? It didn't matter. The students would never know, nor would the teachers, either. The facts darkened the sky like migrating birds; one man might shoot down only a few of them. To teach at all, one taught other people's prejudices and hunches and guesses, one filled books with them, one filled a life with them — and at the end, having helped create this unreal reality of history, one was allowed uninterruptedly to watch the real unreality of TV.

He waved good-bye to the hermit (who, after one suspicious glance, hadn't looked his way) and took his suitcase to his own room down the hall. It was chill and damp. He could remember Norma there, sucking hard candies as she read Jane Austen through the pale summer nights, while he sprawled in silent torment on the bed beside her, embracing the erotic phantoms of fitful dreams. If only she'd chosen Boccaccio.

He went downstairs. His father had made the chocolate too sweet, as usual. Bell drank some of it at the kitchen sink, then poured the rest away. Mrs. Watt was toiling up the back stairs with Grandpa's oatmeal and a change of sheets. Her Romeo had changed costume; he'd put on his Sunday suit, blue serge, and found an imitation carnation left over from some ancient occasion, which he'd thrust into his lapel.

"With your permission, son, I'd like to see Arlene home." Old Aaron strained up on tiptoe to see if Bell would react to the unexpected use of Mrs. Watt's first name. Bell didn't. "The streets are so slippery tonight — and besides, I ought to pay my respects to the family, don't you think?" Mrs. Watt lived with an old maid cousin six blocks away. "I mean, I want to demonstrate that my intentions are honorable!" Bell's father began picking at the scabs on his skull. "One thing worries me, though. Do you think Grandpa would object to our union?"

"No."

"He's too far gone, I suppose. You know, he gets them mixed up sometimes — Arlene and Norma, I mean." Bell's father once more was disappointed by Bell's poker face. He plucked Bell's sleeve. "Listen, Ham. I'm ashamed to ask it, but could you spare me a dollar to treat Arlene to a sundae at the drugstore?"

That, too, was unnecessary. Old Aaron had plenty in the household cashbox. But Bell produced the dollar.

"Thanks, son! Gee, that's swell!" The old swain folded the bill and tucked it into his breast pocket. He smelled heavily of after-shave lotion. "I won't forget your generosity, Ham." He giggled. "And Arlene — well, you know how deeply she respects you. I'm sure she would never expect you to call her Mom."

Bell hid in the bathroom until they left. From the living-room window he watched them hobbling together along the icy sidewalk, arm in arm, his father glancing back in triumph every few steps, even removing his hat to let the lamplight bounce off his dome, and waving the hat a time or two, a great-hearted Byronic gesture inspired by romance — a lover's salute to his son, the neighbors, the town, the world.

Bell telephoned the Lundquist number. Still, no answer. He guessed Mrs. Lundquist would be at her lingerie shop in St. Paul, or at her apartment there. He had the numbers. Should he try to call her there? He really had nothing to report. He kept the receiver to his ear, listening to the distant ringing — was there another noise there, too, in the background? Perhaps he was being too suspicious. "That you, Muller?" he said into the phone. "Can you hear me, boy?" Then he hung up.

The house smelled of his father's lotion. It had even wafted upstairs. Bell checked Grandpa, who was viewing patchwork programs stitched out by his palsy — a roller-skating contest unpredictably alternating with cartoons and an old Nelson Eddy movie. In his own room, Bell fingered his lecture notes. The Rise of Executive Power — the rise of Muller, of Grosch, of Nomad. And when something rises, something else falls. What was falling?

He stared out his window. It faced southeast, toward Detroit. New snow was coming down. All the little blue TV lights were blurred by it. They flickered like spirit gas in a graveyard — blue souls pulsing out of those windows, one after the other. He stood mesmerized by patterns: black night, white snow, blue TV gas. Did form follow function, or was it the other way around? In either case, those houses weren't houses; they were supersize sets, and the families faithfully viewing —

Who was viewing them in turn?

He went swiftly downstairs. Suppose he were Muller — or that ex-halfback Moss — and he wanted to watch the house in case Bell slipped out to lead the way to Lundquist? At the end of the block, across the street, was a service station, now closed for the night. A man in a car there could see the house quite well — and a car was there, all right, parked at an angle to face Bell's way; he couldn't tell whether anyone was sitting inside, but the nearest streetlamp showed exhaust steam rising through the snowflakes; the engine was idling.

Bell got into his coat and went out the kitchen door, through the alley, and traveled a roundabout route so he could come up to the rear of the service station and approach the car from the back.

He jerked the door open. "I'm Bell," he said. "You want me?"

The man inside, startled, had made an involuntary movement toward an inside pocket.

"You're Moss, aren't you?"

"Mister —" The man broke off, alert, puzzled. Bell guessed he had no instructions on how to deal with this.

"Pico said you were asking for me. Well, here I am. What do you want?" Bell was shaking a bit, partly because of the cold.

"Mister, you've made some kind of mistake."

"Maybe you've made the mistake, Moss."

Moss said nothing. His hat shadowed his face. He kept his ungloved hands limber, slowly flexing his fingers around the steering wheel.

"Didn't Muller tell you?" Bell said. "I'm working for Nomad, too. I didn't know it, but I am." He backed off. He'd forgotten his hat, and that Canadian wind was boring into his bald spot. "Drop around Ayle Hall tomorrow about ten, Moss, if you haven't got anything better to do. I'll tell you all about it — the Rise of Executive Power, old buddy. In the meantime, climb off my back."

He turned and walked straight toward the house. As he crossed the street, he heard a discreet click as Moss eased the car door shut. From the opposite direction, a block away, he saw a familiar rotund form hopping snow clods, and to get back inside before old Aaron spied him, he cleared the hedge with a rebound leap, just as he'd done in the good old days down at the gym, and zagged his way among the shrubs, dribbling a dream basketball, and entered the kitchen door again to go ghost-quick up to his room where he sat panting on his bed, smelling those old-house smells curling beneath his door, as melting snowflakes shivered down his cheeks.

H E WOKE FROM a nightmare. All night, it seemed, he'd dreamed of chasing Lundquist. The old prof had legged ahead of him on nimble pins, always within sight, never within reach — a cartoon Lundquist with head on backward, sticking out his tongue at pursuing Bell while running full tilt away. Bell dogged him through a vast slum, tenements built of charcoal, streets of ashes into which he sank deeper with every step, as if being sucked into a subterranean domain of infernal poverty where would live the disadvantaged of Hell. Then he tumbled out of sleep entirely, waking with a palpitating erection beneath the blankets and more lost hair embroidering his pillow.

He left early for the University. The Ford wouldn't start, so he had to stop at the service station — where Moss's tire tracks hadn't quite been drowned by the new snow — to have someone work on it during the day. Halfway to the campus, he discovered he wasn't wearing a tie. That panicked him. He, Bell, forgot his *tie?* He took it as a symbol of some frightful carelessness, and he crossed the remaining streets with extra caution, lest a suicidal urge rush him under wheels.

He hesitated when he reached the library. Within, it now occurred to him, Lundquist had left a trail — his books, forty years of stepping-stones, leading maybe nowhere. Bell went to the special section of the open stacks where the old man's work was kept. All volumes were there. He selected the most recent, published in March — the month the author had gone to Nomad — and flipped through it to find Lundquist's last known address. The book was a study of Spanish-speaking communities in New York, Pittsburgh, Detroit, Baltimore. *Detroit.* Bell went down to the main desk and checked the book out. He'd take it to Detroit, then. Norma and Lundquist together. Or maybe not. Even if he found people who remembered Lundquist, they wouldn't know where the old boy was now. Unless Lundquist had kept in touch. That was possible. If anyone was known in the poverty world, he'd be. He'd roamed it all his life. He'd built up connections. If he was in retreat somewhere, the word might have gotten around.

And what else was there to do? Run classifieds in the papers — *Carl L., come home, all forgiven* — ?

The lecture went badly. In lieu of the tie, Bell had to wear his scarf, which he feared would appear an affectation; the hall was overheated as it was. He caught hopeful glances from sophomores who on Friday had witnessed Bell's substitute, Pico, split the lectern with an ill-advised karate gesture during his discourse on the Supreme Court. Maybe Professor Bell would give them a treat, too. He seemed headed that way. He couldn't tune his voice properly. He either whispered his students forward in their seats or bellowed them back. Some phrases he gargled, others he stuttered. His tongue played tricks. "Normal growth rate" became "norma growth rate." He referred to "grosch national product" and "moss media." (Was Moss auditing the lecture? Bell couldn't see him anywhere — but then, he thought, he'd destroyed Moss's value by pouncing on him, hadn't he? Moss had been compromised. They'd have to send another one.)

His students were restive. They were waiting for him to continue. He'd paused — how long? He hastened to resume. *"The federal executive acts as a mediator between social and economic groups . . ."* Really? Was that true? He was struck not so much by doubt as by wonder. *". . . seeking out and identifying potential conflicts, in order to deal with them before they harden into troublesome realities."* He goggled at his notes. Had he actually written that? Amazing. He couldn't repress a snicker of satisfaction: *heh.* It echoed in the hall. "It's a form of environmental control," he ad-libbed, and almost expected several Moss-Mullers to leap to their feet in consternation. Was Bell beginning to harden into a troublesome reality? He'd better be dealt with, then.

He got through the rest of it somehow. As he was stuffing his notes into his briefcase, a pimpled sophomore approached to ask if he didn't think state government was becoming superfluous. "I don't know," Bell replied. "I honestly don't know. I used to know, but I don't any more. Lots of things are becoming superfluous. Maybe that's one of them." The soph dutifully scribbled notes. "Wait a minute," Bell protested. "I didn't say anything." The soph grinned shyly and mumbled his thanks. He shuffled away, but Bell grabbed his hat and overcoat and pursued him. "You really want something to write down, kid? Go paint the Capitol purple. Then they'll teach government to you — I can't do it."

The soph sidled out with an uncertain smile into the brilliant blaze of sunlight and snow. Bell clapped his hat on and held his briefcase between his knees while he got into his overcoat. Oh, yes. He saw a stranger skulking down there at the base of the steps, a man older than he, with heavy shoulders and a tough face. Descending in a hurry, Bell almost took a header on the ice. He lurched, flailed his briefcase for balance, finally had to broadjump down, ankle-deep in snow crust right in front of the stranger. "Hi, fella," Bell said. "They sent you in for Jerry Moss, I guess." But he guessed wrong this time. It was just the new wrestling coach, heading for the gym.

B Y MIDAFTERNOON, HE was driving east toward the Twin Cities. He'd gotten leave from Professor Glass, but not from his father. Old Aaron had been outraged. Bell knew why. Without him as audience, the courting of Mrs. Watt would

be pointless. His father no doubt had at least a week of fes-
tival drama planned out, an entire comic cycle in which he'd
play all parts in his belled jester's cap, not sparing tears when
called for. But Bell had moved so quickly that all the old man
could do was to bluster at the door, then to feign stomach
pains — "Cancer at last, Ham!" — and finally, as Bell hurried
down the steps toward the revived Ford, to stand panting in
displeasure on the porch, like an old pugdog.

Bell hadn't looked back. He'd timed himself. It had taken
him two minutes flat to carry his suitcase downstairs, break
the news to his father, and then make his exit.

Now he was humming along at a safe fifty miles an hour.
In the back was his suitcase, Lundquist's book stuffed in with
the shirts and socks. The ice-patched highway ran between
dead wheatlands drowned in snow. Was he being followed?
He imagined every trailing car to be loaded with halfbacks.
From time to time he'd stop at a service station or roadside
diner to see which other cars stopped, too, but the few that
did were driven by farmers, by grandmas, by speckled youths.

He kept going. It was like running in that nightmare slum.
He seemed to make no progress. Every mile looked like the
last one; the towns were all the same. The sun seemed frozen
in one place in the sky — and he saw what seemed literal
proof of timeless time: the odometer wasn't moving. It was
stuck at 88,156.4 miles. Had the mechanic broken it when
putting in the new battery, or had it expired by itself of the
cold? Maybe Moss had inadvertently gummed it up last
night while installing the secret beeper that now permitted
them to follow him electronically on the illuminated face of
a magic map in some Washington dugout.

The Ford began losing other faculties. The heater sank to tepidity, the speedometer registered a series of Grand Prix velocities before dying, the glove compartment door flopped open on a ruined hinge, and the engine itself, always noisy, ran for times in sinister silence, then produced a barnyard symphony of moos, gurgles, quacks, and neighs. The car was doing a death dance on the Minneapolis road, with shivering Bell congealed at the wheel.

Each time he had to stop, he was afraid he'd never start again — he or the car or both together. What urged him forward might be precisely as strong as what warned him back. He'd be caught forever in a crazy equilibrium — the Ford and he would rust to junk at the roadside. Darkness came; the headlights worked, at least, though now the heater had declined to bird's breath, and Bell feared frostbite.

He drove all night. Dawn found him red-eyed and blue-jawed, half-frozen in his seat and mad for sleep but still forcing the old car onward. His spirit was willing, but the machine was weak. At a midmorning fuel stop, the Ford quit absolutely. Its pistons popped, it bled bile from its pores, it shuddered under the mechanic's hands, and would go nowhere. Bell had no choice. He left it there for repairs or funeral, and caught a bus.

He reached Minneapolis at 3 P.M. An hour later, he was snoring asleep, naked under a single sheet, in an overheated room of a cheap riverfront hotel in St. Paul. At eight the porter woke him, as requested, and by nine he was in a cab en route not to Mrs. Lundquist's address, but, craftily, to a corner two blocks north of it. He suspected he was being followed. He'd dreamed of it when sleeping, had thought of it when dressing, had become convinced of it while eating, and even hoped for it, as though he needed it to justify his movements. If Muller was trailing him, then he might really be going somewhere.

Afoot in Mrs. Lundquist's neighborhood, Bell made only fitful progress. He strode through the icy mist, stopped short at a store window to cast a sidelong glance for signs of followers, then circled the block, at one point turning abruptly on his heel to retrace his steps — noticing a dozen wandering figures like his own, any one of whom could be whatever he chose to imagine.

"Screw it," he said finally, and went directly to Mrs. Lundquist's address. The shop was dark, but above it, the apartment windows showed lights. Finding the street door locked, he struck a match to locate the buzzer and press it, and after what seemed several minutes heard her voice in the speaker.

"It's Bell," he said. "Professor Bell."

She buzzed back, tripping the lock to let him in, and was waiting for him at the top of the steps, her door ajar.

"Sorry to barge in on you," he said, haltingly. She'd evidently been caught in the tub. She had a scrubbed look, without makeup, and was in a wrapper and slippers. "I didn't phone ahead because — well, I have reason to believe your phone is tapped."

She stared at him. She seemed annoyed and amused at the same time. "Well, come in for a minute then and tell me," she said. It wasn't much of a welcome.

The living room was snug and neat. Bell sat gingerly on a midget sofa, his hat in his hands.

"You haven't found Carl?"

"No." He sensed she was irked by his presence. Still, oddly, she seemed to be on the verge of hilarity, even to the point of suddenly turning away as if to hide an irrepressible smile. Bell felt ludicrous; it vexed him. Was he that homely? "Your information was right, Mrs. Lundquist. He quit the migrant project, I don't know how long ago. He got into some sort of dispute about it — it isn't what it appears to be on the surface — and even they have no idea where he is."

She nodded solemnly, she frowned, she paced about, but Bell had the sensation that she was preoccupied with something else entirely.

"Have you heard anything?" he asked.

"Oh, no. Not a word." She glanced toward the back of the apartment, as though considering whether to offer him coffee. Then, evidently deciding against it, she stopped pacing and sat down.

"Well, you see I'm no further along than I was," Bell said. "Right now I'm on my way to Detroit — "

"That's where your wife is, isn't it?"

"Yes, that's true, and I certainly won't bill you for the time I spend on personal matters, but I have some reason to believe I may be able to pick up a trace there that might help lead to your husband."

Mrs. Lundquist said nothing. She seemed alert to some unseen possibility, perhaps a telephone call. Whatever it was, it appeared to give her intermittent entertainment. He expected her to laugh aloud.

"You don't need money?" she asked at last.

"No, no." (She'd advanced him several hundred against expenses.)

"Excuse me, Mr. Bell. You said something about my phone being tapped — or did you?"

Bell cleared his throat and twirled his hat in his fingers. "It may seem strange to you," he said, almost shamefacedly, "but the project people are trying to find Professor Lundquist, too. When he fell out with them, he apparently made some threats — "

"That's Carl," she said.

" — and they're anxious to find him so they can induce him to return, or at least not to harm what they're trying to do. It's part of a larger work, so I was told by the man at the foundation, Dr. Grosch. They're attempting to develop a mathematical system for handling problems of deprived human groups, like the migrants." He hesitated. Was her apartment bugged? He glanced about suddenly.

"Yes?" She uttered the word insistently, as if to command his attention.

"Well, anyway, they think that I know where Professor Lundquist is. They refuse to believe I don't. It's a bit complicated to explain how this misunderstanding developed, but I've been followed and spied on ever since I left Washington."

"Surely not."

"Absolutely." Restless under her scrutiny, he got to his feet. She rose, too, assuming he was prepared to leave, but he only went to the window to part the draperies and stare down suspiciously into the street. He could see no one. "Well," he conceded, "I can't honestly say they've watched my every move — I don't know that — but I'm willing to bet they know where I am right now, and if you picked up that phone over there, they'd be listening." He prowled about the little room impatiently, thinking that she was skeptical. "I'll bet they've entered that country house of yours in your absence and gone through every single thing. Why they want to find him that badly I'm not certain, but I do know that in order to check on one little part of my story, they flew a man up from Chicago, I guess it was." He felt grim, and looked it, as he came to a stop at the far end of the room before a closed door.

"Well, maybe you'd better leave," she said, in some anxiety, but he still had the impression she wasn't paying much attention to what he said.

He was affronted by her attitude. Didn't she believe him? "This apartment may be bugged!"

"Bugged? Really? Well, that's all the more reason for us not to talk here, then."

It was at that moment and in that mood that Bell heard a noise in the room behind him, beyond the closed door. By instinct, he whirled, and heedless of Mrs. Lundquist's cry — *"don't"* — wrenched the knob and gave the door a push.

There revealed within the room was a plumpish man in his fifties, standing beside the bed with his face contorted in the process of emitting a second sneeze (the first was what Bell had heard), carefully holding a pair of eyeglasses in one hand, the other hand being at his waist, where a bathtowel was wrapped, shielding an otherwise unclothed figure.

Everything happened at once. The rotund satyr in the bedroom executed his sneeze, with a piteous glance at Bell. Mrs. Lundquist gave a despairing whoop of laughter, flopped down in her chair, and slapped her thighs. Bell took an erratic backward step; he almost lost his footing on a throw rug, and, flailing for balance, dropped his hat. The man in the bedroom toddled forward, hampered by his towel, to kick the door shut. "That isn't a spy, Bell," shouted Mrs. Lundquist through her laughter. "That's just Freddy!" she jumped up; her wrapper accidentally parted, revealing mature pink charms. Covering herself, she hustled giggling across the room to the closed bedroom door and called through it, "Stay put, Freddy. It's okay!"

Bell groped for his hat. He'd knocked it under the coffee table. "Don't worry," he gasped. "I'm going."

"No, wait a minute." Mrs. Lundquist had sunk back on her chair again, clutching her side, tormented by laughter, with tears running down her face. "I've got to explain — "

"You don't owe me any explanation." Bell was straightening his hat brim.

She was recovering herself. "Don't be such a goddamned prude, Bell! You've scared poor old Freddy to death. He wouldn't believe you were you — he swore it must be a ruse. He's been expecting his wife's detectives to come busting in with cameras for weeks — !"

Bell was trying to maintain an attitude of sophisticated composure. The word *prude* really stung.

" — and he probably got dust in his nose hiding under the bed!" She gave another yelp of laughter. "If only Carl could have seen your faces when you met!"

"Maybe it's just as well he didn't."

"Maybe you're right. He wouldn't care for Freddy." She got up again, wiping her eyes. "What's he doing in there?" She went over to the bedroom door. "You all right, Freddy?"

There was a muffled response. Bell remained uncomfortably rooted in mid-room. He was perspiring in his overcoat, which he had never removed.

"My God," said Mrs. Lundquist, returning. "I was half-afraid he'd try to climb down by the window." She took a bottle and three snifters from the sideboard and put them on the coffee table. "Take your coat off, Bell. Sit down. I missed half of what you were telling me before about Carl and those people."

"Frankly, the situation doesn't seem quite — "

"Don't be ridiculous," she said. "Take your coat off. Take off that pomposity, too." She poured brandy into the three snifters. "You haven't caught me in adultery, you know. Freddy, yes. He's married — but I'm not." She gave Bell a sidelong glance. Astonished, he sat down on the sofa again, still in his overcoat.

At this point, Freddy emerged from the bedroom, fully clothed in suit and topcoat, hat in hand, transformed into a bourgeois man of business — except that his apple cheeks were overripe and his eyes apprehensively protruded.

"Have some brandy, Freddy," Mrs. Lundquist said.

Freddy wasn't having any. He gave Bell a look of alarm, mumbled something unintelligible to Mrs. Lundquist as he passed by, and at the outer door turned with some dignity to spread his hands in an uncertain gesture of appeal. Then, silently, he left, closing the door behind him.

Bell and Mrs. Lundquist sat without speaking for what seemed like several minutes. Bell downed his own brandy and then, absently, Freddy's as well. Mrs. Lundquist was quietly heaving with laughter. From time to time she muttered: "Poor Freddy. My God — his face!"

She refilled both of Bell's snifters. She hadn't touched hers. "No, sir," she said, finally. "I'm a spinster in the eyes of the law. I'm not Mrs. Lundquist. I'm just plain Rose Neyland."

"Guh," said Bell.

"I guess there's no point in hiding this little fact from you, now that you've found me in *flagrante* whatever. That's why I'm anxious about Carl. If he's had the bad manners to die, then I won't get a nickel of his estate. We'd agreed to get married, you see, to make sure I got my wifely due for wifely duties performed — he knew he wasn't getting any younger — but the selfish old bastard wouldn't take a single afternoon off from his work to go to a J.P. and have it done, and then this migrant project came along and away he went, without making a decent woman of me, damn him." She spoke, however, with no bitterness. "Why should Carl's nephew and his cousins or whatever he has inherit when he dies? They haven't done anything to earn it, while I've managed to live with Carl for some fifteen years, off and on."

"Hum," said Bell, sipping brandy.

"I may have some rights as a common-law wife, but I haven't looked into it. What do you think?"

"Don't know," said Bell.

"If Carl's still alive, then I'll take him to the church in handcuffs if I have to — but suppose you can't find him? Suppose he just doesn't show up? Even for legal wives, there's a long waiting period before a missing man's declared dead — well, you can understand why I've gone to all this trouble and expense, can't you?"

"Sure," said Bell. He was bemused, weary, and embarrassed. Mrs. Lundquist — or Miss Neyland — wasn't being careful with her wrapper. She sat pouting over her troubles, with one plump leg showing, thigh and all. He looked everywhere else — at his brandy, the floor, the walls — but the room seemed too small to accommodate his gaze, which returned, despite his efforts, to that exposed flesh.

She either didn't notice or didn't care. "So, anyway, Bell, you'd better tell me again how things went in Washington."

"Oh, okay, Mrs., um — "

"I'm still Mrs. Lundquist, Bell. You can call me Rose if you want."

He didn't call her anything. He began a rambling account of his adventures with Dr. Grosch and Muller, of his return to the University to find Moss waiting for him, and of his trip by Ford and bus to St. Paul, all the while being aware of her thigh, of her intense speculative concentration on what he was saying — which made him ramble all the more — and of his own befuddlement, the result of the brandy and his lack of sleep. He even told her about his dream, his phone conversation with Norma, and his father's antic courtship of the Widow Watt. It seemed he couldn't stop jabbering. The room became smaller, darker. He was yawning terrifically. Her wrapper, he saw, was as tightly drawn up high as it was shamelessly slack below; he could see nipples projecting. In desperation, he drained his snifter — third or fourth? — and told her everything he could remember about Grandpa Bell.

He awoke to strange sensations. The room was really dark. A dim light was glowing faintly from some other room. There was a considerable weight on his legs, and something small and warm was invading his ear. Good God. He'd dozed off. Now, it seemed, Mrs. Lundquist was attacking him — tongue

in his ear, hot little hand inside his unbuttoned shirt, unwrap-
pered flesh all over him. He, still attired for the street, was
overdressed, but she made up for it.

"Whoa, there," he mumbled, struggling. Together they
sprawled along the mini-sofa, Bell underneath, Mrs. Lundquist on top wrenching at buttons. "What's going on?" he
cried out, weakly. His head flopped back over one end of the
sofa, his legs over the other.

"You know damned well what's going on," she said, un-
knotting his tie. "You spoiled poor Freddy's evening, but
I'm not going to let you spoil mine!"

This was no seduction, it was outright rape. Set to music.
She'd turned the radio on. It sang spooky jazz. Bell could
have tossed her across the room, but he was thrashing feebly
in a brandy fog endeavoring to think of a courteous means of
defense. *Madam, you may have misjudged my intentions
just because I glanced at your thigh.* His belt was whipped
away like a flying snake. Trying to guard his fly, next on her
list, he lost his shoes; she was scampering along his supine
form from head to toe and back again. Writhing beneath
her, he was belabored by knees, elbows, breasts of no negligible
proportions, and always her busy fingers.

Bell's sexual history had few pages. Apart from cold joys
with Norma, he'd broken female flesh thrice only: two times
with prostitutes on boozy college nights long ago, and once
later, when he was a soldier at the aerial photo school, with
a zany navy wife who'd read the Marquis de Sade at Bryn
Mawr and pathetically sought to inveigle Bell into various
depravities (one had required, as props, five towels and an
evening slipper).

Now here, threatened by adultery — he was married, like Freddy, even if she wasn't — he found himself infected by her insouciance. It was outrageous, shameful, an affront to his manhood; also ridiculous. He managed to save his glasses, reaching out to set them on the coffee table, and thus briefly one-armed, was unable to ward off a sudden lipward plunge with a tremendous tooth-tingling kiss, complete with serpentine tonguing and steamy vampire breath. He tried to surface. He felt he needed time to think. Couldn't they take a coffee break and rationally review the pros and cons?

She achieved a neck lock. Bell, seeking to break loose without undertaking grips of his own that might be misinterpreted, worked free by shoving her north as he wriggled south, which involved him in a facial tour of ample contours from chin to hip. There they parted. Mrs. Lundquist took a mild header over one end of the sofa; Bell went over the other.

"Think what you're doing!" he exclaimed, weaving to his feet. He was shoeless, beltless, tieless, unbuttoned, unzipped. His naked adversary was coming at him again, uttering wordless little battle cries. Bell, trying to rebutton, was hampered by outer garments. He shucked off his overcoat and suit jacket, working one arm at a time, needing the other to hold up his pants, as he danced in stockinged feet around tables and chairs, eluding her tigerish rushes. "We've got a client relationship, Mrs. Lundquist!" Unencumbered by coat and jacket, he zipped his fly and began working on his flapping shirt. She charged, he dodged. A rocking chair trod on his toe. The overhead fixture cuffed him above the ear. The whole room seemed rape-minded, too. "I'm a m-m-married man!" The radio hummed up higher, maybe stimulated

by amorous vibrations. Bell roared above it, "Remember —
this place may be bugged!"

"Bug *you*, Bell," she yelled back. But she was momentarily
winded, and had to bend to ease a stitch; in the indistinct light
she resembled a matronly naiad inspecting a pool. Bell took
the opportunity to hunt his belt. There it was, on the threshold of the kitchenette. He stooped to pick it up. She
grabbed him from behind; with one great tug, she brought
his trousers to his ankles, and, as he frantically kicked his feet
free, she downed his shorts as well.

Then he turned on her. *"That's enough."* He howled; she'd
stripped him to his pride. *"Who the hell do you think you
are?"* She was bent on using him, unasked. Damned ungra-
cious. Her form of environmental control, maybe. Grab
everything in sight, regardless. Still, he was a gentleman.
"Sorry," he said as he spun her around and hoisted her under
one arm; no easy feat, for she was massy, if short. Even as he
lugged her off (he had the notion of penning her in the bedroom somehow), she treated him to tweaks, pokes, gooses,
nibbles. The bedroom was quite dark. He lurched against
the bed and tumbled her on it, but she contrived to haul him
down, too, with an earhold and the other hand indelicately
placed.

Thus Bell fell. Like other victims of rape, he could not
stand forever. There were human limits. He was prey to fatigue (he'd battled long enough), prey to admiration (the
little lady never gave up), and likewise to a certain incipient
lust. They rolled and roiled together in the darkness, Bell still
playing the part of stainless knight, but there was a difference
now that began tumescently to declare itself — a columnar

fifth column betraying his rising purpose. Pale thoughts of moral reckonings blew like bubbles through his consciousness. He couldn't stop, though. Didn't want to. She'd unbuttoned him inside, too.

H E LEFT AT 4 A.M. The street was clogged with mist, the lamps were dull. Muller's agents, if any, must have frozen stiff in doorways while he'd been up there. He shivered as he walked, flailing his arms and stamping his feet.

"You okay, buddy?"

A police cruiser had slipped up beside him. There were two officers inside.

"Sure, fine," Bell said. (Should he go with them to the precinct station and make a complaint: raped by a 125-pound redhead, age forty-six, Neyland alias Lundquist?) They were waiting for some explanation. "Actually, I'm trying to find a cab," he said. He told them he'd been out late playing poker.

"Hop in, buddy."

Bell hopped. It was warm inside, and a free ride downtown. The cops examined him en route for signs of larceny, murder, perversion, mayhem, found none, and so acquitted him at the curb in front of his hotel.

The night was young, though, in riotous St. Paul.

"Wanna girl twenny bucks a quickie?" asked the seventy-year-old night porter, as the elevator rose.

"Uh uh."

"Nothin' else?" The porter implied that any request could be filled by whatever walked on two legs or four, had fleece or feathers, skin smooth or scaly, with tail or without, not excluding his own withered self.

"Nope," said Bell.

He napped an hour, woke, shaved, showered. The sun broke upward as if through dirty river ice.

Good-bye, St. Paul. He took a cab to the depot and boarded a Chicago train. Jouncing along on the ratty coach seat, he thought of the middle-aged lady he'd left behind him, a buttsprung victim of his liberated passion. Ah, she'd raised more in him than flesh. Breaking rules, she'd made him break them, too. She'd driven him beyond the borders of his experience into savage country — and he'd thrived there. Still, he wasn't at ease. The taboos she'd made him smash had left some splinters in him. Shame, Bell. Ancestral whispers chilled his veins, cold Puritan mist risen from his hot blood. Norma, Norma. He tried to fix his thoughts on her. His demi-virgin bride had run away, yes, and now he was running after her. Could he help it if his route had carried him into an unexpected cul-de-sac?

No point in denying it, his morals were as rumpled as his clothes; some buttons hung by threads. He felt embarrassed, also like laughing.

"Ticket?" said the conductor.

"It's been punched," Bell joked, but the conductor didn't smile.

He'd brought along a little book on games theory, borrowed from Dr. Slough of Math. Maybe a bit of study would school his thoughts. He opened it and began reading.

As Dr. Grosch had told him, games theory was the analysis of odds. Which horse would win? How many bombers would penetrate the air defenses of Redland? If Player X moved knight to king's bishop's three, what would be the new roster of options available to Player Y? These were conflict situations: Horse A versus Horses B through Z, Player X versus Player Y. The collision of conflict factors — attack move 001 met by defense capability 020 — produced a numerical statement of the odds involved, and the odds on all possible moves were marshaled box-style in a matrix of numbers, the static heart of the Game. Ah, but Slough's little book contained merely simple illustrations. When there were, so to speak, a million horse races in progress, then the giant computers would furiously race as well, galloping up dust clouds of ever changing odds, shifting matrixes of numbers without end, beyond the power of man to count or know.

What a lot of games there were. Military games (Redland versus Blueland); commercial games (marketer versus consumer); biological games (crop versus pests and blight), and industrial games (product versus costs). Now would there be a poverty game, too? Nomad versus the poor? All Dr. Grosch needed was enough relevant data, accurately summarized in numerical form — and what, after all, was the obsession of Americans if not this? Man had begun as a true nomad, an oppressed and restless wanderer gathering what nature had spread on the land. Now his descendants were data gatherers. He, Bell, was busy gathering, too, had been trained to do nothing else, could not possibly avoid it. He was helping shrink human experience into Grosch-form for the computer. Inescapable.

On the other hand, maybe old Grosch was right. Nobody'd been shot or tortured by a computer, had they? To be shoved around by numbers wasn't so bad. Besides, Grosch could deal only with men in the mass; individuals couldn't be gamed. Grosch never would be able to lock him, Bell, into a number matrix. No love game versus Norma, no parent game versus old Aaron, no psyche game (ego vs. id).

Still, suppose that after Dr. Grosch got all his numbers etched onto the tapes and punched the buttons, the best answer to the New Guinea problem proved to be Muller's, after all?

H E ARRIVED IN Detroit late at night. After he checked into a hotel, he thought of phoning Norma, but then decided against it. He needed to find her alone. It would be better to go out there and watch the house until she left by herself, then tail her. But what were his chances — what were the odds? Maybe he could consult a games-theory oracle to learn the optimum program for getting to Norma. He fell asleep trying.

"*Hello, Norma.*"

It was morning. He was practicing before a mirror. By turns, he sought to look soulful, despondent, firm, sincere — and took a crack at being handsome, too, but couldn't manage that one.

"*Hi, Norma.*"

He went down for breakfast, still practicing, giving himself languishing looks in the mirrored paneling of the Breakfast Nook, eyeing the waitresses with reproach, with forgiveness, with steely ardor — one pouted at him, another yawned — and paying his bill with a dollar and a sentimental sigh for the granny cashier. "*Norma, I've come for you at last,*" he whispered on his way out.

Flowers! Candy! He bought roses for Norma, a pound of caramels for Mom, and a fistful of perfectos for Pop. "*Norma, please accept this token of my steam.*" Still, as he rode the bus, he couldn't repress a retrograde thought of his auburn client: how she'd sprawled when he'd chucked her off the sofa, ass-upward. There was an optimum program for you!

He alighted in a gray checkerboard of duplexes, each with scraggy yard, stunted trees, cement walk, TV antenna. Mile after mile it ran, this blue-collar homeowners' paradise. The old union wars that had made it possible were forgotten. On weekends Pop watched ball games on TV, Mom took Cousin Clara downtown to buy a hat — and Norma read *Northanger Abbey* again and smoked a hundred cigarettes.

There she was. Bell had been lurking a block away, clutching his gifts, a conspicuous figure in that scrubby duplex plain. He saw her leave the house — slacks beneath her coat, scarf above — and in excitement he dropped his waxed green paperload of roses.

She was walking in the opposite direction, toward the shopping center. Bell, bending for the flowers, lost the candy, too, then his hat, finally grabbed them all up in order to follow her, and got a sideways glimpse of a third party: a man in a brown overcoat and brown fedora sauntering with elaborate deliberation a block behind him. A halfback for sure. Bell cursed, but went after Norma, wondering as he passed her house if Mom would spy him from the window, recognize him by his height and basketball gait, and run out to squelch him with a mop.

Suppose Norma turned in at the house of a friend? He increased his pace, but she'd always been a fast walker; to catch her now, he'd have to break into a lope, and he felt he was on public show, striding after his quick-legged bride out on this open stage, with a Muller creeping after him (did they expect to find Lundquist *here?*), and a hundred housewives inspecting the tree of them from the windows they passed.

Norma didn't stop. She went to the shopping center. Bell, eighty yards back, imagined a confrontation among canned goods at the supermarket, but she flung her cigarette aside — it still smoked when he reached it, hot from her cold lips — and entered the drugstore. The Mullerman had managed to vanish in the parking lot.

Bell's heart was pounding. *"Hello, Norma,"* he practiced, his voice ragged. His eyes were damp from wind and apprehension. *Be a man,* he ordered. He counted to fifty, took a deep breath, but overventilated, had a momentary touch of dizziness, did it again, again, and pushed his way into the drugstore with a mild bun of oxygenation. He tottered with his roses, candy, and cigars along the jammed aisles among mammoth displays of hair tonic, depilatories, denture pastes, creams, salves, and lotions, which threatened to leap out in hard-sell haste at every passerby and apply themselves to armpits, gums, loins, bald spots. He rounded a corner past a mountain of tweezers hungering, crablike, for excess nasal hair. Then he glimpsed her in a booth sucking a strawberry soda with two straws.

"Hello, Norma."

She gawked up, still sucking. Her jaw dropped slightly. A bead of soda appeared on her lower lip.

And Bell was smitten by the realization that she wasn't alone, after all.

There were three young women in the booth with her.

He stood there grinning foolishly. Norma was mumbling something — introducing everybody? — but he was concentrating on the problem of sticking the roses under his candy arm so he could tip his hat.

They knew who he was, though. Sucked greedily at their sodas, sucked at him with their eyes.

Not friendly.

Bell was reddening, miserable. Time was dead. He'd stand forever there.

"Listen Norma we'll get going," rattled off Phyllis-Alice-Malice Whoevertheywere, flapping elbows, grabbing purses, rubbing their bottoms Bell-wards along the fake leather cushions. Bell recoiled to let them out, caromed lightly off a lady passing by, stuck his elbow among a display of toiletries, watched a dislodged truss complete with cardboard backing topple into his hand-held hat.

"No, I mean," Norma said. Good God, he saw that *she* was sliding out, too, with nary a glance at him. "I'll walk you — *we* will." He was included, then. "Home," she added, as the five of them wrestled air together confusedly in the aisle, and the word *home* pinched Bell's guts — Mom and Pop and Wilbur the dog who didn't like him, either. He longed to seize Norma by her long black hair and cry *shit* to the world, but by the time he got that truss back in place Norma and her pals were shooting along for the cash cage to pay and scram. He had to hurry outside after them.

He was panting, still hyperventilating, sucking in gray wads of Motor City carbon air, crushing the roses to rhubarb. Now he was in the center of the four women, now he was in front, behind, to one side. They were jabbering like magpies, flashing him bird glances to see if he were still there. Sometimes, oh joy, he was directly addressed.

"Do you like Detroit?"

"Wonderful."

"Better than — ?"

"Oh sure."

He couldn't tell them apart. They were all like Norma. Lean hipless young creatures with pale skin and long nervous fingers.

"You teach, um."

"History."

The Mullerman was nowhere to be seen. But there were cars cruising through those duplex streets.

"Well it must be um."

"Very interesting," said Bell.

Maybe Phyllis-Alice-Malice each was equipped with not only a mom and a pop but also a Bell, some crude jerk they'd left. He could almost smell their distaste for him. A staggering thought occurred — *Lesbians*. He rejected it. Never, not Norma. Not in *Detroit*. (But which one *was* Norma? Would he escort the wrong one home — and would it make any difference?)

They began peeling off one by one with asexual strides toward indistinguishable homes.

Bell and Norma were alone. For three seconds.

"Norma, I —"

"Listen, Bell, I'd better let them know you're here."

And off she went ahead.

So vanished his foolish hope that she'd rushed them all out of the drugstore in order to see him alone at the house.

Mom met him at the door. Wilbur looked up at him cross-eyed from between her legs.

"Professor Bell, this is an unexpected surprise."

Bell handed her the ruined roses. That waxed paper was cheap stuff. His sweaty palm was green from it.

"I must express a word of caution," she said, frowning at the gift. "Norma's daddy is not well and the slightest strain or shock — you know? I must therefore ask you."

"Oh I certainly."

"Please do." She meant him to come in. But not for long. Mom was five feet ten, frizzed hair, specs, a one-time secretary to a union local boss. Her clothes were cut by a tinsmith. She despised Bell, envied his learning, suspected him of sneering behind her back. How she glared!

Pop was installed in an armchair in the living room. He looked like a jaundiced baboon; as Bell entered, an expression of nausea soured his otherwise blank features. "Gimme the bowl, Nelly," he croaked, as Bell mumbled hello.

This was Bell's welcome. Norma was hiding in the bath-room. Wilbur squatted panting in front of the TV. Pop drooled bile into a bowl held by Mom's claws. Outside, America lay dying.

"Cigars?" said Bell. But he'd crushed those, too, somehow. *Imperfectos* now. He put their crumpled remains with the box of candy on a table, and, turning out of delicacy from the sight of his father-in-law's silent puking, gazed out the window. Where was Norma? He felt wretched and angry. He ought to leave. He was determined to stay.

Mom maneuvered him into the kitchen. He caught a glimpse of Norma. Yes, that was how they'd handle him: the sight of him made Pop vomit, but Pop couldn't be left alone. Norma would play nurse in the living room while Mom murdered Bell in the kitchen.

"I really wanted to talk to Norma," he told Mom. "That's why I came."

"Well at the present moment you see we're all upset by what may be the matter with Norma's daddy which we simply don't know but you can imagine we think everything."

"I'm certainly sorry he's ill, but if I could have ten minutes with my wife — "

"Norma is awful cut up you know, loving her poor daddy at a time like this I don't see if it would do any good."

"Just five minutes — "

"She's her daddy's baby an only child which I couldn't ex-pect you to understand — "

"I'm an only child, too!"

" — and if I may not have a college degree and all there are certain things at certain times and this simply isn't, Professor Bell."

She'd unwrapped the roses for a vase, but couldn't tell which end to put in, they were that bad.

"I'm a patient man! I'm agreeable!"

"I must really request that no shouting transpire, Professor Bell. Norma's daddy is nothing but protective of the weak sex which if he overheard might subject him."

"Well, I'm sorry, but if Norma — excuse me, is that still too loud?"

"My thoughts are in another room, Professor Bell," she said, to explain her hideous expression.

"I've come a long way to see Norma. If she refuses to talk to me, I'd like to hear it directly from her."

"A child in mortal fear of her father's health cannot be expected."

"She left me eight weeks ago without a word of explanation."

"A bruised flower needs shade."

"Bruised? Bruised?" Bell began to pace the kitchen excitedly. It was offensively clean. No nourishing food could possibly be cooked in it. "I'm bruised, too. Has anybody considered that?"

"Professor Bell, sarcasm is wasted without a college degree."

"*I'm not being sarcastic.*"

"Again I must caution against Daddy's hearing."

"Okay," said Bell. He leaned his forehead against the cold pane in the rear door. Wilbur, released, was defecating in the backyard. Steam rose there. Bell gritted his teeth, turned. "I ask you please — " He broke off. No good. Old Mom had him by the short hairs, all right. How she was enjoying herself! She could hardly keep a leer of triumph off her evil mug. *Why?* He hadn't bruised her goddamned flower. "Tell me," he said softly, "just tell me what's in Norma's mind. What's she doing — just living here or what? I mean, if now isn't a good time, when will she be ready to say something about what she wants from me or doesn't want from me, a divorce or what — "

"As her mother I certainly cannot take it upon myself to speak."

"Exactly. Let me talk to her, then."

"Norma's quite capable of saying anything necessary in her own good time."

Bell heard a liquid noise, surmised that it came from the bathroom a few steps away, surmised further its source. He gave Mom a double fake and dribbled around her for the basket — Norma, emptying Pop's bowl.

"Norma, I'm coming back at eight o'clock tonight. I'll see you then."

Norma flushed the toilet. She looked sick herself.

Mom said from behind him, "Norma baby, you're absolutely free to say and think."

"Eight o'clock on the dot," growled Bell.

"Gee, Bell," said Mrs. Bell, plaintively. "I told Terry I'd go to the movies — "

"*Terry.*"

"She's a girl, Terry Hommler. I mean, if you wanted to go, too — "

"You mean you wouldn't call this Terry up to say some other time?" Bell was sweating in agitation. He thought he might go mad.

"I *promised* her, Bell. It's a Paul Newman picture."

"Oh," Bell said. "I hadn't realized that." He began snickering. "Paul Newman — well, that's different." He wiped his face on a handtowel. "You should have told me that right away."

"You could come," Norma said. They were all mixed up together in the little hallway.

Bell handed the towel to Mom. "I'd love to, Norma, but I've seen all the Paul Newman pictures already. Every one." He'd wandered back into the kitchen, shuddering with laughter. Norma went the other way, carrying the rinsed bowl back to Pop. "Do you enjoy Paul Newman movies, too, Mrs. Hirlinger?" he asked Mom, who was standing within easy reach of the phone, ready to ring for the crazy squad.

Mom said nothing. Her dress was dark at the armpits. She was squinting at Bell, ready for anything.

"It's such a simple question," Bell remarked, smiling broadly. "I'd sincerely appreciate knowing your opinion."

Mom took a step toward the phone.

She'd really call the cops, Bell thought. An American mother will defend her home even if it means she has to kill everybody in it.

"Well, Mrs. H., I guess this wasn't the most convenient time for me to pay a call, that's all." Bell bowed his way out of the kitchen and went back to the living room for his hat, Mom right on his heels, a knife doubtless up her sweaty sleeve. "Some other time, maybe," he said, to no one. Pop occupied his chair as though he'd been poured there. Norma stood behind him, biting her nails. "So long, Norma," Bell said. "See you around." Norma opened her mouth and closed it. "Good-bye, sir," Bell said to his father-in-law. "Hope you feel better real soon, sir." He bowed to Mom. "And my best wishes to you, Mrs. H." He bowed to them all. "Have a happy."

And thus he left them.

BELL ENTERED THE Detroit slums at dusk. Was it dangerous? He didn't much care. He'd already been mugged for the day. If his closure complex had closed, it had closed on nothing.

The streetlights were brighter in the slums. Cops in pairs patrolled not only the streets but some rooftops, too, and maybe the sewers as well. Bell saw blasted storefronts boarded up, wrecked buildings papered with condemnation signs, taxis with steel shields behind the driver to thwart murderous fares, shops selling Soul Brother stickers with no questions asked. Dusk became darkness. The lamps got brighter, as if to bleach everything white. Bell felt the warm weight of light pressing down. He saw few people on the streets; he guessed they stayed inside to escape the lights. The incandescence ate the air. Bell felt light-headed, light-drugged. Here in the slums it was eternal noon. Ten thousand little suns hung everywhere, erasing black shadows, scrubbing concrete snowy, turning window glass to glinty ice.

Bell had a map, and carried Lundquist's book in one overcoat pocket, games theory in the other. When storefront signs began appearing in Spanish, he slowed his pace. Lundquist had walked here. His footsteps had left no echo. Even the people he'd lived with were anonymous in his book. But he'd mentioned a Catholic mission. Might be that one on the corner.

"Excuse me, I wonder if you happen to remember . . ."

Bell addressed a lay brother, a young man with tired eyes and pocked cheeks.

"A sociologist?" The lay brother shook his head. "There are a lot of those. But I wouldn't remember anyway. I wasn't here then. You ought to see Father Burke — he's in the kitchen at the moment."

Bell went, stooping at low doorways, working his way among delicately boned little men who wandered in the dusty corridor as though lost. When he jostled them, they cursed him in soft, deferential tones.

Father Burke was Bell's age but looked younger because he was weighty. He was supervising the making of tomorrow's stew by tasting it from time to time and arguing with the cook. One unshaded bulb cast a feeble light.

"Lundquist?" Father Burke squinted shrewdly at Bell. The kitchen was hot. It smelled of grease and garbage. "I may remember him. I think I do. What's happened to him?"

"I don't know. I'm trying to find him."

"A fierce old fellow. Drank a lot. I can't say I liked him, but still — " The priest pulled out a pack of cigarettes. "Have a gasper. No?" He lighted one for himself and blew smoke into the soup steam. "A *scholar*, you say. I'd never have believed that. Are we talking about the same man? This Lundquist had a limp."

"Yes." Bell produced a snapshot Mrs. Lundquist had given him.

"That's him. Curious — I'd forgotten him, and yet he made quite an impression at the time. An old rascal, Lundquist. If I had to guess, I'd say he was in jail now." Father Burke dipped his finger into the stew for another taste. "Come with me," he said to Bell, and after giving the cook further instructions he led Bell up some rickety stairs to the second floor. They walked past a room where an evening class in English was in progress, and went to a tiny office at the front, overlooking the street. A puppy slept in the swivel chair. Father Burke thrust it out into the hall. He didn't bother turning on the light; the streetlamps illuminated the room.

"Are you from the police?"

"Oh, no." Bell started fumbling for some identification.

"Don't bother. It doesn't matter. But look out there." The priest nodded at the window. "Outsiders don't come here alone. I assumed those fellows were with you."

Bell saw two figures at the edge of a tattered grocery awning across the street.

"Cops, to be sure," Father Burke remarked. "In plainclothes, but you can tell by their hats and their size. Well, what do you want with old Lundquist, if you don't mind my asking?"

"His family is worried about him. He's been gone a long time."

"That man had no family." Father Burke dropped his

cigarette on the floor and trod it out. "At least, I hope he didn't. He had a devil in him, though. You don't see that type often. I felt medieval when he was about, as though there were exorcising to be done. Maybe I should have tried. He put some of the devil in me, Lundquist did." He sighed and rubbed his heavy cheeks. Down the hall the English class was chanting: *I go, I am going, I have gone.*

"Yes, I remember Lundquist," the priest went on, moodily. "Can't say I treasure the memory. I have the feeling I enjoyed my work here before he came — or perhaps I'm being unfair." He coughed and scraped his shoes fretfully on the floorboards. "I mentioned deviltry. Isn't that the word to use when a man's made to see evil in the place of good?"

"Maybe."

"Well, you see, before Lundquist came, I'd welcomed every form of aid and assistance from the outside. In fact, I spent half my time running everywhere trying to get more — trying to interest people to come in with money and programs and technicians. What a jackrabbit I was, hopping all over the city. But he told me I was a fool, that all I was doing was helping gut the community here — and I came to believe he was right, damn his soul. Excuse me, you're not Catholic?"

"No."

"Good," said Father Burke. "Catholics from outside find me offensive — I *am* offensive. Not much doubt of that." He shifted his chair back to the wall so that he was in shadow. The streetlight whitened a tiny crucifix above the desk, which was covered with slumping stacks of pamphlets. "For example, the psychologists and education experts come

into the school to identify — that's their word, identify —
to identify the gifted students, and then they begin pulling
them out, you know, they take them out of the community
entirely into special boarding schools and put them on the
road to Yale or wherever. These kids never come back. Never.
What does it mean? For the kids, it's an escape from slum
life, I suppose. For the community here, it's a dead loss.
These are the future leaders! If the experts with their tests
and their money grants came in with guns instead, they
couldn't hurt us more."

"That's what Lundquist said?"

"Yes. I saw the truth of it at once." The priest made a
moaning sound. Bell couldn't see his face. *Going, going,
gone,* said the English class. "But what's the purpose of
it?" Father Burke asked. "Do they *want* to hurt us? Do they
want to help? God knows. I don't. But I was plagued by
shame and guilt, you see, for I was the traitor here — I'd
summoned up these damned experts, made arrangements,
soothed the people, talked to the kids, and when the first
batch left I was a proud man. I'd saved them, you know.
Damn Lundquist."

"Maybe he was wrong."

"Maybe! Yes, maybe. But the community's the thing,
you know. We haven't got one here. We could have. But
the leaders keep getting stolen — the bright kids by the
educators, the tough kids by the prison system, and the rest
are bamboozled by drugs and drink and welfare qualifica-
tions — and maybe by the Church, maybe by the Church."
Father Burke lighted another cigarette. "What's your
name?" he asked, softly. "What do you do?"

"I'm Aaron Bell. I teach history."

"Ah, well. Perhaps you know more about this."

"I know too little."

"There isn't any history here, I suppose," Father Burke said. "History isn't applicable to these people. They've lost their own, and they can't use ours. No history, no community, no traditions." He made a series of soft clucking sounds. "Isn't that what history's supposed to do, Mr. Bell? To invigorate a community by confirming and explaining its traditions?"

"I'm not really sure," said Bell. He shook his head. He almost laughed. "It's strange. Not being sure. Not being sure, I mean, of what it's for."

"You're not alone," said Father Burke.

"I've always thought of myself as a teacher. More a teacher than a historian. But teaching what?" Bell drew his fingers through his hair. "Teaching tradition. Maybe you're right. Teaching tradition to the children of the only community I know. But if these others aren't included, then the community is incomplete. So the tradition isn't complete, either. And that makes the history a little fraudulent. Doesn't it? I'm not asking you, Father. I'm the one who ought to know."

"You do know."

"Yes. Guess I do." Bell glanced over at the priest, whose face remained shadowed. "You're used to this, aren't you, Father? Hearing confession?"

"Not this kind. Yours is a priest's confession, Mr. Bell. The confession of doubt. It's the kind I make myself." Father Burke blew smoke into the shaft of light. A draft caught it and sucked it high into the darkness. "If you were a Catholic, I'd probably talk to you about God. As it is — " He chuckled shortly, without humor. "As it is, I'd say you'd had a brush with Lundquist, too."

"Not exactly." But Bell thought of Lundquist's wife, the old man's familiar. "In a way, maybe I have," he said. He leaned forward, so the priest could see him smiling. "You mentioned deviltry, Father. Tell me, what do devils do?"

"They possess you."

Bell leaned back, still smiling. He said nothing for a time.

Father Burke resumed speaking about his own preoccupation. "These programs from outside I mentioned. Are they intended to help people live or to keep them in bondage?"

"I don't know."

"Some priests have gone off the deep end, you know. They've become militant and radical. I've shrunk from that. I don't know whether it's a challenge or a temptation. To resist authority? We aren't supposed to do things like that. And yet, if one becomes convinced that authority is hostile and repressive — " He broke off with a wave of an arm, his cigarette end inscribing a question mark in the air. "I've been here four years and I can't even speak decent Spanish. I'm a lousy priest, in short. The only satisfaction I take is that I was a lousy agent of social repression, too — that's what your rascally friend called me — and I've stopped all that nonsense, thanks to him. I don't do anything now, Aaron Bell. I make soup and make confession and keep up appearances, God forgive me, and I'm thinking of dropping those English classes. English is an abstract mechanism of social control. Lundquist again! What a boozer he was. I think he got a girl in trouble, too, though I can't be sure, for she wouldn't say, but anyway he was gone."

"Where?"

"Oh, yes. That's your present concern, isn't it? You can't help me, and I doubt if I can help you." Father Burke sat silently for a bit, smoking. "There is a community of sorts here, actually. I don't know much about it. They don't trust me. They used to, before Lundquist came — or perhaps I'm giving him credit or blame he doesn't deserve. Why should they trust me? I can't trust myself. Maybe there wasn't a community before, either. I thought there was. I thought I had a part in shaping it. I may have dreamed it existed just because there was the Church and the welfare offices and the schools and the playground program and the rest of it. Did you know that two blocks away is a municipal garage housing a riot truck equipped to dispense nausea gas?"

"No."

"Right across from the church." Father Burke got to his feet. "If you'll give me two dollars, I'll be back shortly. . . . Thank you."

Left alone, Bell took another look down at the street. He couldn't see the two men who'd stood beneath the awning, but half a block away a police cruiser had stopped and a man on the sidewalk was bending close to it, evidently conversing with officers inside. Stew smells drifted along the hall, perhaps drawn by Father Burke's opening and shutting of doors. *I have, I have not,* the English class announced. *I should have, I will have.*

The priest reappeared with a little man in a patched army officer's overcoat and a fedora worn far down on his head, shading his features. "Mr. Bell, this gentleman may possibly be able to help you. He doesn't speak English — a matter of preference, I think — but he understands it." Bell nodded in a friendly fashion to the little man, who remained motionless. "He remembers Lundquist, too," Father Burke continued. "Favorably or not, I have no idea. But in any event, he's willing to escort you to a friend or relative of his who's evidently widely connected, etcetera, and — " Father Burke shrugged. "It's that sort of vague arrangement," he added to Bell as the three of them went downstairs and back toward the kitchen. "I do hope for your sake you're really a history teacher." The kitchen was empty. The little man made straight for the rear door. "They'd sense it, you know," said Father Burke. "I couldn't. You seem all right to me. It's a matter of innocence, in a way. You have that quality about you, innocence." The guide made an impatient gesture and stepped out through the doorway. "If you'd rather not, now's the time," the priest went on, hastily. "I make no promises, you know. If you prefer, just turn around and go out the front."

"No, thanks. I'll go this way."

"Hurry, then."

Bell did. The rear door opened on an alley. It was dark. The streetlamps didn't reach everywhere. Bell caught a glimpse of his guide stepping, so it seemed, into the wall of another building. A door was there, and as Bell pushed through, he saw the man far ahead in the hallway, outlined by a distant electric bulb. Hastening, he just managed to keep him in sight. They left that building and crossed another alley, then a deserted schoolyard, skirted the darkest edge of the school itself, then cut across a street where a great tree provided a shadow bridge guarded from light. Bell, striding hard, remained behind the nimble little man in his flapping coat who never once glanced back. They were following a night trail cut through the slums. Men appeared, passed, were gone, without a word or sound. Bell's side ached; he was worried, and perspiration gathered against the lining band of his hat. On and on they went, pursuing a zigzag route behind warehouses, through lots filled with ruined cars and baled junk, under a viaduct, and into a dead-end court where the guide motioned Bell to stop — his first acknowledgment of Bell's presence — as he went inside the closest tenement.

Bell leaned against the wall, breathing hard. Fear had cut his wind, all right. He watched the hundred windows. Most of them were lighted. Families lived there. Bell could smell food cooking, hear murmuring voices. *Praack* — some kid with an air pistol popped a streetlight bulb. Bits of glass shivered down, a dog howled, a cat-sized rat galloped across the court.

From the doorway of the near building, a man made a two-step exit and waved Bell in. "Who, me?" said Bell. There was no one else. The man didn't wait. He went back inside, and Bell followed. *Praack* — another bulb. Stairways rose like ladders, three old winos sat glugging on the cement floor that was chalk-marked for hopscotch, a pretty girl in a red wrapper was chattering into the pay phone, radios blasted through every inch of air space. Bell hot-footed it after his guide, but it wasn't the same one. He was following an old geezer in a hunting cap and black raincoat, who, when assured Bell was dogging him, set off scrambling crook-legged like a spider along the shotgun hall, down a flight of steps into a basement area where Bell couldn't see a thing but could hear lovers moaning in some corner. He hesitated, fuming and uncertain. Then he caught the snick of a door opening — black on black straight ahead — and went quickly that way.

Outside again. And there was the raincoat racing through a dwarf forest of waist-high weeds. Bell went stumbling after, sending varmints scuttling aside. Tenements towered all around, patchworks of crazy window eyes. Bell tripped on something, knelt impromptu, rose and rushed on mumbling curses. What, were these little men going to run him all night in relays, to wear his long legs down to their size? Maybe it was a joke. Two bucks entry fee for the cross-slum marathon. *"Hey,"* he shouted. But his guide kept going.

It seemed like hours. The two of them — the pace-setter some twenty yards ahead, ungainly Bell floundering behind — flashed in and out of buildings, descended garbage hills, climbed junk slopes, skated along grease-paved alleys, crossed sinister back streets where sharpshooters had dimmed the lights and Spanish Normas strolled in rabbit-trimmed coats, swinging meager hips. Once Bell thought he smelled Father Burke's stew. Another time, rounding a corner, he spied a distant movie marquee — would Paul Newman be there? But he had no time to read the neon letters. The guide had hustled ahead on the nowhere trail. *"Hey."* No answer. Bell ran after.

The slum became an anti-Bell machine, an obstacle course

full of pitfalls and pratfalls, Bell barking his shins, stubbing toes, snagging clothes. His ankles were mantled with weed burrs, which itched. Threading his way through some pitchy mews, he'd jostled slop cans and gotten a shoeful. His agile guide was untouched; Bell caught hell everywhere. Environmental control, where was it? He figured he'd covered miles back and forth, in and out, up and down. He might have been tricked into hoofing to Chicago, for all he knew. *"Hey."* This was too much. *"Stop."*

Around the next corner, Bell saw black raincoat at a dim doorway, mumbling to someone there. Bell approached slowly, sweating hard, and winded. "This it?" he croaked.

His guide just turned aside, squatted down, and took a puff on a cigarette cupped in his hand. Bell was left facing a black man, darkly dressed, who leaned in the doorway, vaguely outlined by light from within.

"What you want?" the man said.

"I'm looking." Bell had to stop to clear his throat. He mopped his face with his handkerchief. Somewhere not far a woman was sobbing. "Looking for a man named Lundquist. Maybe you know him? An old guy in his sixties with a limp?"

"I knew him."

"Trying to find him," Bell said. "I'm not a cop, nothing like that. I'm a friend, friend of the family, just want to get in touch with him, that's all."

"He ain't here."

"Right. Didn't expect he'd be here, exactly. Just thought somebody might have some idea. Thought somebody might have, um, heard where, you know." Sweat was sluicing down

Bell's back, chest, arms. "He sort of, well, disappeared during the summer."

"Ain't seen him."

"Right," Bell said again. He wondered whether he ought to offer money. That might be a wrong move, though. He had no idea what might be a right one. Except maybe to cut and run. "I'm just trying to check around, that's all." He was under hostile inspection, sure. Not just from this man. All around, eyes.

Suddenly the black man leaned forward, tense and angry. "Listen, you know where you are, man?"

"Pardon?"

"You some damned fool to come 'round here. Know that?"

Bell said nothing.

"People here cut your white ass crossways. You know that?"

"Maybe so."

"I mean, man, you some kind of crazy fool."

"Okay, but I just came to ask —"

"Don't care what you come for." The black man's voice was rising. He had his fists clenched. "Where you been at, anyhow? I mean, you must be dumb's you look, come in here. It ain't guts you got, man, it's just stupidity, ain't that so?"

"Maybe," Bell said. He kept his eyes on his inquisitor's face, but caught movement to one side. His guide was edging away; not a reassuring sign.

"That old man, Carl. He come here, but that was two years back, man. Two *years*. Hell, even tough old bastard like him, he'd have sense enough to stay away now. I mean, don't you know where you *are?*"

"Well, I just — "

"You better shag ass and pray, man. There's people here don't care. I mean, they don't *care.* I tell you I don't much care my own self, but I mean you say you some kind of friend of Carl's but I swear if you don't get gone right fast I may forget that — "

"Okay." Bell didn't move, though. Something stubborn rose in him. He wouldn't run. "I just came to ask about him. If you're sure you haven't — "

"You crazy fool." The black man took a short step forward. "By God, you are. Listen. Carl was in Chicago two months back. So I heard."

"Chicago."

"He ain't there now. He went back south."

"Where?"

"I don't know no more than that, man."

"Okay." Bell turned. His guide had had enough, anyway. The little fellow was starting off. Better go after. "Well, thanks," Bell started to say, turning back, but the doorway was empty now, and he didn't wait. No time for politeness. Send a thank-you letter later. He got his legs working. They were stiff as stilts. Everything in his body was running scared, and he was a little dizzy with the effort of keeping himself from breaking into a panic dash. *Walk fast, with dignity.* A tough prescription. It made him pant. His footsteps sounded like jackhammers. Where was that damned black raincoat? Ah. There. Up ahead.

The way back was shorter. It was a different route. Bell

could tell that much. The streets seemed almost deserted, but from the shadows they were watched. Dogs ran patterns around them, sometimes pebbles stung past their heads, whispered curses swarmed in their wake. Once at an alley turning a window at hat level bloomed light to show a huge old black Aaron with mad eyes spread-eagled with shaking fists, howling with silent laughter as a bucketful of clotted waste slathered down from above, spackling Bell's hat and shoulders.

It was a silent night, misty, full of fumes. Bell moved as in his dream, so stunned with fear and tiredness that he couldn't feel his feet drumming that treadmill alley. His guide was a mechanical rabbit he'd never catch. Run to dawn. He was trapped where his senses didn't function. Couldn't see, couldn't feel. He might be running in a closet, might be running in a dark corner of his own confused mind —

Then they broke out, clear at last. The guide was gone, but Bell didn't need him now. He'd emerged into the blaze of one of those noonlike avenues. Two cops strolled across the street, sticks swinging. There was a taxi stand with three cabs waiting.

He had to catch his breath. He stood puffing beside a low playground fence where, under glaring lights, a gang of lean black youths in their teens played basketball, shooting at a new-netted hoop. What a mess he was. His hat was antiqued, his shoes were mudpies, his coat festooned with sewage.

Hearing a familiar series of signals approaching as if rising from memory, he turned instinctively in time to see the loose basketball bounding his way and to grab it as it cleared the little fence.

Just chuck it back? Hell, no. This was his game.

He swung his long legs over the fence and began slowly dribbling the ball toward the basket. Would those black boys show him a zone defense? They didn't do a thing. Bell drove in, overcoat flapping, hat askew, and sank his lay-up unopposed except by silence and, he guessed, contempt. He decided not to give a damn. If any one of them had so much as moved a hand, he'd have passed off his rebound, but they stood still, just waiting for him to get tired and quit and leave.

He didn't. He put on a show. Dribbling through them left-handed, he began working off his overcoat without losing control, switched hands, sank a jumper at twenty feet — *swish* — flung his coat out of bounds, scooped up the unclaimed ball again, and hit seven in a row from all angles and distances — hooks, jumps, one-hand sets, lay-up stuff-shots. He had the touch tonight, all right. Even when he missed he was close, and tipped them in with All-Conference follow-through. Yow. He was a hot-handed forward on a superscoring spree, a whirling dervish slithering among those black statues in the bright slum night, magic fingers making the net suck and sigh. The cops had come across to watch, and the taxi drivers were approaching, too, but Bell was so possessed that he saw nothing but the ball, the net, the court, the trapped sullen boys.

Then one Bell-sized kid made a quick steal as Bell ranged past. Bell stole it back, but now a game was on. They ran him ragged, they taunted him with their moves, they set up screens to block him, they wrestled rebounds away, but, by God, they played him. Without a word. No referee, either, and no times-out. When Bell got elbowed climbing air for the backboard, he elbowed back; when a fast set of finger-nails drew bloodlines across his dribbling hand, he returned the favor. Drive, shoot, rebound — he still flashed and fought, still sank a few, blocked others, stole, broke out of tie-ups, faked them dizzy except for one goateed six-footer who stayed with him like a shadow, outjumped all but a rail-thin kid with Sudden Goose ladderlegs. Thus they played: seven black boys and one white Bell, twisting and leaping in a silent midnight game. Gone Norma, gone Lundquist, gone Nomad, all gone.

Until, as if by prearrangement, the kid with the goatee got the ball, turned, and loped off the playground, with the others straggling after. And they were gone, too.

Bell leaned gasping against the support posts. Gasping and laughing, sweat skiing down his cheeks.

Then he picked up his overcoat, found his hat, and went rubber-legged toward the cabstand.

Sᴏᴍᴇᴛʜɪɴɢ ᴡᴀs ᴡʀᴏɴɢ. Bell knew what as soon as he opened the door of the house, even before he was greeted by Mrs. Watt, her broad face plaintively swollen, or saw old Aaron tottering down the stairs with one pudgy hand splayed across his glasses, being supported by Dr. Bierman, the family physician who lived down the block.

The TV was silent.

"*Son.*" Old Aaron slumped against Bell, who dropped the suitcase to grab him. "It happened just an hour ago. His heart. It stopped." The old fellow sobbed against Bell's stained coat. His tears dampened the crusted spots Bell hadn't been able to brush out.

"Your grandfather," Dr. Bierman said, as though to make certain Bell knew it wasn't the TV they were mourning.

"Well, Dad," Bell muttered, hugging the old orphan, and, with Dr. Bierman's assistance, maneuvering him into the living room, where they eased him down on the couch. Mrs. Watt meanwhile was treading her way back upstairs. Bell's father lay moaning and whimpering his grief and beating his temples with his palms, first having removed his spectacles and handed them to Dr. Bierman.

Bell went swiftly upstairs, passing the widow near the top.

Grandpa was stretched on the bed, looking hale and fit. Death had brightened him. His hands had been folded on his chest, above the sheet, and his eyelids had been closed, but one had popped back open by reflex action so that he appeared to be making a wink of infinite duration at the ceiling.

"So long, Grandpa," Bell whispered. He felt no sorrow, no surprise. He put his hand on the top of the TV set. It was cold. He noticed that someone had unplugged it, perhaps an act of respect.

Mrs. Watt shuffled in. "It was during the Art Linkletter show, Professor Bell," she said, putting forth one speckled hand to relid Grandpa's eye. "He always laughs. He didn't today." She rattled interior fibrous tissue with a mournful sigh. "And it was really a good show this time, you know," she added, seeming still vaguely puzzled at the old man's silence. "But he passed on with a smile, your grandfather did. I thought you'd like to know that."

"Yes, thank you, Mrs. Watt." Bell wondered how long Grandpa had sat there stiffening before his co-viewer had checked him. Did they have to pry the channel changer from his hand? "That's a comfort to hear," he added, backing off. Grandpa wasn't smiling now, though. He seemed expectant, almost eager in repose, as if awaiting the end of a commercial.

"I'll stay with him," Mrs. Watt said. She lowered herself heavily into her accustomed chair, which had not been moved. It faced the set. Bell quelled the impulse to tell her: *Go ahead, turn it on. He'd have wanted it that way.* Instead he said, "Thank you," and asked, "Has Anderson's been called?" Anderson's was the funeral home. Mrs. Watt nodded.

Bell changed suits and phoned the cleaner to ask for a

rush job, especially on the overcoat. In the living room Dr. Bierman was administering a sedative to old Aaron. Bell was famished; he made two peanut-butter sandwiches and ate them standing by the sink, listening to his father's far-off groans. A death in the family. The last one had been Bell's mother, a quarter century ago. Grandma Bell had died young, too, before Bell was born. It wasn't a lucky family for women. Maybe Norma had sensed that, he thought, as he returned to the living room.

"I failed him, failed him!" The elder Bell lay writhing in his fat. "Everything I did was failure! A wasted life — all gone!" He spoke as though he'd died, not Grandpa. Dr. Bierman drew Bell into the hall to discuss details of funeral arrangements, acting in the capacity of family counselor rather than physician. Old Aaron kept lamenting. He didn't require an audience this time. The cosmos was enough. He was in a tantrum of grief, drumming his chest with fat fists and thrashing his legs.

"He'll be asleep in two more minutes," Dr. Bierman assured Bell. "Anderson's will move your grandfather out then. It'll be better that way."

"He set impossible standards," came old Aaron's voice, somewhat weaker. "But he wanted a son to be proud of! Instead — a washout, a flop, an emotional cripple!" He bayed anguish that ended in what seemed to be a snore, but when the man from the dry cleaner's arrived, he sat bolt upright on the couch, and seeing Bell in the hall hand over the overcoat and suit with limp dangling trousers, he shouted "No" in a wild voice, then sank back down asleep.

Bell spent a dreary hour telephoning: newspaper, University, family lawyer, minister, a scattering of Grandpa's surviving colleagues, remote cousins, friends. Mr. Anderson and his sons came with the hearse. The sons lugged Grandpa out while Mr. Anderson talked business with Bell in the dining room. It still smelled of cat piss. At dusk Mrs. Watt went home, and various friends began dropping by to console the bereaved. Bell's father by this time had regained consciousness. He sat blinking on the couch, racked by tremendous yawns, tears running down his cheeks as he munched gifts of pies and cakes. The visitors kept saying what a great figure Grandpa had been, which made the unworthy son weep the more.

The weather had been milder. Much of the snow had melted, refrozen, melted again, become mixed with sand spread by the street crews. Bell's hallway was gritty with it now from sympathizers' galoshes. The phone kept ringing. Professors Glass and Pico paid a call. "I'll never forget your grandfather on the westward movement, Bell," said Professor Glass. "It inspired me." He made an eastward movement, toward the sherry bottle on the living-room table. Pico ate a whole pie there. Bell felt disoriented, as though he'd lost his glasses. Two neighbor ladies were tidying up the kitchen, exchanging significant glances as they uncovered fresh caches of grime. Mr. Anderson returned. Bell wondered hazily whether he'd come to take the TV set, but he had only brought some papers to be signed. Bell wandered from room to room, accepting handshakes and back pats. Old Aaron had fully recovered from Dr. Bierman's dope. ". . . Father spent his golden years in quiet reflection," Bell could hear him enunciating to a gathering of gaffers who themselves could be counted on to hobble home in time for the Channel Three monster movie.

The phone again.

This time it was Dr. Grosch, long-distance.

"Professor Bell? Is this the young one?" Dr. Grosch seemed confused and in haste. "The operator said there were two of them."

"There's only one now," Bell said. "My grandfather died this morning."

"Good Lord."

"He was eighty-eight."

"Oh, well," said Dr. Grosch impatiently. "Listen, Professor Bell, I'm calling to ask about our, you know, our mutual friend. Any word?"

"Nothing."

"Oh." Dr. Grosch made a clucking sound. "Are you sure? I mean, you can speak freely to me, you know."

"I don't know a thing, Dr. Grosch."

"I'm calling from a public phone, Professor Bell," Dr. Grosch said, in a wheedling tone.

"Well, I'm not."

"That's true," Dr. Grosch conceded. There followed a pause of sufficient length for Dr. Grosch to receive further instructions from Muller, if, as Bell thought, that were the case. "Um, let me speak frankly, Bell," Dr. Grosch resumed, in a more forceful voice. "This is no petty matter, you know. I'll tell you what. I'll send one of my personal representatives up to see you for a little private conversation, and you can tell him everything in strict confidence."

"I won't tell him a damned thing."

"You won't?"

"No."

"Why not?"

"Because I'm damned tired of being followed about all over the country, that's why."

"Oh." There was another pause. Bell thought he could hear a mumble of voices in the background.

"Where are you calling from — Washington?" Bell asked.

"Eh? What's that? Oh, it doesn't matter where," said Dr. Grosch, in a pettish and distracted manner, and then the line went dead.

"Hello?" Bell punched the telephone cradle a few times. "Hello?" He hung up.

His father was sitting alone on the couch, cake crumbs on his chin. Everyone had gone except for one fanatic woman still scrubbing the kitchen, and for Pico, who was treading majestically toward the bathroom, magazine in hand.

"Well, Dad." Bell clumsily gave his father a hug. Old Aaron received it passively. His face puckered, but he had no more tears. "It's over," Bell said. "Don't feel too badly. Listen, after the funeral, we'll take a little trip." He had a vision of the two of them as Groschian nomads, berrypicking in the southern hills. "Or something," he added. His father seemed genuinely broken-spirited. His silence was almost alarming. "Look, Dad," Bell went on, trying to cheer him, "suppose we take a beer upstairs and watch *Son of Kong?*"

"It wouldn't seem right, Ham."

"Guess not." Bell could hear the mop slavering across the kitchen floor. Pico was whistling mood music in the bathroom.

"I hated Father," old Aaron said. He wasn't clowning. He looked shrunken and fearful. Bell held his hand, not knowing what else to do. "That's a terrible thing to say, isn't it, Ham? But it's true. I thought every day of my life, if only Father'd died instead of Mother. She was more like me, you know. I mean, she was afraid of Father." He looked into Bell's face. His eyeglasses were askew and his eyes didn't seem to be focusing properly.

"Don't brood about it, Dad."

"He was a selfish man, Ham. You never knew him in his prime. He'd come into a room and you'd feel like hiding. I don't mean he was cruel. He was just so full of himself there wasn't room for anybody else. He denied me, denied me. For a man to hate his own father — that's frightful, isn't it?" He gave a little gasp. "But you, Ham. You don't hate your father. No, no." He whipped his glasses off with his free hand, as if they impeded his study of Bell's face. "Ah, but maybe it's worse than that, what you feel. *Contempt.*"

"Dad — "

Pico came back in, like a regiment. He'd neglected to re-buckle his belt. "You fellows come over to the Pico house," he said, in his trombone voice. "How about it?"

"No, thanks, Pete," Bell said. "We'd better get Dad to rest right here."

"Don't bother about me," Bell's father said suddenly. "You and Peter go on out and have a good time somewhere. Just leave me alone with my memories!" The old sly look had returned. Bell was somewhat relieved. He and Pico got blankets and a pillow, to make a bed on the couch. There were too many ghosts upstairs. Bell's father let them help him into pajamas. "I'll be next to go," he announced, in a sickly manner, although his color had much improved. "Next year it'll be a shroud, instead of pajamas. The big sleep!"

The neighbor woman had finished the kitchen. She'd worked three hours, and entered, a sated martyr, to fetch her coat.

"Mrs. Finn," cried Bell elder, snatching blankets over his nightclothes in a show of modesty, "a million thanks to you!"

"I'll be over in the morning to make breakfast," Mrs. Finn said. Her face was stiff with Presbyterian joy.

"Never! It's too much! Kind lady!" Old Aaron wriggled in his blankets.

At a sign from Bell, Pico left with Mrs. Finn. Bell went around the house turning off lights and checking windows and doors. His father had fallen asleep by the time he returned to the living room. A single lamp there cast a pale glow against the curtains. Bell went out on the front porch in his shirtsleeves. The night was clear. The stars were bright. The streetlights here didn't hide them. No starlight in the slums. He remembered then that he hadn't notified Norma of Grandpa's death. Ah, he'd send a wire in the morning. No doubt Mom would interpret it as a trick to lure Norma-baby back. Bell spat into the yard. His legs and back still hummed from that basketball game — Detroit All-Stars 68, Bell 30 — but at least in that one he'd scored.

It was cold. Bell shivered. He heard the night train screaming unseen across the steppe. Even now in some lonely farmhouse, an old Swedish husbandman, heir to the Jeffersonian dream, would be trudging with glazed eyes to pick the pig knife from the barn door. The night train screamed again. Bell's thoughts frantically boarded it, fleeing the bloody pillow where the farmwife lay grinning. At Chicago, where the slums blazed in consuming light, he switched trains, headed southeast —

He went inside. Locked the door. Before he went upstairs to bed, he stopped in the living room. Slowly, gently, he bent low, bowing, to kiss his sleeping father.

THREE MORNINGS LATER, as Bell was leaving the house with his father and Mrs. Watt for the funeral, the postman came by and handed him a letter from Norma. Bell put it in his pocket. Later, in the church pew, he surreptitiously ripped the envelope open. It sounded like pants splitting. "I am the uh Resurrection and the uh Life," the Reverend Torgeson intoned. *Dearest Bell,* wrote Norma. Bell put the letter away again, and set his mind on Grandpa, stiff and tough as a TV dinner in that big black casket. ". . . he uh that believeth in uh . . ." For this occasion, Mrs. Watt hadn't spared the powder. She sat like a floured cake. Bell's father both wept and bled; he'd cut himself three times while shaving. He'd chosen unmatched socks to show how distracted with grief he was. *Dearest Bell.* ". . . whosoever liveth and believeth in me shall never uh die . . ."

It was windy outside. Birds were flying south. Bell was afraid his father would make a scene at the cemetery and stayed close to him. Most of the mourners were gray-heads or bald. Pico stood among them like Mount Rushmore. The clods were thrown. Old Aaron, afraid of death, didn't howl or faint or jump on the casket. He just picked at his razor cuts. *Dearest Bell.* Grandpa's pickled body lay in satin; Grandpa's electronic soul zipped among technicolor clouds. Leaving the cemetery, Bell passed one envelope to the Reverend Torgeson and kept the other, Norma's, bunched in his pocketed fist. He saw a stranger inspecting headstones and doing tension exercises with the palms of his hands. "Ever tackle that guy?" Bell asked Pico at the graveyard gate. But the stranger had strolled behind the caretaker's hut.

Dearest Bell. Bell read the letter finally at his office, where paperwork was stacked high on his desk. *I hope you understand we were all awfully upset when you came because of Daddy who's really very sick and may have to go to the hospital. Honestly Bell we wouldn't have wanted to offend you for the world, my mother included, and it certainly wouldn't be like that again I can promise you that. In haste, love. Norma.*

Bell squeezed the letter into a ball and tried a left-handed hook for the wastebasket, twelve feet. Missed. Tough shit. Norma'd had time for Terry Hommler, Paul Newman, and Phyllis-Alice-Malice, but not for dearest Bell. Why hadn't she emptied her daddy's puke bowl on her hubbie's head? He'd asked for it, skittering up there with his roses and candy. So her letter opened the door for him to creep back again. No, sir. He wouldn't. Norma would have to make the moves now. No more Mr. Nice Guy. He scowled down at student essays, bloodying them with red-pencil strokes. He skipped lunch and did thirty push-ups instead, then flogged more essays, and at his senior seminar on Public Service Ethics, he unethically cross-examined a Norma-like girl so harshly that she reddened and her eyes got damp. But what did ethics mean in an age of Muller and Mom? "Government ethics aren't matters of morality but of fashion," pronounced Professor Bell, a hungry cynic. His seniors swallowed yawns. In his office down the hall, Professor Glass refreshed himself with colonial readings. Real ethics then, on the burned-witch issue.

Later Bell got a telegram. DEEPLY GRIEVED PASSING OF GRANDFATHER BELL SORRY DADDYS ILLNESS PREVENTED COMING LOVE NORMA.

This time he sank his shot.

The clock in the hall struck five. Bell's door opened.

"Dr. Bell?" It was the graveyard stranger, sandy-haired and blue-eyed and smiling. He entered with tiny steps, showing teeth, his hat slowly atwirl on one finger.

Bell said nothing. He sat shirtsleeved and granitic, elbow-deep in essays.

"My name's Brant, Dr. Bell," the smiling stranger said. "Personal assistant to Dr. Grosch."

"Sit down, then," Bell said, unkindly.

The stranger sat. "Dr. Grosch said you ah might have some information for him." He was smiling enough for both of them. Bell guessed his age to be twenty-five. "Or might not," Brant added, smiling even more.

"Yep," said Bell, cryptically. He gave Brant a savage stare.

Brant, well trained, didn't wilt under it; he seemed to blossom instead, but Bell noticed he had begun tension exercises with his fingers. "No, listen," Bell said, suddenly deciding. "I'll tell you everything I can. I want to be helpful."

"Super," said Brant, pulling out a pen.

"First, though, tell me. Where'd you play?"

"'Scuse me?"

"Your college team, I mean."

"College, oh. Well, I went to the University of Idaho."

"Football?"

"Well, no. I was swimming captain, matter of fact." Brant's smile was perplexed. Bell was writing all this down, ferociously, in giant red letters. "State diving champ in high school," Brant added, uncertainly. Bell wrote some more. "Um, that's all," Brant said.

"I'm helping a colleague collect data," Bell said, again giving Brant the hard look. "He wants to find out what happens to old college athletes, how they carry that rah-rah spirit into civilian life, you know. What about Muller? Where'd he play?"

"Gee, him, well, I'm not sure exactly." Brant was working his smile back up. "Maybe I could ask and drop you a line."

"Great. You do that." Bell had the impression that Brant's feet, hidden from his sight by the desk, might be engaged in tension combat, for Brant was wiggling slightly in his chair. He had a little notebook ready.

"Now, as you were saying before — "

"Check. The man you want is located at 327 North Butterfly Street, Seattle, Washington."

Brant happily wrote that down.

"It's a rooming house," Bell added. "He's doing a study on destitute salmon fishermen. He'll be there at least until December first."

"Oh, boy," muttered Brant, scratching away. He gave Bell a grateful look. "Ah, could you tell me the source of this info, Dr. Bell?"

"You bet. Man I met in Detroit last week, name of Dred Scott, 1857 Decision Street."

A look of doubt passed across Brant's face. It lasted only an instant. "Scott with a double *t?*" he asked.

"Right." Bell guessed maybe Brant had stayed under at that Idaho pool a bit too long. "That's all I've got for you, Mr. Brant."

"That's plenty, Dr. Bell." Brant glanced hungrily at Bell's phone as though he were considering asking permission to use it. Then he got up. "Can't thank you enough for your help, sir. Dr. Grosch will really be glad to have this."

"Any little thing I can do," Bell said.

By the time Bell got home, at seven-thirty, Brant was waiting on the sidewalk, having had time to go off somewhere for his phone calls.

"'Scuse me, Dr. Bell, but I guess you played a little joke on me."

"Didn't you find the man?"

"There isn't any North Butterfly Street."

"Well, that's a shame, Brant."

It was too dark to see Brant's face, but Bell guessed he wasn't smiling.

"That stuff about Dred Scott and all — well, I just wonder why a man in your position would do a thing like that."

Bell's anger burst out. "Okay, now you listen to me. I told your buddy Jerry Moss to climb off my back and now I'm telling you. You're not going to get a goddamned thing out of me. Understand that?" He'd taken a step toward Brant, who stood his ground, tensing his fingers, thumb versus pinky.

"We advise you to cooperate, Dr. Bell."

"And I advise you to splash off, champ." Bell turned through his gate, and went up the steps and into the house.

At nine, he told his father he was going out for a walk. The street was empty. Brant was disguised as Mrs. Finn, a dark female shape at a window across the street, on watch. Bell tipped his hat her way — she'd sent over a pot roast for supper — which made her vanish in confusion, a nosy neighbor observed.

Bell had no object in mind. He walked. This was the town he'd been born in, grown up in, won (and lost) his bride in, and he paced its streets as though he were seeing it for the first time, or the last. That wind was colder every night. Winter came in several stages there, each one rougher, and number two was on its way. Bell could smell snow coming from a thousand miles north. They'd be buried in it two days hence. Brant would have to turn in his water wings for skis.

He stopped at the Northland Delicatessen for cheesecake, which he ate standing at the counter. The cheesecake was shipped frozen from Minneapolis three times weekly. Roseman, the proprietor, was three-fourths Dutch. The Chinese restaurant down the street served chop suey following a recipe from the old country, i.e., San Francisco, and the Scandinavian eatery couldn't offer a decent smorgasbord, being too far from the sea for fresh fish.

The melting pot had melted everything down to goo. How could a history teacher teach goo? Pico was right: all they really wanted was sports. Brant, who'd probably been a dean's list man, had swallowed Dred Scott, but if Bell's Detroit fiction had been baseball-based — George H. Ruth, 60 Homer Drive — the swim champ would have known it right away. Games, games, all games.

He walked kicking old icicles to chunks. The streets were almost empty. The good people preferred to gather around a nice hot TV to watch dramatic tension exercises. At the Gadfly Bookmart he examined the titles in the window and the mustaches of left-wing grad students, also on display inside. Those intellectual gamesters were antigoo, maybe, but if they were given the choice of doors by Father Burke, how many would take the alley exit. Why had *he?*

Went back south, the black man had told him. He'd sought the word, and that was it. Lundquist had gone back to Nomad, but on the outside this time, a real nomad, maybe.

He shivered. That wind came unbroken. The steppe lay open. Men wandered there, lived, died, but each winter their tracings were buried by those seas of snow, blasted by those towering north winds. It was a land without history. Any wonder, then, that his own roots there were so shallowly sunk, so easily blown loose, to make him a tumbleweed man, a sort of nomad too?

PART II

PART II

They moved him to a cot, but his senses were so bewildered by the drug that it seemed he was lying also on the floor and sometimes on the ceiling, too. The room appeared to be full of prone Bells stretched out head to toe everywhere, even in mid-air.

"Tell us, Bell . . ."

Someone was sitting not far from his head, but he was too tired even to try turning.

"Tell us how you found Lundquist, how you first found him, tell us, Bell, tell us. . . ."

They'd given him some sort of truth drug, he supposed. It kept him on the cot, made the room blind-black, jumbled his thoughts and the voice he thought he heard.

". . . how you first found him, found him . . ."

The drug was working, he suspected, for he wanted very much to speak. Yet there were so many truths. Which one did they want?

"Inside," he whispered.

"What's that?"

"Inside of me, that's where."

"Inside you, Bell?"

"Right." His voice was stronger; his thoughts were breaking loose. "There were two Lundquists, understand."

"Two?"

"Yes, that's the answer. Two Lundquists. And the important one wasn't exactly a man, an individual man, but more like — well, the condition of being a man, you might say."

"Bell, that's not very clear."

"You're right. It hasn't been clear to me, either, not until just now, when you asked me about it, and I'm grateful for that, because it was troubling me." He really felt grateful. He even smiled, to show his appreciation. "Well, although I didn't know it, there were these two Lundquists, as I said, and I had to find the first one before I could find the second one — and I kept having the sensation that I was getting closer to Lundquist all the time, you know, but it bothered me because I had no reason to believe I was closer, none at all — "

"Closer to which Lundquist?"

"I was always thinking of a single Lundquist, you see. That was my mistake. For example, about the time my grandfather died, I had the feeling that I'd made real progress in my search, and yet there wasn't anything to support such a feeling. Nothing, that is, which could be justified in terms of a single Lundquist."

"Bell, you mean to say you'd begun to identify yourself with Lundquist?"

"Well, no, not that."

"Did you at any time suspect that you yourself might be Lundquist? Is that what you're saying?"

"No, no, that's crazy. Sure, I'd concentrated my attention

on Lundquist, but it wasn't anything like that. Look, what I
call the first Lundquist sort of superseded the second one —
and he wasn't a man, as I say, but more a state of being.
Within me. That's what I felt was coming closer — me
toward it or it toward me, I didn't know — and I still thought
of it simply as Lundquist. I got excited and sometimes sort of
happy, even when I didn't have much to be happy about."

"Bell, this is all very interesting, but it seems to me that
you're describing your own internal emotions and whatnot, am
I right?"

"I guess so."

"Well, you see, we're more concerned about what you refer
to as the second Lundquist. Our hope is that you'll be able to
recall the exact and precise circumstances under which you discovered, or were assisted to discover, his whereabouts."

"Oh, that. Well . . ." Bell was a little discouraged. They
didn't care about the first Lundquist, but that was the important one — he'd told them so himself. "It was on a train," he
began.

"A train?"

"Well, no, not exactly. Let me think." But he was obsessed
by the idea of the first Lundquist and he knew he couldn't dis-
regard it, no matter what else they would prefer him to talk
about, and since they weren't interested in that part, he kept
quiet about it. It lasted a long time. They came and went,
and hours went by, it seemed, but still Bell lay telling truths to
himself alone.

IT TOOK BELL a whole morning in Roanoke to locate the Nomad field headquarters. The address Muller had given him weeks earlier in Washington was no longer valid, if it ever had been — Muller's Butterfly Street, maybe. Bell had to quiz his way among several municipal bureaus and state offices to obtain a location, get directions, and have them verified independently elsewhere, before setting out in a rented car.

The place was known as the Joint Ecological Studies Center, twelve miles north of Roanoke in hilly farm country bounded by low blue mountains and a sulky sky. It was a degraded rural landscape. Old barns lay foundering in weedy fields, and abandoned farmhouses slumped among rusted antique reapers where fieldmice played. The roadside *Jesus Saves* signs were riddled by worms. By contrast, the Center gleamed sharp and brisk; it was a group of low flat buildings, surrounded by shrubs and gray-green turf and reached from the road by a winding pebbled drive.

Bell had determined to see the headquarters director no matter how much bluster might be needed. None was. He was expected, which surprised him, although it shouldn't have, inasmuch as he'd made the whole trip openly, never once bothering to look back, and had used his own name at his motel and in asking directions at the offices he visited back in Roanoke.

The uniformed guard at the entrance escorted him along a corridor to an office at the end. *Dr. J. B. Franklin, Director* — so said the letters on the frosted glass, which Bell had barely time to glance at, for the guard opened the door at once, without knocking.

"Professor Bell? A pleasure, sir." That was Dr. J. B. Franklin coming swiftly around his desk. He pumped Bell's hand, dismissed the guard with a wave, helped Bell dispose of his hat and coat, and offered a chair. "I'm asking a friend of yours to join us," Dr. Franklin remarked, resuming his seat. "He'll be here in a minute. How about some coffee?"

"All right," said Bell. "Sure, thanks." He was confused and suspicious. The director's office was windowless. There were paintings on the wall (snowy northern scenes of loggers wrestling giant pines, of red-eyed wolves circling a wounded caribou) but no windows. Dr. Franklin, too, presented an unexpected aspect. He was slender in build, abrupt in gesture, keen in manner, and quite black in skin.

Another little surprise. Dr. Grosch entered, looking very white.

"Hello, Professor Bell."

"Hello," said Bell.

They chatted for a bit. Dr. Grosch seemed somewhat shrunken. He didn't explain why he was in Roanoke instead of Washington, and Bell didn't inquire. Dr. Franklin did most of the talking; Dr. Grosch toyed with his pince-nez, and

Bell listened to minute vibrations of some remote automatic system, possibly that of computers, gossiping.

"I won't mince words, Professor Bell," Dr. Franklin declared finally. The coffee had been brought in. Dr. Franklin was ready for business. "We'd like you to be associated with us in the project. We'd like to have your special skills available to us on a consulting basis." His eyes remained unwinkingly on Bell. "Now we don't know whether you have any other outside commitment which might create, let us say, a conflict of interest situation" — he paused to emphasize the words — "but I can assure you that we are seeking to engage you to whatever extent of time you may wish to give us, over and above your regular university duties."

Bell glanced at Dr. Grosch, who was polishing his pince-nez on his sleeve.

Dr. Franklin continued. "I have in my hand a consulting contract in your name, Professor Bell, a contract under which you would provide the Joint Ecological Studies Center with your part-time services for the period of one year, renewable at your option." He pushed a printed contract form across the desk. Bell didn't pick it up. "How much time it would take you to provide your special services would be up to your discretion and your judgment," Dr. Franklin added, "but if, for example, you were able to complete a particular job of work for us within — who can say? — a month or even a week, your compensation would continue for the full contract period, even if you did nothing further. We guarantee all reasonable expenses, too, needless to say."

"That's a really fine offer, Bell," put in Dr. Grosch in a lackluster voice.

"You bet it is," Dr. Franklin said energetically. "We'd be happy to consider increasing the stipend, incidentally, but in that case we'd need some evidence on your part that you'd be able to meet your obligations."

"I don't have any evidence," said Bell. He didn't. Just something an angry man had told him in a dark slum doorway. Still, he was troubled by the sensation that he knew more than that, much more, and that maybe Nomad had been right all along — he'd been in touch with Lundquist somehow, and now he alone of the three of them would recognize signs of Lundquist's nearness, as though the old man's face might take shape for him among the frozen slash in that logging painting. "I don't have any evidence," he repeated. "I don't have any obligations, either."

"Of course not. We don't expect you to sign this immediately. Take it. Look at it. Think about it. We're here to answer your questions."

Bell picked up the contract. The amount of compensation astonished him. It was higher than his annual salary at the University — and presumably they were convinced he could earn it at once, just by scribbling down a certain address, the right one this time. "Why do you want Lundquist this badly?"

"Many factors," Dr. Franklin said sharply. He seemed both annoyed and relieved that Bell had mentioned Lundquist's name openly. "For one thing, Lundquist wantonly damaged certain property belonging to the project. Vandalism, malicious mischief — whatever you want to call it. Now, we could prosecute, but we'd never do it. He's too big a man. At the same time, we can't forget that he's a potential fugitive from the law. We have no present intention of swearing out a warrant, but if we had to do that, then anyone who deliberately withheld information leading to his apprehension would be getting into a pretty sticky situation himself."

"What, are you threatening me?"

"Not at all, not for a minute!" Dr. Franklin and Dr. Grosch exchanged glances. When the director resumed, he adopted a milder tone. "Our object is to persuade Carl to rejoin us here, of his own free will. No man in America has his knowledge or his contacts. We need those very much. Carl has pioneered for forty years, and the most valuable part of his findings he's never bothered to publish, we suspect."

"He's written a dozen books," Bell said.

"Yes, but there are elements referred to but never really developed in any of them, and presumably this is because his work wasn't complete. In short, he is still in the process of gathering material."

"What elements?"

"Those having to do with the organization of social forces throughout the poverty stratum, to the extent this may exist." Dr. Franklin got up, evidently in an excess of nervous energy, and stood drumming his fingers on the back of his chair. There was something military in his bearing. "We know a good deal about poverty structures for the simple reason that we've created them — I don't mean we as a project but we as a society — but what about the structures we haven't created, that have grown up spontaneously? Are there any? What are they?" He stood in a parade-rest position, hands locked together at the small of his back. "As far as I'm concerned there *is* no world of poverty as such, except for a kind of distorted mirror image of our own society, but there may be something there that we haven't quite come to grips with yet, and we'd like to know more about it, if it exists. If anybody knows what's going on there, it's Lundquist."

"And you want to know, too," Bell said.

"Right."

"Why?"

Dr. Franklin seemed surprised. "Why? Because it's our business to find out such things. It's your business, too."

"Not mine."

"Oh, it may not be your specific field, Dr. Bell, but generally speaking, your job is to gather and analyze data concerning the society we live in, and that's what we're doing here. Right, Grosch?"

"Yes, yes," said Dr. Grosch, without enthusiasm.

"I don't know what you're doing," said Bell.

"True, you don't," said Dr. Franklin. "You're quite right there. You can't be expected to go into something you don't know anything about, can you? Of course not." He sat down behind his desk again. "Obviously, I'm obliged to tell you about our aims and our purposes, our programs and our plans — but of course I would very much like to have your assurance that, at the very least, you don't reject the possibility of working with us. Granted, you can't commit yourself right now, but — "

"I'm not committed to anything," Bell said.

"Excellent," said Dr. Franklin. "Now, concerning our work, as I believe Dr. Grosch may have indicated to you earlier" — he gave Dr. Grosch a quick look, and Dr. Grosch managed a sickly smile — "we play games, Dr. Bell. Mathematical games. There isn't anything particularly unusual about this, except that the mathematics tends to become rather complicated, and of course we use computers, but as far as the games themselves are concerned, we're simply doing what every other literate creature in our society does — and as you yourself do, in your profession of teaching history."

"That isn't a game."

"Ah, but you use the properties of games. You teach by building abstract models of reality, don't you? You have to. You can't show your students the reality itself. That's impossible. You're dealing with a tremendous complex of events which is over and done with, vanished, gone forever, and so to resurrect it in a manageable form for teaching purposes, you construct a highly selective and miniaturized model, don't you? Five pages of printed text tell the story of the Treaty of Paris, let us say. Eight different textbooks and thirty lectures constitute a teaching model of the French Revolution, right?"

"All right," said Bell.

"Now, then. Our games are models, too." Dr. Franklin's eyes had darkened; they were almost whiteless, as though the intensity of his gaze had swollen the pupils. "We build abstract models just as you do, and our purpose is similar — to show in model form the essential elements of some real situation or problem so that we may comprehend it, analyze it, perhaps do something about it. Well, if a textbook is acceptable as a word model of the French Revolution, then you shouldn't object if we make our models of numbers — or of clusters of magnetic dots on a computer tape."

"I don't object."

"All thought is abstract," Dr. Franklin went on, "as opposed to the immediate and direct impressions of the senses. And as man is a thinking animal, he is devoted to the process of abstraction. We live in a world of abstract models — a simple piece of correspondence, an ordinary interoffice memorandum, a newspaper, the very language we speak, the letters of the alphabet — these are all abstract models and game elements." He spoke rapidly and with assurance, as though he'd gone through the same explanation many times. "As life has become more and more complicated, we have been forced accordingly to rely more and more on life models in order to cope with it. We are trained to handle the real problems of our society, yes, but it is only through the proper use of models that we can effectively manipulate these problems. We need to master the models, not what they represent — we haven't time for that any more. An engineer can design a perfect dam without needing to inspect the site — and a games theorist can devise a perfect bombing pattern without ever having seen a plane or a bomb."

"You mean that the reality is unimportant."

"It is *irrelevant*. Or rather, those elements of a particular reality which are essential must be abstracted into the form of a model — and then the model becomes the reality, the only meaningful reality. As games theory, Nomad is a culmination of the abstraction process. At least, we have hopes it will be. We're experimental here. We've got a long way to go — research, lab tests, field trials. But we're not just playing around with games, Dr. Bell. We're endeavoring to place the most abstract force of all — mathematics — at the highest service of man, by building numerical models of human realities." He was perspiring a little. Almost angrily he wiped his forehead on his sleeve. "Our object is to be able — in the not too distant future — to construct models of world problems so that corrective action may be undertaken on a scientific basis and with a minimum of violence."

"No violence," echoed Dr. Grosch, weakly.

"Let me try to illustrate this further for you," Dr. Franklin resumed, speaking more composedly. "There are many ways of categorizing games. For present purposes, I will divide them into two types — closed and open games. In what I call a *closed* game, the persons involved — and let me call them players — the players are well aware that a game is in progress and that they are playing it against each other. We are playing such a game, in a strategic and political sense, against the Soviet Union. Further, to be *closed*, such a game requires that the players be of roughly equal skill and that they pursue the most rational courses of action in their moves. But now look at the other kind of game — an *open* game. In an *open* game, one of the players does not recognize that a game is in progress. In effect, he declines to play — or, rather, he does not play according to any rational system. As his rational opponent, you may force him, through your superior skill, into a position where only one logical move is possible, and yet he may not make it; he may very well do something else even though this seriously damages his interests."

"That would make it a short game, then," said Bell.

"Ah, but it isn't that simple. I wish it were. You may be visualizing this in terms of a chess match, say, in which your opponent is a blind man who has never so much as heard of chess before and therefore cannot conceivably make rational moves. All right, I'll accept that analogy if I can modify it for purposes of illustrating the American position with respect to various world problems. Take the example of famine. Obviously, we don't consider starving people to be our enemies. At the same time, we must recognize that their failure to develop orderly and productive societies places an extra burden on us, to the extent we are obliged to feed them and police them. 'That isn't fair, is it? Of course not. Well, they've got to be guided toward rational solutions. They've got to be shown how to manage their affairs so they don't impinge on us as co-inhabitants of the same sphere. Speaking in a game sense, every loss on their part becomes to a certain degree a loss on ours; that is, we have to make up some of their losses for them. Let me put it more precisely in game terms. Suppose that the penalty for the loser in this open chess game of ours is death — but that there is also a penalty for the victor, namely the amputation of an arm. Now, this changes the game, doesn't it?" Dr. Franklin was smiling eagerly, studying Bell's features. "You certainly don't want to lose — but you don't want to win, either. Your object now is to avoid ending the game. You want to establish a commanding position on the board in order to control the play, but without being forced to take too many of your opponent's pieces or risking your own, right?"

"Guess so."

"The chief danger, therefore, is not the skill of your opponent — he hasn't any, remember — but his irrationality and incompetence. If you were pitted against a player like yourself in a closed game, you and he would quickly arrive at a *modus vivendi* in order to stabilize this dangerous situation (as we have, to a large extent, in our game with the Russians). But you are in an *open* game now. Your reckless adversary — who does not seem to realize he's in a game at all — appears to be bound to die and in the process to make you lose an arm. So, what must you do?"

"You've got to play for him, too," Bell said.

"Exactly! Or, to put it another way, you must somehow impose rational play on him. For this, you must play another game — that is, a second game within the framework of the first one. You've got to penetrate the irrationality of your opponent. There's a pattern there, even if it appears to be a random and nonsensical pattern which he himself doesn't understand, but to discern it, you must study *him*."

"Two billion blind chess players," muttered Dr. Grosch.

"Quite so," said Dr. Franklin. "Clearly, you can't analyze each one of them. You have to take samplings, which you hope will be reasonably representative, and you've got to keep running the facts you find from each sample through a comparative sorting process — a computer, naturally — which from time to time will disclose certain elements which appear to be common to every sampled group. This is a painstaking operation, to say the least. And subject to error. But let's assume that you do begin to collect some results which appear valid. This becomes the initial basis for your game-within-a-game. You are ready then to begin translating the impulsive and unpredictable irrationality of these two billion chess players into the language which you are accustomed to, the language of mathematical abstraction — and this, in turn, will permit you to predict with increasing confidence what had been unpredictable, and adjust the pattern of your own chess play accordingly."

"But you've simply learned to play their game. You aren't forcing them to play yours."

"Correct." Dr. Franklin seemed pleased by Bell's response. "That's just the first step. You must now go on to teach them, to maneuver them, to influence them — and you've already gone a long way, because the very fact that they are becoming more and more engaged with you in play, and you with them in the process of comparative analysis, means that there is an interchange of reactions, yours and theirs. Just as you slowly begin to perceive them accurately, so you gradually force them to recognize you and the board and the chessmen. And of course there is only one way to play chess. *Your way.* They may hate you. In fact, their hatred may be desirable. From their hatred can rise the determination to defeat you — and to do this requires that they become expert rational players, which is actually your hope, too."

"You want them to become like you."

"Yes indeed! Oh, not all of them can. Only some, at first. The rest will continue irrational play and must be kept in check — or rather, *not* in check, since we're using the chess analogy. Do you see what I'm talking about, Dr. Bell? We're fighting for humanity here. We want to *save* them by exercising the privilege of our leadership! Right, Grosch?"

Dr. Grosch stirred suddenly in his chair. "Oh, yes," he said, uncertainly. He seemed depressed. His eyes were heavily bagged. "Um, another point is that games theory is not an isolated phenomenon, Dr. Bell. It merely expresses in a mathematical way an approach to life problems which has come to be characteristic of our, ah, modern society. But our games are desperately important ones, Dr. Bell — *your* games, too, you know. You're one of us. You have a social duty, just as we do. Don't you, um, agree?"

"I have a social duty to get Lundquist for you, is that what you mean?"

"In specific terms, yes," said Dr. Franklin.

"That's a pretty profitable social duty," Bell remarked. He folded the contract and thrust it in an inside pocket. "I'll study the matter, right? But there's one essential thing. I don't want to be followed any more."

Dr. Franklin shrugged his shoulders.

"I mean that," Bell added. He stood.

"Do join us for lunch," said Dr. Franklin.

"No, thanks. I'm going back to Roanoke." That window-less room was making Bell feel suffocated. He eyed the paintings on the wall. He could almost see Lundquist leering from the trees — not quite, but almost. "I can't decide about the contract right now, but I'll talk to Dr. Grosch privately this evening."

Dr. Grosch gave him a piteous look, but Bell was firm.

"Dr. Grosch alone — seven o'clock at my motel. I guess you already know which one that is, don't you?"

Dr. Franklin shrugged again.

Dr. GROSCH ARRIVED by taxi at the appointed time, agitated and suspicious. He put his hat down as if it were a bomb, and when an owl in the pine grove behind the motel let out a hoot, he shuddered.

"Have a drink," said Bell. He'd bought a bottle of bourbon and a sack of ice cubes.

"No, thank you. Just plain water, please."

"How come you're in Roanoke now?" Bell made a weak drink for himself. Dr. Grosch glugged down his water. He kept glancing all about the room. Bell had to repeat his question.

"Oh, that." Dr. Grosch leaned forward as though he were about to impart a confidence. "I was transferred," he said, but so loudly that Bell recoiled. "I, um, much prefer it." His gaze roved the walls, the TV set, and came to rest on the little steel box attached to one of the beds which, when primed with a quarter, made the mattress vibrate to soothe tired travelers. "It's wonderful here," Dr. Grosch continued, virtually shouting. He got up to refill his glass from the bathroom tap, and on his way back bent close to the little box. "I couldn't be happier in my work!" he declared into it. Then he sat down and gave Bell a look both defiant and beseeching.

"Listen," said Bell. "What does all that crap about two billion blind chess players add up to, anyway?"

"Dr. Bell, I won't hear a word against the project," Dr. Grosch interposed hastily. He began fumbling in his pockets.

"You may not approve of it fully, you may not completely understand it, but take my word for it, it's a thing of b-b-beauty, and um — " He had pulled out a pen and a note pad and was busily scribbling. " — very democratic, too, in its potential applications." He ripped off the page of notepaper and flashed it at Bell. He'd written: *everything bugged.* Immediately he crumpled the page, dropped it into the ashtray, and set fire to it, scorching a finger in the process. He moaned and thrust the finger into his mouth, but at the same time he started writing another message, printing it clumsily with his left hand, for the burned finger was on his right. "But actually," he said in the same unnaturally loud voice he'd used ever since his arrival, "my main object in visiting you this evening, Dr. Bell, is to encourage you to, er, sign that little agreement Dr. Franklin gave you this noon, and to, um — " He was perspiring in his efforts to speak clearly while sucking his finger and simultaneously printing his second note. " — to provide you with any information I can which would, ah, lead you to conclude that, um, by signing the contract you would be doing all concerned a big favor."

He flashed his second message. *Don't sign*, it read. *Go home. Don't come back.* Swiftly he crumpled this little page, too, and Bell helpfully applied a match to it. Infected by Dr. Grosch's example, Bell spoke in a booming voice: "I'm not going to sign that contract!" He assumed this was what his guest hoped he'd say, but he saw by the stricken look on Dr. Grosch's face that he'd erred.

"Surely you don't mean that," Dr. Grosch cried, seizing the pen in his right hand and writing rapidly, wincing with pain.

"You can hardly come to such a decision so, um, quickly, can you?" *Say yes but don't sign,* he'd written this time.

"That is, I won't sign it tonight," Bell amended. Again paper flamed in the ashtray. The room was becoming smoky. "Tomorrow would be good enough, wouldn't it?" he added. "I could mail it in then."

"I'm sure that would be satisfactory!" Dr. Grosch seemed somewhat troubled by the jerky pattern of their conversation, for their dialogue had been broken by suspicious silences as they sought to convey their real meanings. "Guess I'll have another glass of water, Dr. Bell, if you'll excuse me!" Dr. Grosch pointed, however, at the bourbon; then he stamped his way to the bathroom where he ran the tap full blast and returned with an empty glass. "This Virginia water is the purest and finest obtainable!" He eagerly watched Bell pour the bourbon, then fell to writing again, took time out to drain his glass at a gulp, said "yum" sotto voce, and displayed his latest note. *Take train to NY tonight. Outwit them. Then fly home.* Bell obediently burned the message, but when he moved toward the curtained window with the idea of letting out some of the fumes, Dr. Grosch made frantic negative gestures.

Bell's patience was ending. "Listen, Dr. Grosch, let's go get something to eat, how about it?"

"I never eat at night! I sometimes take a bowl of cereal!" Dr. Grosch got busy with his pen again, but Bell brusquely took it from his hand, popped his hat on his head, and tugged him to his feet.

Dr. Grosch submitted to this show of force, but even in Bell's car, driving toward the center of the city, he was fidgeting in anxiety, and, having recovered his pen, thrust a new note before Bell's eyes at a stoplight. *Car bugged, too.* Bell, undaunted, found the downtown lot of the national rental agency he'd used, and, as Dr. Grosch lurked uncomfortably in the background, switched cars.

Dr. Grosch wasn't completely reassured. As Bell drove off in the new car, he was aware of Dr. Grosch whispering in his ear: "They've got devices — pick up conversations blocks away!" Dr. Grosch snapped on the radio and the heater, intermittently jangled a handful of coins, and remained close to Bell, cupping his hand to Bell's ear to transmit his words. Thus huddled together like lovers, Bell and his companion drove about Roanoke and its suburbs, windows closed, heater humming, whispering at each other through a storm of hillbilly music.

"Squa . . . ru . . ."

"What's that?" Bell couldn't make out what Dr. Grosch was saying. The old fellow kept casting glances to the rear.

"Strange things are going on," Dr. Grosch confided, his bourbon breath hot in Bell's ear. "Some of the migrants are making trouble. They're squatting instead of migrating. I mean, they just won't move on like they're supposed to."

"Where?"

"Up at Camp Two. That's Ross's Farm, as it used to be known, about thirty miles north of here. Those migrants ought to be down south with the others by now, but they simply won't go, and then just this week we got a report from Camp Three — that's even farther north, up near Staunton — that about a dozen migrants have shown up *there*, where they have no business to be at all because it's completely out of season, and frankly it's rather disturbing."

"Well, what does it mean?"

"We can't be sure. Muller thinks it's Lundquist's work, naturally. We all expected Carl to make a public denunciation of Nomad through some muckraking newspaper columnist or perhaps a Congressman, but there's been nothing of that sort. As far as these squatters are concerned, who can tell? It may be spontaneous. They may have decided that the camps are an easy mark for handouts — why should they walk their legs off if they can settle down somewhere and cadge meals from project scholars?"

"Is that all they're doing?"

"Yes, except — well, actually, some of our recent depth probes have been unusually counterproductive. A depth probe," Dr. Grosch explained, "is what we call a full battery of tests conducted in such a manner that the subject doesn't know he's being tested. It's virtually foolproof, but, dammit, we've been getting, as I say, a rather sharply increased percentage of nonsensical and improper responses, such as dirty stories, and we haven't yet been able to program it out to see if there's a definite pattern. It's annoying, but not damaging. The system can accommodate itself and adjust," he said, with a note of pride in his voice, and then he added nervously, "I'm sure we're being followed. Do you think there's a camera capable of filming my lip movements?"

Bell swung the car into a drive-in restaurant lot and parked. He couldn't tell if Dr. Grosch's fears were justified, but he was hungry and ordered two hot dogs. Dr. Grosch chose a Dixieburger with Rebel Yell pepper sauce.

Later, as they were touring again, Dr. Grosch continued: "There've been a lot of rumors lately about Carl's whereabouts. He's been reported in a dozen cities in the U.S., Canada, and Mexico. Even Havana, which was very hard to check out. It's almost as if these rumors are being planted deliberately, simply to badger us. Your little joke about Carl's being in Seattle was taken as further evidence that you're in cahoots with him, you see."

"What does Dr. Franklin think?"

"Him? He's of no more importance than I am," Dr. Grosch said, moodily. "He's trapped, poor Franklin. They put him in as a front man because he's a Negro — and because he's a Negro, they don't fully trust him."

"Who are 'they'?"

"I don't know exactly, Bell. I'm just a humble programmer now. There seem to be, however, two factions within the project. Those, like myself, who are dedicated to the ideals of Nomad, and those who would make compromises. They'd use truth drugs on the migrants, for instance, which is a form of violence. Those people are American citizens, after all. I mean, when you surrender to violence and stealth and sneaking around, doesn't it deny the very purpose of your work?" Dr. Grosch was speaking vehemently now, heedless of lip movements. "They're perverting Nomad by their very presence, these people! They're impatient. They say they want immediate results!" He gave a little moan. "The only reason they jumped at the Nomad concept in the first place was because they saw it as a shortcut weapon — a weapon! That's how they've always referred to it! And now the shortcut isn't short enough so they want to shorten it some more. They might as well go out and machine-gun all those squatters. That's the only shortcut they really have faith in! Honestly, Bell, I don't much care for some of the features in the depth-probe system — hidden tape recorders and undercover scholars posing as migrants and all that — but one has to draw the line definitely at drugs. And they keep pressing and pressing for action. Now we're supposed to develop a counterinsurgency game plan for experimental use in a certain country by the end of the year! Incredible! It's like asking the Wright brothers to build a supersonic jet!"

"Is that a military game plan?"

"No, no. They've got those. This happens to be a plan to neutralize disaffected elements by removing potential leadership. The idea is to prevent the buildup of a cohesive and organized antigovernment force which might later prove hard to handle."

"I wrote something like that recently," Bell said abruptly.

"How's that?"

"*The* um *federal government* something something *seeks out potential social conflicts* um *in order to deal with them before they harden into* ah *troublesome realities.*"

"Yes, that's our general idea, all right."

"I taught that!"

"To be sure," said Dr. Grosch. "Quite sound doctrine. The point is whether the job is done nonviolently."

"Let me guess," said Bell. "You identify key future leadership and send them to Yale."

"To Yale?"

"Never mind."

"No, no. I think I see what you mean, Bell. The notion is that you grab these people early and promote them into your leadership structure and in so doing separate them from the disaffected groups they might otherwise organize against you."

"Like Dr. Franklin."

"Dr. Franklin? But he's not an example. I'm not talking about the United States at all. This particular assignment will be an open game for a certain government to use as a policy tool with respect to its own disadvantaged citizens. We have nothing to do with it at all, except to send down top advisers and observers and field men. Naturally we'll supply the equipment, too." Dr. Grosch had begun speaking with brisk optimism, but his mood changed again. "But they're rushing us into going off half-cocked. We're bound to make a blooper. It'll make the theory look bad. You can't force-feed basic research like a goose. Do they *want* to ruin Nomad? That thought has occurred to me. These policemen — that's fundamentally what they are, Bell — they don't have any use for any solutions except for their own. But I won't quit on Nomad. I won't walk out. I'm still fighting for it — from within." Then he sighed dolorously. "I'm not really fighting, you know," he said in a small voice. "I'm just putting in my time. I'm too old to fight. They won't let me find out what's going on outside my little cranny anyhow. I can't see the big picture any more. Maybe nobody sees it. There may not even *be* a big picture! Maybe there never was! Just these security types creeping around opening one's mail. You know, Bell, not long ago I proposed a wholly new approach to my colleagues. I suggested that we go to the migrants themselves with open arms and explain to them how we wanted to help all humanity with mathematical analysis, and I was certain that once the purpose of Nomad was made clear, then the migrants would respond enthusiastically. They'd be proud to assist us. They'd rack their brains to remember the slightest detail that might be useful. Well, do you know what the reaction was to this idea of mine?"

"Tell me."

"They laughed. It was humiliating. And ever since, I've been the recipient of certain glances, as though my brains are addled. Which may be the case by now. They even check on my drinking habits. It's true that I'd nerved myself with a few snorts before broaching my plan, but —"

"Listen," said Bell, to cut short Dr. Grosch's flow of talk, "you've advised me to go home and forget all about this. Don't you want Lundquist found?"

"Maybe I don't. But I was thinking chiefly of you. No good can come of your further association with this project. These people aren't trustworthy. Don't you agree? What do you think of them?"

"I don't like them. They sometimes remind me of myself."

"Do they? That's strange. You seem different. Carl was, certainly. *He* was trustworthy. When Carl said he'd kick a man in the shins, he did it." Dr. Grosch polished his bald dome with his handkerchief, blew his nose, then began absently cleaning his pince-nez. "Sometimes I think of Carl as really being in Mexico or wherever," he continued, in a dreamy voice, "but then again I have the feeling that he's very close, very close indeed, almost around the next corner, and I have this horror of bumping into him without any warning. I wouldn't be up to such an encounter."

Bell had returned to the center of the city. He pulled up near a cabstand.

"If you do find him," Dr. Grosch said, "kindly give him my regards." He looked at Bell sadly. The winking neon glare from store signs fluttered yellow light across his puffed old face. "Do be careful," he said. The light emphasized first one feature, then another. Dr. Grosch was an abstract patchwork of pince-nez, double chin, spacious brow, then pince-nez again. "And what's going to become of *me?*" he asked, but without waiting for a response, he quickly shook Bell's hand, climbed wheezing out of the car, and went over to the nearest cab.

Bell drove back to his motel.

H E HAD TROUBLE sleeping. Dr. Grosch's obsessions plagued him, too. Once he got out of bed and unplugged both the mattress vibrator and the TV set, checked pillow, shower stall, toilet tank, and even the Gideon in the drawer, found no wires or mikes, and lay back down to lull himself to sleep by reciting in his mind all U.S. Presidents, including dates served, going backward toward Washington but stumbling on Arthur and Fillmore. Which served when? Was Arthur the one before the Civil War? He fretted himself asleep, and woke when a rooster crowed the answer: *Fillmore first, Fillmore first.*

He peeked through the curtains as though he expected to see a halfback platoon entrenched and waiting. Nothing.

Just a Virginia dawn with blue mist shivering on the highway.

The migrant camp was thirty miles north of Roanoke, Dr. Grosch had said. Bell studied his map. Three roads led north. One passed the Joint Ecological Studies Center. He followed another one.

There were little farms by the dozen in the hills. Some were abandoned, soil leeched senile by tobacco, and plowed to death. Others were held by city men for weekends of hunting and boozing. Bell saw stands with pumpkins for sale. Halloween was a week away. *Southern Fried Chicken,* a sign said. But this wasn't Deep South; it was hillbilly country. That hillbilly general, Stonewall Jackson, had marched his army north this way, trying to keep Dr. Franklin in bondage. If old Stonewall had lived, he might have brought some history north of Iowa — battle of St. Paul (1867), rebel ironclads on the upper Missouri, a Jeb Stuart raid through the Black Hills!

He was in a lazy maze of country roads. The hills got higher. There were turkey farms and orchards and raw reaches of burned-over pine woods, stony slopes quarried by sheep, and rickety roadside farmhouses with spider-webbed windows and chickens strutting in the doorways.

"Ross's Farm? No, sir, mister, there ain't no Ross around here."

He asked everywhere. He stopped at crossroads stores and one-pump filling stations, jumped ditches to speak to farmers in their fields, questioned school-bound kids, the rural postman, even a slick state trooper wearing sunglasses.

Bell wasn't in any hurry. He had no real idea what he'd do when he found the place, but he wasn't using his time to think, he was just nosing around the hills watching sunlight climb through pine branches and cows chug out of barns. The country air smelled of new straw. He heard frogs grumbling in the creeks, and saw mist drifting down the cold rills that notched the blue mountains on the West Virginia line. It was back country, all right. Nature had endowed it for nomads only. After Great-Great-Grandfather Ross showed up with his ax and mule and began hacking pines and pulling stumps, the thin earth had started washing from under his feet, and when the old fellow arose one spring morning after an all-night downpour to discover half his land boiled off into the creeks, leaving him a fine crop of subsoil stones for his family to munch on the rest of the year, what a look of outrage and betrayal must have frozen on his face. He hadn't much left to pass on except that look. It was still there. Bell had seen it all day on those pale faces. The air was fresh, but the land, ruined long ago, was still paying off the mortgage of disaster. The country people had been eroded, too, down to bitterness. Bell could smell their hatred. They hated everything — him, too, for coming there with his new car and suit and hat and a face that wasn't sullen or sly. Some pretended they couldn't understand what he was asking them, scratched their ears in puzzlement, and fouled him with snuff breath or slimy looks from rheumed eyes — cunning, hostile people who maybe knew damned well where Ross's Farm was but wouldn't tell him out of sheer meanness.

The sun was moving through occasional clouds. Bell drove faster. The land looked a little different to him now. Something sour about it. Generations had sown pebbles and reaped stones. A poverty landscape, sure. The mountain hardwoods were high enough for October frost to have burned reds and yellows among the pine green, but beneath them were desolated shacks and fester-back mules and men with scarred plowshares watching chickweed grow in the gullies. Nomad country! Up ahead Bell saw an old country-man shuffling like a bear, one leg alimp. He pumped his brakes and let the car creep up on his quarry — but then the old boy turned a half-wit face and gaped both teeth, and Bell drove on. Lundquist's spirit was taunting him — Dr. Grosch had sensed it, too — but the flesh wasn't to be so easily captured.

He stopped for gas and lunch: stale crackers, a candy bar, a bottle of lemon pop.

"I'm looking for the farm where the migrants work. Used to be called Ross's Farm."

The attendant obviously didn't understand the word *migrants*.

"Agricultural laborers," said Bell, aware of his northern accent. "Transient farm workers. They work and then move on somewhere else."

"They's a place two mile north got a new fence on the left-hand side maybe that's it."

It wasn't. But at a crossroads a little farther Bell saw a small blue marker, arrow-shaped, labeled *Camp Two*, presumably to guide replacement sociologists. He went where it pointed. The road narrowed and turned into a graveled track that rose, twisting, through hilly woods.

There was a gate, hospitably ajar. A gatepost sign read *Ross's Farm, workers employed in season*, and then, in smaller letters below, *Camp Two*.

Bell drove through and up a rise to where the trees ended, then stopped and got out of the car. The farm was spread below him.

It was an apple orchard, mostly. The bare trees were ranged in rows along a slope that dipped out of sight into a hollow. Here and there were patches of worked earth marked with tiny pennants, perhaps agronomists' test plots. To Bell's right the orchard ended at a downhill creek; to his left it stopped where the ground steepened at the pine line. The farm buildings were at the edge of the woods: a two-story frame house freshly painted in white with black trim, with two automobiles and a pickup truck parked in front; beyond was a small barn, and some hundred yards farther was a long low structure which Bell guessed was a bunkhouse.

He couldn't see anyone, neither squatters nor scholars. Far off among the pines he thought he spied rising smoke, but the trees breathed such a haze into the afternoon sun he couldn't be sure.

No help for it. He guessed he'd have to pay his respects at camp headquarters.

They'd heard his car coming. Two stocky youngish men in blue jeans and parkas stepped out on the porch of the house to watch him as he drove up.

Bell chatted with them there. They were polite, but didn't invite him inside, even after he introduced himself and said no less a personage than Dr. Franklin had the previous day offered him a project consultantship. They might at least have given him an apple.

"Thought I'd have a look around before I decided about the job," he went on, inviting himself. Still they didn't budge.

He hadn't caught their names. One was a soils specialist, the other a social anthropologist; they looked as though they could do fifty push-ups without sweating.

"Heard there were some migrants still here," Bell said, prodding a lagging conversation.

"Who said that, Dr. Bell?"

"Forget just who," Bell said, scanning orchard, creek, pine clumps, "but is that true?"

The two husky scientists looked at each other. "Well, there are a few of them in the woods," the anthropologist said, reluctantly.

"What, sleeping there?"

"That's right. We closed the barracks when the season ended. Technically those people are trespassing," the anthropologist went on, "but we're not making a stink about it yet, as long as they maintain good fire discipline and keep their area policed up. It'll be too cold for 'em soon. They'll have to move on."

"How do they eat?"

"We're giving 'em canned rations in exchange for some odd jobs around the place. We don't want to get into the position of driving 'em off, you see. That might create a bad image."

"You bet," Bell said. "How many are out there? They in platoon strength?"

"Just a couple squads, Dr. Bell," the anthropologist replied, and then, as if caught off-guard, he gave Bell a sober glance. "Maybe twenty men," he added, sulkily.

"You fellows wouldn't object if I paid a visit to your squatters, would you?"

"You're welcome to do it if you want to, but we wouldn't recommend it." The soils man did the talking this time. "That's a pretty rough bunch of joes in those woods, sir. I don't mean they'd harm you or anything, but the two of us don't go in except twice a week when the supply guys come and can sort of give us some back-up, you understand, and even then we carry shotguns like we're hunting rabbits, which we do, but I mean to say there's some ornery characters in that lot, and that's the truth."

"Gotcha," Bell said. "I'll take my chances." He went down the porch steps. "Mind if I leave my car where it is, fellows?" They didn't mind. "See you around," Bell said, squelching the impulse to ask how big the anthropology department was at West Point. He might need some help later.

No telephone wires, he noticed, as he started barnwards. No power line, either. He guessed they had their own diesel unit for electricity, plus a radio-phone (with which to let Dr. Franklin know he'd come). That barn was probably a camouflaged computer, and every tree would be bugged, a mike in every pine cone. They didn't have to worry about squatters. Every time a migrant farted, Dr. Franklin could study a graph of the sound waves.

He was whistling, but not feeling too chipper. He wasn't dressed for this occasion. With blue suit, street shoes, topcoat and hat, all he needed was a briefcase. And what would he do when he reached these rough joes, anyhow — fill his hat with pine needles to make a basketball and dazzle them with left-handed hooks into an owl's nest?

He was entering nature's slums. There were squirrels instead of rats, rivulets instead of sewers, and in the tenements here the windows were open all the time. He stopped to listen. He heard nothing. Even his own heart was muffled by woolen Yankee underwear.

He wasn't lost, not yet. He'd passed the bunkhouse and was about fifty yards beyond it in a woodland labyrinth, but he could tell directions by the slope of the ground. Left went uphill to Lord knew where; right went down to the orchard. He peered all around, sniffed the air, studied the ground. His senses told him nothing. He wasn't much of an outdoorsman. In summer he sometimes went fishing with Pico, and in winter he skated on the river — last Christmas he and Norma, courting, had skated arm in arm at midnight between great bonfires on both banks! — but he didn't hunt, never watched birds unless they watched him first, hadn't scouted or camped, had seen his first fox in a zoo, was an old expert on landscape features (but only from falcon heights, this being the lore learned in army photo-intelligence school and not too useful at his present altitude of six feet three), and knew trees not by name but for their usefulness in providing paper for books and basketball floors for gyms.

He marched on. It was chilly. The sunlight came down in patches. He wished he'd brought his earmuffs. The farther he went, the less jaunty his steps became. Those all-American environmentalists back there went visiting with shotguns, but all he had was a ballpoint pen.

Something had moved up ahead. A man, a squirrel, a feathered friend? He couldn't tell. That something had melted away into nothing. But he'd come across a sort of path, a trampled way leading uphill, and, following it, he encountered evidence of human presence: a rusted bean can, crumpled by somebody's hands. Wow. Really crumpled. Could he, Bell, do a job like that even with his own outsize mitts? He tried to console himself; probably it was a cheap can. But it bothered him.

He strode forward nonetheless. Climbed a little knoll. Crashed through a brambly thicket. Jumped a path-blocking bough like Pico's Ojibway high hurdler, Broken Crotch. Skirted a nest of turds, probably human. Then stalked between a pair of bosomy boulders, fitted with lichen bras.

And found himself right in the middle of the squatters' camp.

They were all around him, watching him in silence.

Bell completed his last step. He made a slow turning movement, keeping his fists clenched so his fingers wouldn't fall off. Yes, sir. He'd found the place. There were rough joes aplenty giving him animal looks — steady, remote, cold.

He cleared his throat and raised one hand to tip his hat, figured it would be a dandified gesture under the circumstances, and instead wiped his nose, which needed it.

They weren't being silent out of respect, that was sure. He looked from one face to another, seeking some sign of acknowledgment.

Nothing. They were giving him a treatment. Sweat, stranger.

Some leaned against rocks, others sprawled on makeshift twig mattresses or squatted on their heels beside the dead ashes of their lunchtime fire. A mountain breeze informed Bell of their odor. It was tragic, that smell.

He got worried waiting. His legs were turning to cotton. Where was that old-fashioned Virginia courtesy he'd read about?

"Peace," he croaked, trying the lighthearted approach. No reaction, not so much as the shifting of a tobacco wad. *Don't show fear*, he advised himself. To keep his legs steady, he began a dignified tour of the campsite, studying each man he passed to see if *leader* might be written on one forehead.

The migrants were all sizes, ages, colors. Blackberry, ginger brown, bile white, whiskey red. Old and young. One had a pegleg, another was minus an ear, most sported whiskers, and as for clothing, it was a ragbag array of castoffs and military surplus brightened by two derbies and a set of spats. Bell stared; they stared back. Once he thought he saw a familiar face — a young face dressed in a cornsilk beard — but couldn't place it.

All of a sudden he found himself flat on the ground. Two pairs of hands had yanked his ankles in mid-step from behind. He lay with his hand-heels dug in dirt. His hat had hopped a yard ahead.

They were laughing now. He heard them. Snickering and snuffing all around. But when he slowly got up, retrieved his hat, and brushed himself off, the chuckles died out and they began playing possum again.

"I'm looking for — " he began, then something hit him between the shoulder blades. He turned. It was an empty can of beans, uncrumpled. He picked it up and gave it all he had, doubling it, damned near flattening it, he was so furious and scared, and he felt a little better. "*Lundquist*," he shouted. He hooked the bean can thirty yards into an unseen basket. But there weren't any court fans in this mob. No cheers.

"Man named Lundquist — I'm trying to find him." Now he was being hit by pebbles; little ones, but they stung his wrists and ankles, where they were aimed. Nobody was trying for his head. Not yet. He never saw who was pitching. He'd turn one way and get potted at from behind. When he edged back to a boulder, he got peppered from the sides. "*Lundquist*," Bell roared, as if he expected old Carl to wriggle out from a dead log and put a stop to all this nonsense. He lost his hat next. Some prankster crept around on the other side of his boulder and swept it off with a stick. Bell went for it, but a grubby hand snatched it first, and the hat went whirling around the squatters' circle, chucked from one man to another. He started to pursue it, topcoat flopping, but decided that's what they wanted him to do, and so took up his old center position, bareheaded, ignoring the hat when it appeared on the end of a stick, just out of reach.

"Listen, my name's Bell! I've got nothing to do with the project! All I want is to find a man named Lundquist! If any of you — "

He had to stop for breath. His rage was fighting his fear, leaving not much energy for public announcements. Those pebbles were flying now, and the marksmen weren't being too careful. One struck his cheek, another bounded off his bald spot. He took his glasses off, cased them, and put them in his pocket. A pebble hit his forehead. They wanted to see him cut and run, they wanted to see those long outsider legs chop a new path in the forest — and he could, he could — he could go booming out of there downhill and in ten minutes he'd break into open orchard space, provided his astigmatism didn't fetch him into an oak.

But he'd be damned first.

They'd drawn blood. He felt some on his cheek, his brow, his chin, too. He swung around, searching the faces, now very slightly blurred.

"I came here to ask some questions, I didn't come here to fight." He caught one pebble in his hand and shook it like a die, ready to throw back. "I can't fight twenty men, but by God I can fight one."

Something he thought he saw. Weird. One of those crouched migrants seemed to be doing tension exercises with his palms. Bell, marveling, squinted harder that way.

Then one man arose. The pebble storm ceased. The squatters seemed to relax a bit. No more silent treatment. They began scratching and gaping, hawking, spitting, stretching, passing a few comments to neighbors, all the while lazily keeping watch on the man who'd gotten up and now, as he came closer to Bell, was getting bigger.

"You kin fight *one?*"

That's what Bell heard the fellow say. It depressed him — but what had he expected, Band-Aids? He made no reply. He stood his ground, puffing. The man was approaching so slowly he had time to give him an eye frisk. No knives in evidence, but these rural knights were said to carry them in their sleeves and hats.

"Kin you fight *one?*"

Check, Bell agreed — but this one was like a dozen. He wasn't so tall as Bell nor so bulky as Pico, but he had a face on him that would make a hangman faint, a face like a crowd of faces, all raging; a jigsaw face stitched by scars and wart-buttoned — purple cheeks, gray lips, nose bashed in, un-matched ears, beard bald in the scarred places.

"Here's *one* for ye."

It didn't make matters any worse, but the purple-cheeked man happened to be wearing Bell's hat.

This was Test Two, Bell figured. He hadn't run from pebbles; would he run from this?

Those fists looked like young pumpkins. How many jaws had they broken? *Watch the eyes.* Bell bent slightly at the knees. *Don't hit first.* But he might not survive long enough to be second.

Ten feet apart, then five. The man in Bell's hat grinned, moved his elbows out, came shuffling forward inch by inch.

"Ain't no Carl Lundquist here, Shorty."

He growled that from three-foot range, then made a jump Bell's way, arms wide for grabbing.

Bell skipped backward — or rather, tried to.

Another little joke. Someone had slithered out on hands and knees behind him, and he went crashing back full-length in the dirt.

He rolled quickly into a crouch, but his antagonist was swaggering back to his place and the whole camp was hee-hawing with laughter and chucking pebbles again, not at Bell but at each other, in pure high spirits.

What next? This was a Roman circus, Bell as gladiator. Maybe they'd get tired of jokes and start heaving boulders. He didn't have to stay. He'd shown guts enough. Besides, it would get dark before long. The sun was slanting down far-ther every minute. And hadn't old Purple Cheeks himself assured him Lundquist wasn't around?

"What you come here for anyhow, Shorty?" That was

his late partner again, bellowing from across the way. "We just a bunch of pea pickers. They weren't no call to come a-showin' off them fine city clothes 'n make us pore folks feel small, now was they? We just humble as cow-pies out here, Shorty. No rich man in his right mind wants to mess with us." That voice whined like a fire siren through ruined snout and huge ashy lips.

Someone raced past Bell and showered him with a handful of dirt.

"Reckon you done wanted to have a look at real honest-to-Jesus *poverty*," the spokesman went on. Bell shook dirt down. "Well, Shorty, we's 'bout as *impoverished* a lot of mothers you'll ever see, so you better take a good long look — "

Bell's topcoat was yanked hard from behind. He swiveled on his heels, but his attacker scrambled back out of reach. In the meantime, the pegleg had stumped out and flung a dipper of what Bell hoped was just water, which splattered against his shoulder and trickled down inside his collar.

" — got us 'nother country out here, Shorty. Ain't no 'merica where you is now. You done crossed the line — "

Bell couldn't go after a cripple, but he swore he'd maim the first complete man who came at him. Sweat was storming down his sides. He could hear his own voice — "huh, huh, huh" — singing a small song of closure madness — he'd die first, die first — and still could hear that great whining purple ox mocking: " — this here's *poverty* nation, Shorty, 'n when some outside mother pays a call like you done, well, shit, man, you got to *conform* to the local customs — "

A black man came dancing out with flailing arms. When

Bell made a move toward him, he feigned terror and bolted, hopped onto a boulder and sat there grinning.

" — got us just a hole in the woods here, but that's good 'nough. Don't need no fine homes out here. Don't need no city hall, no sheriff, neither. We a bunch of free starving mothers in this nation, Shorty — "

Bell was prowling around the circle, daring some bastard to come at him. They just lay there grinning from their boulders and holes. Got him sore, all right.

" — got no idea how *free* we be. We ain't got *nothin'* that ain't free. We got free speech, we got free religion — the good Lord he's directly overhead, Shorty, 'n he washes our sins away each time it rains — "

Bell, watching from man to man for movement, saw what he thought he'd seen before. Damned if he didn't. That young squatter with the silky fringe of beard was doing tension exercises, palm vs. palm.

" — even got us a free press. That's me. I mean to say I'm the local *newspaper*, seein' how we ain't much for readin' here 'n I got a voice on me capable of mighty wide circulation! They call me Jesus, Shorty, that's my name, for my daddy he was one of them wetback greasers swum hisself to Texas — they's a lot of greasers calls their kids Jesus — 'n my mamma, she some old Kentucky lady, half-nigger 'n half-white 'n half split in two pieces, Shorty, when *I* got borned, for I come out 'bout the size of a buffalo calf feet first 'n ready to run, 'n *Jesus* was the first thing I heard, for my ol' mamma kept hollerin' *Jesus Jesus* with me a-bustin' her in two — "

Bell studied that silk beard. It had to be young Brant, the swim champ. Had to be.

He raised his arm and pointed at silk-beard. *"You,"* he said. He beckoned. *"Come out here, champ."*

Silk-beard had no choice. He got up and came out slowly. Bell backed off to give him room.

It was Brant. No doubt of that. He was keeping his distance from Bell, who now didn't know what to do, and all the time Brant's eyes were blinking desperate messages and his head was shaking no-no-no.

"— 'n when *I* hollered back, why ol' Jesus Senior, my daddy, he *run* all the way back to Messico, 'n the midwife she fell dead 'n folks miles 'round was struck deaf!"

Both Bell and Brant were aware of the central fact. All Bell had to do, to win these poverty hearts, was to denounce the spy. Brant's Idaho accent and uncalloused hands would be proof enough.

"— so they finally had to shove my loud-mouth ass down in Texas where I could holler all day to the coyotes 'n rattlers 'n such — "

Be tough on young Brant. But Bell didn't owe him anything. Let Brant be gladiator for a while.

"— punched them steers twenty years, a goddamn cowboy, 'n I mean to say, Shorty, in them days it was a *privilege* to engage in that profession — why, we et cactus boiled 'n sometimes fried on weekdays 'n prairie-dog steaks Sundays — Cowboy Jesus, you bet your white ass! Now say there, what the *shit* is you up to, Shorty, goin' to dance a *waltz* with that young feller or is you fixin' to creep aroun' behin' him to cornhole him or what? Let's you 'n him get to fightin'!"

The squatters were getting impatient, too, shouting and throwing dirt chunks. The two reluctant battlers shuffled together and grappled like pro wrestlers, with sham ferocity.

"Sure hope you won't peach on me, sir," Brant muttered in Bell's ear.

"Don't worry." Bell, furious, felt betrayed by his damned sense of honor — and he knew Brant wouldn't trust him, not after Butterfly Street.

They staggered back and forth amid shouts and clods. Brant was as fresh as a brook trout. He had Bell's arms locked and was making him rumba.

"Better let me whip you, Dr. Bell. Tell you why. If you won, sir, then prob'ly some other guy would come out to fight you, understand?"

Bell understood, but he didn't give a damn. He'd deck them all, one after the other. Let them come. He heaved loose from Brant's grip — his coat seams split — and lunged at him, seized air, saw the camp dart heavenwards, and found himself stretched flat, with Brant on top, pinning him.

"Great, Dr. Bell," Brant whispered. "Now push me off and we'll do it a few more times to make it look better."

Brant knew judo, it seemed.

Bell was almost helpless. The swim champ had him crawling in air, floundering in dust; he handled Bell as gently as a mother might, even making him look good — and all the time kept encouraging his performance with muted words of cheer. "Doing super, sir." Bell was huffing out dry sobs of rage. "Putting on a real show there, Dr. B." Bell lost count of the falls. Sometimes Brant managed to slip under him as he toppled, sometimes Brant let out a howl of pretended pain, and once when Bell by chance smacked his nose with an elbow, Brant gave a genuine yip. "Winged me on that one, sir."

On and on they rolled, kicked, thrashed, grunted up and down, but Bell wouldn't quit. "Judge it's 'nough, sir." Brant was getting a bit winded now himself. Bell was deaf, blind, dumb. "Last pin coming, Dr. B.!" It came. Bell just lay there and took it. "Try to see you later, sir." Brant's parting message. Then he was gone.

Bell didn't quit even then. He got right up again — or thought he did. But it was darkening now; night was slipping fast into the woods. Two men were building a big cook fire; others played cards; a ragged tenor whimpered a mountain love song while punishing a homemade guitar. Bell had been flung down like a dirt rag for God knew how long. They'd let him lie undisturbed. That was something, anyway.

Then he realized that his shoes and socks were gone.

His wallet, too.

They'd left him his wristwatch only because he'd lain with his arms doubled under him.

He just sat there—barefoot, smeared with dirt and spotted with dried blood, huddled in his ripped and ruined topcoat, voiceless, a rung Bell wrung dry. But he was still there, wasn't he?

He shivered, and rubbed his naked feet. A damned outrage. His whole body ached from Brant's massage. Nothing broken, everything bent. He worked his way backwards on hands and butt until he reached a rock to lean against.

Woodsmoke was coiling up like cottony guts as the cooks forced the fire down to coals. Cowboy Jesus, beyond the fire, threw his head back to drink from a bottle. Bell heard his donkey bray above the racket of the camp: *"Hot shit."* He began hopping and capering, fanning his mouth with Bell's hat, fending off with elbows two squatters anxious for the bottle, took another pull, whooped again, grabbed his crotch, skipped around the fire — *"ride 'em, cowboy."* When one of the would-be topers got too close, Cowboy Jesus knocked him flat; having made his point, he handed down the bottle.

It was then that Bell remembered. He'd said *Lundquist* only, hadn't he? But Cowboy Jesus had used the first name, too. *Ain't no Carl Lundquist here.* And there was more than just that. Lundquist left his mark on men — and the Cowboy was marked, almost as if it was Lundquist's hat he wore instead of Bell's. That wild hybrid with skunk cabbage cheeks had surely sucked in from Lundquist some of what he'd been jabbering out at Bell. Ought to double-check it, maybe. Ought to listen some more. Or maybe it was time for a little self-preservation. Nobody but a fool would stay longer. He ought to wheel around that rock and scamper twinkle-toed downhill to safety before his feet froze or his throat got cut. He still had his car keys, glasses, and Nomad contract. He could drive barefoot to the Center and get a nice cash advance. He'd have earned it.

He went around the rock, but only for bladder relief. Pebbles gnawed his tender feet. The forest was black now; sunset trails wandered far above, fading fast, racing above that cell at the Center where Nomad had its black man trapped, above the computer zoo where Dr. Grosch frantically fed numerical chow into each cage, above campuses where future Brants splashed in heated pools, loosening up for Muscle History.

Meanwhile, Bell was pissing in the wilderness. It ran downhill. Why didn't he?

Lundquist was playing him off the board in an open game. Bell was the blind man here. A hoot owl quizzed the night. Who? Fillmore first, that's who. Ah, but had old Fillmore ever sat barefoot in October woods? Bell heard the owl, farther off. The fieldmouse would squeak like Garfield did when the bullet hit him. Nature's machine was oiled by blood, but it still squeaked. Owl ate mouse, Muller ate Grosch, Fillmore ate Taylor (1850), Arthur ate Garfield, and now somebody, everybody, was eating on Bell.

Wouldn't squeak, though.

He padded the length of the camp to reach the fire. Rabbits and chickens were spitted there. Beans were bubbling in a pot.

"How come you still here, Shorty?" The Cowboy was squatting like a red-eyed frog. "You aim to stay for supper? We ain't no goddamn Salvation Army."

Bell kept his hands shoved in his pockets and squinted around at the faces painted by flames and smeared by smoke. Sparks tumbled up.

"Reckon maybe you come slummin' here, Shorty. Figure you get a free meal maybe. Well maybe you done figured wrong. Just 'cause folks is poor don't mean they handin' out roast chicken to ever' mother come stompin' in. Shit, you strip folks down to bareass poverty 'n by Jesus you find out how motherin' *mean* they really is. I'm tellin' you, Shorty, *you* done taught me poverty 'n meanness, you done taught me *good*, 'n I'd be an ungrateful critter, Shorty, if I neglect to let you know how well I learned."

There were snickers and a murmuring from the darkness beyond the fire. Bell felt his stomach tighten and turn.

"My little brother — my half-brother, like, outa my

mamma by some ol' Indian — anyhow, *he* gettin' an advanced de*gree* in state jail up at Frankfort. Yes, sir, you really educatin' that young feller!" Cowboy Jesus took Bell's hat off and spat into it and put it back on. " 'N as for me, you done put me on the cross down in Texas, Shorty, if you 'member when I was s'posed to be foreman but you tol' me I couldn't 'cause I was a nigger or a spick or greaser — I mean, you couldn't figure out 'xactly *what* I was, I so goddamn all mixed up — but anyways when I got a mite fractious, why you like to have me lynched right there, Shorty, you was so disappointed, 'n it wound up I give two years of my life to the state of Texas a-helpin' them other slow-learnin' sons-of-bitches improve the county road system!" He got up. Two strides brought him face-to-face with Bell. "I built them roads for you, Shorty. Ain't that enough? You want my roast chicken, too?"

Bell kept his jaws clamped so his heart wouldn't jump out. He'd come over, like a fool, but he'd come to listen.

"You aim to help me, Shorty? That what you 'bout to say? You going to *ameliorate* my condition?" The Cowboy was speaking spit flecks that spattered Bell. "Shorty, you done ameliorated the shit out of me already, 'n now you anxious to practice on me some more so you can ameliorate some other poor fuckers in some motherin' other places you reachin' out for? Well, Shorty, got to beg yore pardon, but this cowboy has done *seceded* from yore union." He was glaring at Bell with a grin, eyes fleshed tight to points that caught the light of the fire. "You scared, Shorty?" He almost whispered that. "You never et fear before? Taste it, Shorty. Taste it good. You done served plenty — you should ought to have tasted it before you served it."

There was a knife in his hand. The point of the knife was touching Bell's coat at the stomach.

"*Taste that!*" He roared right into Bell's face, and for some little time he and Bell stared into each other's eyes like beasts, like brothers, enemies, like one man studying his image in a mirror, as the stars exploded silently overhead and the fire died low and the other men there stood with their mouths filling with saliva and shuddering with a strange hunger.

Then Cowboy Jesus stepped back. "You shore is one cold mother, Shorty." He shut his knife and pocketed it. "Some melt, some freeze. You the freezin' kind, I reckon." He went back to where he'd been before and muttered something to one of the cooks. The others relaxed, disappointed. The man with the guitar began tormenting it again. Bell made his mind up he'd stay standing. Wouldn't fall. His jaws ached, but he clenched them all the tighter.

"Now, we ain't rich but we ain't poor neither," Cowboy Jesus went on, squatting down, "'n we shore don't want to deny a meal to a feller who's come so far for it. Just hol' yore hands out, Shorty, 'n you get yore share."

The cook was coming toward Bell with a pan.

"Hol' yore hands out," the Cowboy repeated.

Bell did. The cook emptied the pan into them. What came out felt cold and slimy. The other men, crowding around for a look, broke into laughter. Bell had gotten the entrails. They dripped and oozed through his fingers. He couldn't have held them if he'd wanted to.

He turned and walked stiffly away from the fire. Some sport scooped up a handful of what he'd left and flung it after him, decorating his back and shoulders.

He kept going. When he reached his rock, he sat down and began rubbing his hands in the dirt to clean them. He kept his eyes on the squatters, who were milling around the fire to get the food being handed out.

Bell was out of the light and alone. He stayed where he was, taking a long time to work on his hands, and thinking of nothing much else but that.

Iᴛ ᴡᴀs ᴘᴀsᴛ midnight when he woke. He studied the luminous markings on his wristwatch for some time, having trouble because he was shaking so. Must be near freezing, he thought. He couldn't feel his feet. The cold had come shoving right through him.

"Dr. Bell — "

That was Brant, tapping his shoulder. Brant wanted him to get up and go somewhere.

"Dr. Bell — "

The campfire sighed and grumbled in its coals. The migrants were fanned out around it, snoring like donkeys. One lone fire guard remained up, wrapped in a blanket, throwing pine chunks into the coals from time to time and watching the sparks snap high.

"Got your shoes and wallet, sir. Here."

They'd gone some eighty paces off into the woods. Bell's legs rippled with cramp. He couldn't stop shivering.

"I figured if I didn't take them, Dr. B., somebody else might."

"Socks," Bell said. "No socks. Socks gone."

"Darn," Brant whispered. "Somebody stole your socks? Gee, if I'd thought of that, I'd have taken them, too. You just can't trust those people, sir. I'm real sorry — but here, I've got a little brandy. It'll warm you up some."

The campfire was a rose smudge far off. No light of moon or stars came through the branches. Bell couldn't even see Brant's pale face.

"Listen, Dr. B., when you're ready I'll guide you down to the farm. They'll have some coffee and chow for you." The brandy was defrosting Bell's interior; he could feel it boiling in his belly and sending radiant feelers into his arms and legs. He poured some into his hands and rubbed his feet with it. "That's where I went," Brant continued, "to find out what they figured we ought to do with you, and we sort of decided the best thing would be for you to break off contact here."

"Oh, yeah?" Drunks don't freeze, Bell thought. He hadn't eaten since those crackers at noon; already he felt a bit boozed.

"With all respect, sir, you sort of compromised your position coming in like that, asking openly about the man we're trying to find, you see, and it's better if we coordinate — I mean, we really appreciate your having protected my cover — but my mission here might be jeopardized, you understand. Oh, I've got a candy bar for you. And a sandwich. Ham and cheese."

Bell was nearly comfortable, leaning against a tree trunk, sipping brandy and eating the sandwich. He pocketed the candy bar.

"It's not my idea, Dr. Bell. I mean, Major Reuss is the one in charge here."

Bell guessed that Major Reuss would be the West Point anthropologist. But how could Major Reuss be in charge of Cowboy Jesus? Ridiculous. "What's this about a mission, champ?" Bell asked. "You trying to get religion into these migrants or something?"

"Ha, ha. Well, no, sir. It's communications. I plant these electronic bugs on them and we trace their movements that way. They're really marvelous little things, made up special for us, in the exact same size and shape as wood burrs, so a man won't realize what it is actually sticking to his cuffs or on his hat or wherever I manage to fix 'em. I mean, what's a wood burr more or less to these people? They give off signals like little pulses, as I guess you're aware, sir, and then you triangulate on 'em and so you can follow a man generally in this way by electronic means."

"What, you mean you've been creeping around putting wood burrs on these guys?"

"Right, sir. I've just been here a couple nights, so I've got quite a batch to do still. You've got to be careful in this kind of operation. A few at a time, you know. I'd have gotten some more done tonight except I had to get down to the Major to clue him in about you. We feel kinda responsible for you, Dr. B."

"You're tagging the migrants like birds?"

"Ha, ha. You might say that. Never thought of it like that,

sir, matter of fact. Listen, whenever you feel refreshed, we'll hike on down to the farm. I kinda promised to have you there by one o'clock."

"Hang on a minute, champ. Tell me, what results have you gotten?"

"From the bugs? Well, nothing much. It's a little early to tell. There's a lot of traffic here — two or three new men show up each day, and two or three leave — and they've got no security at all that I can tell, which made it easy for me to kinda slip in and play dumb, you know, just another guy drifting in to help chop wood for his beans — well, anyway, the first trackings just showed a few men going in to Roanoke, and the results were pretty disappointing."

"Where'd they go?"

"Oh. Well, when the Major's people performed actual field follow-through, they traced these subjects to some, well, some pretty disreputable locations."

"Whorehouses?"

"Matter of fact, sir, yes."

"Still wearing their burrs!"

"Check. Um, you 'bout ready to leave, Dr. B.?"

"Hold it. Can't use my feet yet." Bell was brandy-merry but alert. He concentrated on wiggling his toes. "But apart from these whorehouse expeditions, you predict ultimate electronic victory, do you?"

"Not sure, sir. My own opinion is that the man we want isn't within a thousand miles. I mean, I've been analyzing every scrap of info I've picked up around here hour after hour — we're trained in this work, you know, Dr. B. — and there's not the slightest indication, not a clue."

"That so?" Incredible, Bell thought. Brant would never know, nor would Major Reuss, nor Moss, nor Muller, nor any of them, never. It took a closure-ridden fool like himself, with a fantasy wood burr bugging his brain. "Tell me, champ. How come you got into this project business, whatever it is?"

"I got hired on campus, sir. A recruiter came — "

"No, I mean what's your, um, sense of purpose in your chosen work?"

"Oh, that. Well, Dr. B., the way I see it, I'm helping defend our heritage. You know what I mean, sir. You teach history."

"You've got me there. You sure put your finger on it." Bell sat straight and took one last sip of brandy. "Didn't quite realize it before. I mean, I don't teach so much history as heritage. By God, I'm a professor of *heritage*."

"Check, sir, and not so loud if you don't mind. Heritage is right, and those of us who are privileged to attend college, if we learn nothing else we learn to value this heritage and that we've got to keep other people from taking it."

"Brant, you've got it wrapped up, right there." Bell burped and yawned. He capped the flask. Had to stay sharp now. Those wood burrs were no joke. He'd have to dispose of young Brant somehow. "Champ, I have never known a man with such moral certainty as yourself."

"Say, thank you, sir. 'Preciate that a lot." Brant rustled leaves as he stood. "Guess we better start down now."

"Uh uh."

"Sir?"

"Not me. I'm not going. You go."

"I can't just leave you here alone, Dr. B. The Major instructed me — "

"Forget it, Brant." Bell tucked the flask in his coat pocket. "Forget the mission, too. It's finished. No more wood burrs."

"What do you mean?"

"I mean I'm closing you out, champ. You're through up here. Go back to the farm and report in, that's all."

"Gee, Dr. B. You can't do that. I mean, I've been *assigned*. You can't prevent —"

"Damned right I can. And I will, if I have to. I protected you this afternoon, kid, but if you stick your nose into that squatter camp again, I'll tell them exactly who you are and what you are."

"You will?" Brant sounded appalled. "I mean, I can't believe you're serious, sir. They told me you'd decided to work along with us."

"They're wrong, Brant. I didn't. And I'm not kidding you. Shove off."

"Listen, Dr. B. If I have to drop out, the Major'll only send somebody else."

"He'd better not. I'll put the finger on anybody he sends. Tell him that."

Soft sounds near Bell's ear indicated that Brant, analyzing the situation, was aiding reflection with tension exercises. "I'm really surprised at your attitude, Dr. B. I really am. I just don't see why you'd want to side with these people out here."

"I'm not siding with them. Go on, Brant. Get back to the farm."

"Listen, Dr. B. You understand you're putting yourself in a pretty bad position by this, don't you?"

"So long, champ." Bell got to his feet, wincing with pain. He moved off a few steps, testing his legs.

"I mean, I'm going to have to report fully to the Major, and he's going to be darned upset, particularly without you offering any sort of reason."

"Just tell him I've decided to guard his heritage in my own way," Bell said. "And thank him for the sandwich."

BELL RESOLVED TO set up his own camp. Suppose Major Reuss sent Brant back with a brace of two-hundred pound agronomists and a strait jacket? Suppose the Cowboy stopped joking and started whittling in earnest?

He blundered north, following the ground rise. It was dark as a closet, the underbrush as dense as suits hung inside. He went one hundred paces, not counting lurchings into tree trunks, toe stubbings (he carried his shoes, his feet having swelled), or one unforgettable yielding tread upon a fecal bundle — still, it seemed, slightly warm — and then he hand-raked a mound of pine needles behind an outcropped rock elbow, where he lay shuddering until dawn, dozing off, then waking in terror of throat-ripping catamounts or eye-fancying owls, and in agony from leg cramp.

Sunup found Bell a wreck, with a brandy hangover on top of his other vexations, chief being a terrible hunger. Brant's

sandwich had long since been burned away. The candy bar
tantalized him. He couldn't eat it now, though. It was all he
had. For breakfast he merely smelled it through its wrapper,
and then washed that down by licking the inside of the unscrewed cap of the brandy flask, not taking so much as a drop.
Thus refreshed, he reconnoitered. He couldn't see the squatter camp, but he could sense where it was. Someone had
thieved a pig during the night. They were roasting it now. Its
aroma made him weep, and in torment, a new, wild Bell
leaped up, grappled with the old one, flung him to the ground,
and seized the candy bar and gobbled it down in two ferocious
bites; then, moreover, it had the effrontery to take a healthy
swig of brandy and sit there smirking and rubbing its ruined
feet while smoking a morning cigarette with blissful in-
solence.

Bell stayed encamped all day. He found a scalable tree
from which, at twelve-foot elevation, he could observe a corner of the squatter camp. He heard wisps of laughter, muted
shouts, sometimes a breeze-borne Cowboy Jesus headline, and
saw from time to time men strolling off on sanitary errands,
staggering (he thought with longing) under digestive burdens
of ham, pork, bacon, spareribs. If he crept down during siesta,
could he scavenge the ears, hoofs, tail? For lunch, he ate his
thoughts. The Donners, snowbound (1846), at least could
nibble one another, whereas he was alone. Could a starving man eat, say, his own foot? Rats were said to be capable of
autoingestion in a pinch. A nice long juicy tail! One little nip
and it would be off. Too bad he hadn't brought Pico along; a
man could live on Pico for a month.

". . . *my only sunshine* . . ."

Bell hugged his pine trunk harder. He must be dizzy from hunger. The singing seemed to be coming from up the mountain, not from the camp.

"... *make me happy* ..."

It was coming from the mountain, all right. Bell squinted hard that way from his coniferous perch. There — he glimpsed the wandering minstrel threading his way through distant patches of brush.

"... *never know, dear, how much* ..."

The singer was heading for the camp. Man walking down from the north — and what lay north? Real wilderness: owls like eagles, unicorn deer, Indian ghosts, cannibal hillbillies haired like apes, maybe.

Descending, Bell split his pants and ripped out half his topcoat lining — from which, however, in pioneer spirit, he fashioned crude socks. By removing the laces, he was able finally to wedge his shoes on, and thus shod, limped over to where he'd seen the new man go by.

It might qualify as a trail. Bell put his glasses on to inspect it better. The way was lightly marked by ruffles in the forest flooring, and a few scars on the pines where passersby had plucked plate-sized pieces of bark. Should he follow it? He didn't, he couldn't, he was too famished. Ravenous, he crept campwards with the dusk, ready to gnaw roots, crunch pine cones, swill tree sap, lick pork-greasy migrant fingers, anything. The campers dined on beans and bread and chocolate bars, unaware of Bell salivating like a freshet thirty yards away. Spying out where the stores were kept, he waited until the cook left it unguarded, and then slithered close — eat or die! — to grab and slither off again.

He didn't stop until he'd regained his own estate. Then he realized what he'd taken. Two cans of beans. Tremendous. But how to open them? He had nothing but pen and teeth. He broke down, beating his fists in the dirt. He'd worn his knees and elbows through cloth to ragged flesh for this! Raging, he began to pound one can against a sharp jut of rock. It boomed like ax blows, so he quit that, in fear of rousing the squatters, and more prudently used his coat to muffle the sounds, and hammered, hammered, hammered until his arms went weak and he fainted or dozed off, then woke to bean smell with his coat and hands sticky with liquid from the cracked can, and fell to feasting there in the darkness, panting now with joy, a battered scholar of the American heritage, bareheaded and kneeling in the Appalachian midnight as he gobbled beans and guzzled bean juice, cutting his lip on the can and so feeding on his own salt blood as well. That night the presence of Lundquist drifted around him like the cold mountain fog, taunting him in his dreams, sidling silently up to watch with eyes that glistened like remote stars —old man of the mountains, rollicking in fog forms by night but changing at sunup into the mountains themselves, looming above the men who sought him in vain, not knowing what it was they sought nor why they searched.

THE SAME SONG woke him. "*You are my sunshine . . .*" He'd all but buried himself in dirt, leaves, needles, and sat up with skittish caution, like a wild turkey cock rising from its nest. "*. . . please don't take my sunshine . . .*" He fumbled out his glasses and clapped them on. The man who'd descended yesterday was singing his way back up now — and with him was someone wearing Bell's own hat, the Cowboy without a doubt. "*. . . much I love you . . .*" Bell leaped to his feet. They were heading for Lundquist. He was certain of that. He thrust his provisions into his pockets — the second can of beans and the flask, now only a quarter full — and went hobbling off in haste before he lost sight of them completely.

He was afraid to dog them too closely. If either turned and saw him, they'd both rush back to grab him — kill him, maybe — and he was too weak to fight a squirrel. Nor could he follow their way directly; they might have assigned a third man to lag back as guard, and Bell would be caught from behind. He had to watch both ways and himself stay hidden. It seemed impossible. He went through the woods on a course he judged was parallel, pausing from time to time to listen, wild with fear. The minstrel still sang — but that was no reassuring sign, for they might already be aware of their clumsy pursuer and could be luring him to some convenient spot for ambush.

The slope increased. The woods thickened. A dozen times

he was sure he'd lost them — and lost himself, too, for he'd never find his way back now — and then he'd spy movement far ahead or hear Cowboy Jesus curse in his stentor voice, or find evidence, as once he found a fresh and gleaming gob of spittle swinging like a spider from a twig.

They seemed to be in no hurry, but Bell was getting spavined keeping up. He had to thrash forward, stop and listen, then rush on along what he guessed was the right course, and so as the two migrants climbed the wooded range at leisure, behind them gasping Bell tore zigzag gaps in brush, scrambled through stony thickets, snapped tree limbs, fought briars, warred with creepers, lurked in dread around sudden boulders anciently rolled down like marbles from disdainful glacial thumbs, expecting to find on the other side a pair of grinning faces and the glint of knives.

At noon the woods dwindled, then abruptly ended. Bell found himself at the edge of a wind gap, a waterless pass scoured down by the winds of ages — and there they were, the two men, tiny figures far ahead, toiling across. But he dared not follow yet. He'd be exposed to sight for miles there. The gap broke down into a tiny valley marked by vague traces of the ruin of several old homesteads. Above it and beyond, more blue mountains swelled, backed by darkening clouds. Even now, a scattering of rain blew in Bell's face.

No help for it. He'd have to descend the gap on the other side, then climb back up to where the trees began again, and hope to pick up the track. He was tipsy with hunger, though, and numb-tired, a nomad out of season, with no berries to pick or nuts to gather. The way down was easier than he'd imagined. He tripped and fell, began rolling, and let himself roll, almost dozing as he spun down through the brown wind-grass. He came to rest in a cluster of deadwood where he slept the fantasy sleep of hunger, his face pelted by rain gusts, but it occurred to him then, for the first time, that he might die out there, might really die — he, Bell — and so he broke out of the skeleton embrace of branches and began his ascent.

It took him an hour to reach the woods again and find where they'd stopped. They'd lunched. The dirt they'd kicked over their fire still was warm. Bell crawled about searching for crumbs, then spied a squirrel twenty feet over-head lounging on a branch to finish off a bread crust. He rushed the tree like a madman. He'd shinny up and wolf down crust, squirrel, branch and all, and chew old bird nests with a seasoning of bark lice, but he had no strength, no time, he had to keep going or surrender all he'd fought for, and as he pressed on into the heavy woods, the bean can in his coat swung mockingly against his thigh. He couldn't stop long enough to beat it open, and might starve in mid-step with salvation locked in his pocket. He could drink, though. He paused for a swallow of brandy; then lighted a cigarette — had two more left — and wandered on, flask in one hand, cigarette in the other, like a guest strolling at some incredible garden party.

Later the rain came stunning down. He tried to find cover — surely the men up ahead wouldn't be moving much, either — and staggered, drenched, into a beaten way tunneled in the brush where he stared for one enormous moment into the sorrowful face of a great buck deer, not four strides away, before each, man and beast, pushed hastily in opposite direc-tions. Water-soaked, Bell's clothes had gained nearly what he'd lost by his diet and open air exercise. His guts were gas-filled but his spirits were empty. Even the sight of a muddy bootprint on a creekside stone didn't encourage him. He was still on the track, but they could roam the hills for days until he fell from famine or exposure.

He stepped into the creek. It boiled chunkily at his knees. The rain stuttered against him. Halfway across he felt it harden into hail that swarmed and sang and stung, and he stood in mid-creek in bewilderment, bowed like Job before the malicious fury of creation, his hands raised to shield his face. Beaten low, he bent and took a step, slipped to his hands and knees, and crawled in pain and fear at what savaged him until he reached rocks on the other side and lay gasping there. The forest smoked with hail. The creek fired up jets of spume. The mountains that reared all around had turned from haze-blue to storm-white, crumbling into shattering ice, hurled down so thick Bell couldn't breathe or see. He rolled beneath bare bushes but found no protection. The old man was scourging him, scourging him.

The hail stopped, the rain resumed; then the rain stopped, too, and a bitter wind came shaking down the cut where the creek ran. Bell drank half the brandy he had left. Then he started on again into the forest where the late day now was dusk. He was soaked through, freezing except for the sullen brandy in his veins, his ruined coat pressing down on him like the weight of sleep. He had no idea where the others were. There was no sign. He was lost in this wilderness.

Ah, he knew he couldn't come through a night like this. Darkness was falling fast. A desire to survive beat up in him like a lover's sickness, a yearning so poignant it made him sob. He needed fire to live, but the forest slash was wet. Still, turning over pine-needle beds as thick as peat, he found a layer near the bottom that wasn't soaked, and by stripping wet bark away from deadwood twigs and branches, accumulated a heap of fuel that might burn. With his cold-blistered hands he dragged sections of half-rotted fallen pines to use as fire dogs and later as logs. He built his fire then, touched off the twigs and needles with his cigarette lighter, watched it spit and snap, die almost to extinction, then catch, blaze, and hold. He stripped his clothes off, wrung out as much water as he could, and tried to dry them on sticks above the flames, one item at a time, as he danced around in his skin, feeding in more damp wood. Everything got scorched. His underwear browned like waffles, his suit jacket steamed from a forgotten pocketful of water, and his topcoat plunged down once like a giant bat, almost smothering the fire before he could whirl it off. One shoe sidled in and burned its tongue off unnoticed as Bell hammered away at his bean can.

What a greenhorn he was. He squatted amid fireside branches in his fried underwear drinking warmed beans, hands and feet swollen and red, long white shanks glittering in the firelight, and heard the gathering frost snap in the trees unseen around him. He moved closer to the flames and put on his smoke-blackened shirt.

Shades of old settlers slipped up in the shadows to watch him, amused. He'd survived by luck for a night, perhaps, but they'd held the old man off whole winters; generations of them starved and stormed at, crops blighted and animals lost, sickness melting their bones and lonely terror their minds, yet they'd stayed, living and dying but staying, and then there were those who'd tramped where the snows drifted up to the height of the trees and the only trail was the blood of men ahead — George Rogers Clark who'd gone overland to Kaskaskia, and Arnold who'd crossed Maine to Quebec. But that was paper heritage. The real nomads weren't these schoolbook heroes. They weren't even the tough old whites whose descendants now cooked grits at roadside diners and pumped gas, but those who had no history — the red nomads who'd roamed the mountains with the deer, and the black ones brought in chains to a wilderness bleaker, more cruel. Nomads without names, who'd borne the old man's fury and torn their years from his grip; their very lives had been victory. Ah, and for all this, they were excluded from the heritage. Heroes numerous beyond counting, their deeds forever lost. Their torment had made the earth ring — but there were no echoes now. Bell, cowering by feeble flames, sensed gathering in the darkness the ghosts of those forgotten men. What had his hunger meant, what else could the storm lash have been, if not rebuke? Of all the crimes against them, his was the last, the cheapest — to have ignored them, to have supported the lie that barred them from acknowledgment, the lie not that they were good men or bad but that they had never existed.

The mountains hadn't finished yet. Snow came now. It spit into the fire. The old man wouldn't let him alone, would keep him up through the night protecting his fire — greedy mountain devil bent on turning him to stone by sunrise for hunters to find, all rags and bone, some summers hence. "Snow down, then, you bastard!" Bell roared. Sure, let Lundquist bury him in snow. Maybe the old man had won that right: Lundquist, whatever else he'd done, had listened to those dying echoes; he'd spent a lifetime wandering among the children of poverty, hadn't he, a lifetime with the only heritage those ghosts had left — a history written in the hieroglyphics of scars on starved faces? So let him blow that cold wind, that rain, hail, snow, everything. Bell shook his fist. He howled, "You won't kill me, you old prick!" But Lundquist kept him hopping, all right. First to keep from freezing, then to grab up more fuel and build that fire high. So Bell ran whooping and cursing back and forth in the snowy forest, shirttail flapping, hairy legs flashing in and out of the reach of firelight, laboring in a snowstorm with the taste of poverty in his mouth.

Toward dawn the air stilled. Bell could hear his stomach roaring. The woods seemed as empty as he. Rising, he seemed to lift like a spirit from his body, and although he had a practical object in mind — to sight the campfire of the other men before sunrise masked it — he moved with the languor of a sleepwalker. He was becoming detached from his predicament. Was it the first sign of exposure sickness, he wondered, to be slightly bored by the approach of one's death?

He followed the rise of land. When he reached a high

point, he tried to climb a tree. It was dressed in ice. His swollen fingers found no purchase. But in the sky was the morning star, hung in the east. North was at his left hand. North was the way still, he supposed. He saw no campfire, but as dawn broke, he struck an old way cut in the woods — a wagon track of early times? — and followed that for miles until the woods thinned.

Another wind gap. The valley there was scarred on its sides by old coal mines. Its slanted floor had been farmed once; the gullies were choked by the mottled jackal growth that fed on dead earth. And there were houses down there. He counted a dozen.

It took Bell an hour to reach them. They were shells, rotted and crumbled. He found a graveyard by what he guessed had been the church and schoolhouse, but the stone markers had weathered so that the inscriptions were illegible. Nameless settlement, nameless dead. When the coal ran out and the soil washed away, the people died, too, and now lay in this forgotten hollow of America where the only prowlers were rabbits, foxes, and occasional deer.

One hut still had its roof. It was set apart from the others. Bell approached it cautiously, his heart drumming. Yes — footprints, leading away. The two men had spent the night sheltered there. It would be empty now.

He hobbled inside. There was an old iron stove, still warm. Wood chunks were piled against one wall. A pair of army cots held stinking blankets. On the plank flooring were cigarette butts, crumbs, empty soup cans, a drained pint of whiskey. He hunted frantically for food, found nothing, routed out a clan of mice, lunged to grab one, but plucked splinters instead. Then he leaned in the doorway, staring dully out toward the far hills.

Something caught sunlight in the sky. An airplane. He squinted up at it. It was a little one, just poking along up there. It flew over the valley, then banked and flew back again. Bell had a vision of Major Reuss at the controls, goggled like von Richthofen, with Brant beside him strapping on a chute. Crazy, but he'd forgotten about Brant's wood burrs. Was his agony recorded on some electronic map? Had he damned near died in the woods, just to lead them to Lundquist? He whimpered in rage. *Wood burrs.* He stripped off his clothing and went over it inch by inch. Rags and ruin, comedy clothes shredded and smoked, but burr-free. He examined his shoes. They'd been in Reuss's custody for hours. The heels were loose. He pried them off. Nothing. So he was bugless, anyway — but what about the two men ahead? The sunshine singer had entered the camp after Brant left, but Cowboy Jesus might be tagged.

He hurried into his clothes and pulled his deheeled shoes on. The sky was empty. A cold sun glittered down on the thin, melting snow.

He started at a run, but couldn't keep it up. He was dizzy and feverish. The hidden ground was treacherous; it tripped him in slick spots and sent him tottering, thrashing, sometimes falling. When the ascent began again, he sometimes pulled himself from tree to tree. Sunlight burst up from the snow to blind him. Once he followed a deer track by mistake and had to go back to pick up the bootmarks again. He was turning numb, dozing as he walked, tramping head-on into trees, waking as he sprawled face-down after sleepwalk tumbles, staggering death-drunk across silent clearings, hearing his own footsteps sounding miles away, imagining himself ant-size creeping through an endless forest that towered to the clouds.

Was it day or dark? He wasn't sure if he still walked. His hands and feet had lost feeling. He wondered if he wasn't dreaming movement while lying stiff in snow. He turned to study his own tracks, as if they would inform him, then turned back, afraid that somewhere he might have confused his course and be heading back toward the empty hut.

He was weeping. He knew he'd die. He tried to think of his loved ones — who were they? were there any at all? — tried to think of his short life, his few pleasures, his tiny triumphs, of river skating with a girl on his arm, of his last basket in his last senior game — a running one-hander at the final buzzer —

He wasn't trudging any more. He was rolling, gathering snow. A flicker of delight. He was back home, a kid playing in the snow. But it was dark now. Time to get up. Time to go home.

Out of the darkness someone was running toward him. His mother?

Grabbed him and gave him a good shake. He accepted it sheepishly and let himself be guided toward the house.

When the warmth hit him he thought he'd split. His head rang so he couldn't hear. He saw faces around him.

One was purple-cheeked. Ah, yes.

"Wood-burr bugs," he tried to say.

Another face there he knew, knew well.

Bell, a sagging tattered half-dead giant in the doorway,

grinned. Stepped forward toward that face, that ferocious white-bristled scowl.

Stepped forward, but his legs gave way. He went to his knees but still, by God, stayed straight. And, before he let himself pass out completely, spoke to it:

"*Dr. Lundquist, I presume?*"

PART III

"You're still not being very helpful, Bell."

"Guess not," Bell said.

"You've put us to an enormous amount of trouble, you know. The least you could do now would be to try harder. That's really all we ask. . . ."

Bell was still on the cot. He wondered how long the drug lasted. They'd put their truth in his veins, but his own was already there, maybe stronger.

"Listen," the voice behind him said peremptorily, "do you know where Lundquist is now?"

"Um, think so."

"You do?" The voice was eager. Then, more cautiously, it added, "Don't be hasty. Remember, you swore up and down earlier that you didn't."

"He's here."

"Here. What do you mean, here?"

"In this place right now. Can't you tell? He's in this room, in me, maybe in you, too — "

"You know that isn't what we mean!"

" — he's in Detroit, too. I found him there, you know. And

in these hills all around where he's been, he's still present, you see —"

"Bell, are you mocking us?"

"No, no. It's the truth. You want the truth, don't you?"

"Not those truths; they're worthless."

"Not to me they aren't. I happen to think they're pretty important."

There was a mumbling conference somewhere in the room. They were frustrated. Bell the liar was almost better than Bell telling truths.

The interrogator resumed. "Bell, we're starting to have some doubts about you."

"Hmmm?"

"You never did find Lundquist."

"I found him, all right."

"You think you did. But you didn't."

"I found him."

"You became obsessed with the idea of finding him. Then, the hardships you endured tended to weaken your hold on reality — we're not blaming you, understand, we're trying to figure out your problem, that's all. You never found him, but you couldn't admit it, even to yourself."

"I found him."

"You were pretending all along, weren't you? First, you let us believe you knew where he was. Now you're trying to persuade us that you actually found him —"

"I did."

" — for reasons that evidently are basic to your own personality structure. You can't face failure, can you, Bell?"

"Didn't fail!"

"You're convinced of that, naturally. But these obsessions play tricks, you know. That squatter named Jesus. A fellow in your circumstances could easily lead himself to imagine that Jesus was actually Lundquist — "

Bell just shook his head. He was tired of this. The drug was wearing off. The urgency to tell them everything had gone. But he wouldn't let them know that.

" — because of surface resemblances in manner. When you left the farm, this Jesus fellow was the one you followed, and he was the one you finally found. . . ."

This went on for quite a while. Bell lay patiently, trying not to listen.

Bell was fogged in for days. They took his glasses, which suited him fine. He was just as well off without them; he wasn't looking at anything. "And who the hell are *you?*" Lundquist had roared at him, a question repeated over and over in different ways night and day, even after they'd taken the wallet and examined its contents; then, when it became obvious that he was just a human log, they rolled him into a corner.

He'd done some talking at first, but only on the subject of wood burrs. Once he was satisfied he'd explained that little problem, he said farewell and sank down into himself for hibernation. The sight of Lundquist had closed a tremendous circle for him. He felt purged, content, free to meditate on an achievement that had nothing to do with Lundquist personally, for it had been something else he'd been chasing through the slums and trees — a vision of himself, which he'd caught up with at last, and now in his fever and weakness, he wanted merely to be left alone with it, Narcissus on honeymoon. He didn't have any curiosity about Lundquist.

"I found you, by God," he exclaimed once when Lund-

quist's shaggy white head came blurring close out of the astig-
matic shadows.

"You're nuts," the old man grumbled at him, drawing back
annoyed. Bell heard him shouting somewhere, "That's a crazy
man there!" The voice was high-pitched and frenzied. He
went stomping around the place. "Bonehead idiots!" The
other men shrank sullenly down on their heels. "You let a
maniac get in here — !" His pacing was jazzy, syncopated by
his limp. Bell didn't care. He snuggled deeper into himself.
Lundquist's roaring was like a mother's lullaby to him.

He lay on a blanket, wrapped in his topcoat. The air piling
up between the floor planks was warm, and he remembered
that at some point they'd hauled him up into a loft. It smelled
terrible. He'd lacked the strength to totter down and out, so
he'd been forced to unburden himself in a corner.

"You tell me why you're here." That was the old man
again. Bell could see him only as a shape. There weren't any
windows up there. "Good God, how it stinks. You crapped
up here!"

Bell tried getting to his feet, partly out of courtesy, partly
to see if he could. He couldn't. The sloping ceiling was too
low. He smacked his head on it and sat down abruptly.
"Christ," he moaned.

"You crapped!"

"Guess so," Bell conceded. He'd really banged his head. He
rocked back and forth, rubbing it with his hands. Lundquist
was the right height for the loft. He stood over Bell, cursing
him, still wanting to know why he'd come. "Oh, that," Bell
muttered, dizzy from the knock he'd gotten. "Well, sir, I've
written sort of a book, see." It sounded ridiculous but he

went on anyway. "Has to do with, um, governmental mechanisms, including a chapter on poverty — "

"Don't play games with me!"

" — which I'd sure appreciate your looking over when you get the chance."

"You're with Nomad."

"Sorry to say, don't seem to have brought it with me, though." He remembered. The manuscript was in his suitcase in the back of the rented car he'd left with Major Reuss.

"You even had your contract in your pocket."

"Doesn't matter," Bell went on, still referring to his book. "Guess I'd have to rewrite it anyhow."

"You're a Nomad man!"

"Nope."

Lundquist burst into a tirade. ". . . *rotten lousy liar* . . ." Bell yawned. The old man gave him a kick, and threatened to cut off his food, to throw him out into the snow to freeze, to let Cowboy Jesus chop him up for the foxes, all of which didn't trouble Bell much. He'd been through that. This old fellow was really just a pint-sized version of the one he'd wrestled in the wilderness, so he endured his rage patiently, and even when the sunshine singer and another hillbilly climbed up later to twist his arms and slap him around, he wasn't too perturbed. He'd won such a victory at such a cost that he felt mystically disengaged, and sat yogalike apart observing the vexation of his flesh. Alone once more, he lay almost contentedly where he'd been dumped, listening without comprehension to voices — Lundquist's and the Cowboy's — from the room beneath. An argument. It made the whole cabin jump but wasn't enough to keep him awake.

Later — an hour? a day? — he managed to descend the loft ladder.

Lundquist was alone in the main room of the place. The Cowboy had gone; the others, too. The old man got up when he saw Bell. There was no mirror, but Bell could guess what he must look like.

"Where do you think you're going?" the old man said. He wasn't quite so tough now.

"Bathroom," Bell said. Lundquist jerked his thumb at a door. It led outside. Bell stood uncertainly on the threshold, confronting pines and snow patches. *"Shut that door!"* Bell stepped out. He was barefoot. His ruined feet had swollen like footballs. Standing on the top step, he wrote his name in yellow letters on a slate of snow below.

Lundquist was in front of the fire. To one side was a splinter-legged table holding papers and a whiskey bottle. "Have a shot," the old man said, nodding grudgingly at the bottle. He kept his hands behind him, as if gripping a poker to use in case Bell got frisky.

"Your health." Bell downed a mouthful. The cabin was a mess. It stunk of rotten blankets and burned food. "You've got a nice place here," he remarked, replacing the bottle. He padded off out of poker range, and eased himself to the floor with his back against the wall. "Planning on coming back to the University pretty soon, Professor Lundquist?"

The old man simply grunted. He'd let his hair and beard grow. It looked as if he'd plunged his head into a dirty snowbank.

"People up there getting sort of anxious about you, I mean."

Lundquist glowered at him. The single window was almost blind with cardboard patching. Only the fire illuminated the room. Its flames made sunsets in Lundquist's hair; his face, turned toward Bell, was dark. "When did you join the project, Bell?"

"Didn't join." Bell waited. No response. The old man stood there respirating ferociously, but Bell suspected he might be worried. An old bear with dull claws, maybe. "Didn't join, didn't sign," Bell said. "You joined once. How come you left it?"

"*I'll ask the questions here.*"

"Dr. Grosch thought you might come back. By the way, he sends his regards." Lundquist took a big swig from the bottle. "He's in Roanoke now," Bell added.

"You maintain you're not with the project?"

"Stands to reason, doesn't it? Would I have come here alone?"

"I don't remember any Bell at the University." Lundquist belted down another drink. "Wait. There was one, but he was an old-timer."

"My grandfather."

"Maybe. All right, who's history chairman, then?"

"Glass."

"Anybody could look that up." Lundquist began walking around restlessly. "Doesn't matter a damn anyway." He cast quick glances at Bell. "So, what are they saying about me at Roanoke?"

"They say they want you back with them."

"Those bastards. They lie."

"That's what they told me."

"Listen, Bell." Lundquist stood over him, sending down whiskey steam. "You don't know a damned thing. All they want is to get their hands on me. Sure they'd let me work for them. But they know I wouldn't, and they're ready for that."

"For what?"

"They'd lock me up somewhere to die."

"They couldn't do that against your will."

"They could for a while. It wouldn't be too hard." The old man's eyes caught the glint of firelight as he squatted down not far from Bell. "Particularly if they had the cooperation of the only other member of the immediate family." He cocked his head at Bell shrewdly. "I mean my wife," he said.

"But you're not married."

Lundquist spat on the floor. "So that's what she told you."

Bell wiped his face with his sleeve.

"She really played you for a sucker, Bell. That little bitch."

"Don't quite get you, Professor Lundquist." But he was beginning to understand.

"How much is she paying you, Bell?"

"Fifty bucks a day plus expenses."

"That's cheap." Lundquist creaked up and backed away, on the prowl again. "I don't have to guess. She needed a good story to tell you so she said she wasn't married but wanted to be — I know that cunning little slut, Bell — and you didn't bother to check. Or maybe you've been playing her game all along?"

"Wasn't playing any game."

"I don't know when I've met a bigger fool, Bell. You swallowed that story of hers?"

"Sounded okay at the time," Bell said.

"We've been married fifteen years. Nomad has guaranteed her I don't know how much bounty — so she'll get two estates out of me, won't she? One now, the other a little later, when Nomad finishes me off. Couldn't they do it? Damned right they could!"

"But you have friends — "

"I don't have any friends. Not that kind."

"Just a minute. She isn't working with Nomad. She would have told them about me."

"No, she wouldn't. She hired you on the sly. Guarding her interests. What were you supposed to do if you found me — phone her?"

"Guess so."

"Then she'd fly down and be in at the kill, just to be sure she got every last nickel. She tried it in the summer with a private detective, except he got scared early and quit on her." Lundquist stumped over and handed Bell the bottle. "Have a snort. I guess you earned it. Never figured somebody like you'd make it this far — how come?"

Bell didn't answer. He drank slowly from the bottle.

"Well, she wasn't ever dumb," Lundquist said. "She knew a fool when she saw one."

Bell set the bottle down.

"What a bitch," the old man said. "What a bitch." He had lost whatever worry he might have had about Bell, for he turned his back contemptuously. "I shouldn't complain. I thought she'd become tough, but she turned tough and nasty, too — "

The cabin door opened. The two men who'd beaten Bell

earlier came in with sacks slung over their shoulders.

"Leave him alone, he's all right," Lundquist told them, as they gave Bell hard looks.

"Okay, Cap," said the taller one, the sunshine singer. They clumped on through to the back room and began unloading their sacks there. Groceries, Bell guessed. He wondered where Cowboy Jesus had gone, and whether he'd return. Something strange about Lundquist, though. He seemed to stiffen when the men came in, and they hadn't exactly tugged their forelocks to him. That *Okay, Cap* might have been a bit sarcastic. Maybe those hillbillies weren't too happy running errands through the woods.

"How far's the nearest town?" Bell asked.

Lundquist just scowled. He sat down at his table and fiddled with the papers.

Bell tried again. "The Cowboy coming back here?"

"*Shut up.*"

A sore point, evidently. Maybe Lundquist was wondering about it, too. Bell remembered the argument he'd dimly heard: the two men roaring at each other before the Cowboy went tramping off.

He took another drink. The hillbillies came in later and began cooking supper on the fire, snickering back and forth, giving Lundquist an occasional amused glance. Bell couldn't hear what they were whispering; neither could Lundquist. The bit of glass in the window browned out in dusk. Lundquist shuffled his papers and scribbled notes. Bell, half-crocked, half-asleep, had the impression that the old man was just pretending to work. The two men squatting by the fire were communing in private — having a bit of gossip about the Cowboy, more than likely — and Lundquist wasn't included.

Then the tall one got up, stretched himself, and crossed the room to pick up the bottle from where Bell had set it down. "Say, Cap," he said. "Mind if Lester 'n me have a little drink?"

Lundquist grunted something. He didn't look up from his papers.

"Sure thank ye, Cap." The man tipped the bottle up. "Here, Lester." He passed the bottle. "Now don't forget, Lester. You thank ol' Cap."

"Lester thanks ye, Cap," Lester said, and the two men grinned and winked and kept the bottle moving back and forth.

Lundquist didn't say a word. He sat there, one hand shading his face from the firelight, the other moving a pencil slowly across paper. Bell watched him, watched the others, too, saw the greasy smoke coiling up the chimney, and the wisps of it that drifted out into the close fetid room, and he was uneasy, and more than that, felt a touch of pity to see the old man mocked.

Lᴜɴᴅǫᴜɪsᴛ's ᴠᴏɪᴄᴇ woke him.

"Bell? Bell?"

Bell was in the loft again. It was night.

"*Bell.*" Lundquist had climbed up. He was there some-where. "Wake up, damn your hide."

"I'm awake. Watch out. You'll step on me."

Lundquist grunted as he eased himself down onto the plank flooring.

"Here, damn it. Take this."

It was a bottle. Bell took it with blind fingers. What, had the old fellow come up for a chat? He took a sip. He didn't really want any. He had a headache from what he'd drunk be-fore downstairs, and the smell of the cabin was so bad he had slept with his nose jammed against a chink in the wall that let the outside air in.

"You bastard, Bell. You sold me out, didn't you?" The old man's voice was thick. "With my own money — that bitch paid you with what *I* earned!"

"Here, take the bottle."

"You damned traitor. Take a man's money and hunt him down with it."

"Take it easy," Bell said. Was this Lundquist's idea of a so-cial visit? "I'll pay you back, if you want. Just give me enough to get home on."

"Go to hell."

"Listen, I didn't figure I was doing you any harm by this.

I'll go back and tell her I couldn't find you, that's all. I don't even know where this place is. Look — if I'd wanted to sell you out, I'd have sold you to Nomad."

"Maybe you have."

"They'd be here by now if I had."

"Those dimwits. You'd have to lead them by the nose. Yes, and that's what you'd do, wouldn't you, Bell?"

"Wouldn't. Didn't. I told you about the wood burrs, didn't I?"

"We didn't find any. Maybe there weren't any to begin with."

"Oh, Christ," said Bell, discouraged. "What makes you worth finding, anyhow?"

Lundquist didn't answer that. "They think anybody who doesn't work with them must be crazy. Well, maybe they're right."

There was a silence while the old man drank. Bell could hear him gulp. It was depressing. Would he be snowed in all winter with this suspicious old boozer?

"They think I know the answers." Lundquist was mumbling. Bell couldn't hear what he said next. From below racketed up the snores of Lester & Co. ". . . structure of poverty!" Lundquist laughed. Again, a glug at the bottle. Bell shivered. Icy air drilled through the weathered boards. He imagined hunting parties lolloping silently toward the cabin, like wolves: Lundquist's bitch-wife, hairy halfbacks from Reuss-Ross's Farm, with Brant a pup romping beside them. "*Isn't any structure.* I told them there wasn't but they wouldn't believe me — " The wind drummed up over Lundquist's voice, chattering a loose outside board.

"They said you destroyed something of theirs."

"Damn right I did. I destroyed their goddamned certainty. That's what I did. Men never forgive that."

"You ought to get some sleep."

"They think I'm hiding something — but it doesn't exist! Listen to me, damn you." Bell heard the old man hunching across the floor. "Poverty structure — they've thought about it so long they're convinced it's real." Bell smelled him now, through all the other smells of the place. "It ought to exist — that's what they think. They can't find it, so they think I've got it under my coat somewhere. That's why they're hounding me, Bell. They want to set up Nomad in the slums. Not just one project, but a dozen! They want my expertise, my knowledge, my contacts — where to start, who to see, how to do it right! They think I'm the key to it all! They got angry when I told them how crazy they were — not just stupid, but crazy, too. They're searching for a formula for managing people. It comes down to that. Isn't that insanity? If I took them into the slums, they wouldn't see men and women there. They literally *would not see*. They'd see what's stamped into their brains already, some damned abstract of dots and lines and God knows what. They'd see *units*. They'd see *forces*. They've drugged themselves on stuff like that! They're committed to it! They believe in it! That's the reality for them! Listen, Bell, the old teachers I used to work with years ago developed some of these notions about social structure, and then some idiot started calling them conceptual tools — tools! By God, that was the first mistake, calling an idea a tool. A tool is something you can pick up in your hand, goddamn it. And after that, these self-important human crumbs began making up more nonexistent abstract tools and acting as though they really had something! You can measure a tree, but not a man. But they didn't care about men any more. They had to prove the value of these damned tools of theirs — so they began running around pretending to measure things that couldn't be measured and convincing each other it all meant something."

"Some of them, maybe."

"Most of them! More all the time! They've forgotten they're supposed to be studying living men. They don't want to be reminded of that. They've withdrawn behind a wall of technique — and they've lost their humility."

"And I suppose you're humble!"

"I am humble, damn you. There's a difference between humility and meekness. 'Man can't be reduced to graphs,' they say — but they don't believe it. Their whole careers are built on the thesis that you can treat men like machine units in a factory — they don't admit it, they deny it, but by God that's exactly the way they act, and there's a bureaucracy of them now, fighting like devils to justify themselves and to get in on the big money that's spent by the war crowd."

"Some of it's useful."

"Useful, hell. What do you mean, useful? Computers and adding machines and their goddamn social-profile indices? Useful for clerks — and that's all the best of them are, glorified clerks. Don't be an idiot. Have a drink."

"No, thanks."

"They talk about numerical models of reality and all that garbage but they wouldn't recognize reality if it came up behind them and bit their ass. A man isn't a man to them, he's a collection of functions, and life is just a series of problems. They're in love with numbers because numbers are easy. People are hard — but if you can change people into numbers, then people are easy, too. You know what I told them? I said I wouldn't work with any man in their outfit who didn't first spend six months on the migrant route picking peaches and pulling carrots, and it was like a fart in church, they were that shocked. They pretended it was just another eccentricity of mine, but they were scared, and they knew I was right, and they hated me for it. God, if they had the guts to try it, it would shoot half their lifework away. They don't want to study men, they just want to study math. 'Life is too complicated,' they say. 'We've got to use numbers.' It's the same old game, without the brown shirts. Numbers! Sanitation! Castration! Our balls are being sawed off by the universities and the mathematicians and these poor creeps who pretend to be humanists but have managed to turn themselves into half-assed mathematicians — and if you want to test that little notion, then just take a look at what it is they want as the end result of their numerical humanism."

"They want everybody else to be like them."

"That's right! You got the message, Bell! Exactly! And *what* are they? They're corpses. And that's what they're working toward for everybody else!"

"That's extreme."

"You don't know anything about it. This stuff with the migrants is just window dressing, to keep rabbits like Grosch happy. They're working out anti-riot and guerrilla-control programs. That's the real job. Their world is a prison system, and the wardens need to know how to deploy their tanks and troops. Grosch talks about nonviolence — they all talk about nonviolence — but what they really want is noncontact. Just let some lousy stinking migrant come in from the fields and suddenly all these saints have to run off and take a bath. They don't even do much direct interviewing any more. They justify it by saying they get more genuine results by snooping and drugs, but the fact is they can't stand the smell of working-men. Frightened of it! I got so fed up I finally stopped wash-ing. That's what got them. Not that I insulted them or got drunk once and took an ax to one of their damned computers — and I did do that, by God, smashed a big box with a fire ax — no, sir, it was because I stunk like a polecat from crotch and pits."

"You're no flower," Bell agreed. He couldn't see the old man in the dark, but his presence was powerful. Had he come up to give Bell the same treatment, too? No, it must be loneliness. Lundquist had been cabined too long with Lester and Fester. "Listen, Professor Lundquist, what are you going to do?"

Lundquist didn't answer. He seemed to be brooding. Bell could hear his guts storming.

"Like to help you out, matter of fact," Bell said.

"*You* help me!" Lundquist almost screeched. When he got excited, his voice climbed high. "You deceitful bastard — "

"Ease off," Bell said.

But Lundquist wouldn't ease. He raged at Bell until his voice whined up into the rising night wind, and Bell, hearing no longer words but only sounds, fell asleep.

". . . just a word, that's all it is." Bell woke to the old man's grumbling. It was still dark, still storming inside and out. "Wasn't any poverty back then, when people were poor. Poverty — that's a conceptual tool the rich invented to ream poor people with. How the hell are the rich to know they're rich, unless poverty is defined? Otherwise, they're just people with money, and they don't want to be people, damn their souls, because people stink and die. They're afraid to die! So they're afraid to live! They want to be numbers. They want to deny their humanity — theirs and everybody else's. Hear that, Bell?" He gave Bell a nudge in the ribs with one boot.

"I'm listening," Bell said. What kind of crazy seminar was this with Lundquist haranguing him in a cruddy cabin loft in some lost Appalachian valley? The old man kept erupting. Didn't he ever sleep? No wonder he'd worn Grosch out.

"Think I want to work with a bunch of cadavers like that? Teach their stillborn kids? The universities — they're graveyards, the professors are a crowd of mummies. The only decent things to come out of them are sports and riots. Hell, the teachers don't teach, all they do is pass intellectual gas. They haven't *got* anything to teach. What do you say, Bell?"

"You bet." Bell was amazed. The old boy was yammering out some weird cram course for his benefit. So it seemed. Was he supposed to take notes?

"Structure! They invented structure — another goddamned nonexistent abstraction, and they spend their time playing around with that, while everything else goes to hell and their police and priests and case workers go around wrecking the slums."

"Oh, hell," Bell said. "It's not that bad."

"What do you know about it?"

"A little."

"Nothing! You know it like the foetus knows the placenta — it feeds you and keeps your ass warm, that's all you know! To know what something's like, you've got to stand outside of it. You've got to fight the bastard! You've got to be at war with it. Its smiles don't mean a thing."

"Hard to fight it," Bell muttered.

"If you're a coward, it is."

"Who's a coward?" Bell was feeling pressed. "Just because you booze it up and stink like a goat doesn't mean you're so goddamned brave. How come you're hiding away in the woods if you're such a hero?"

"I'm not hiding from anything!"

"Hell, yes, you are. You said so yourself. You're afraid of Nomad."

"You're a fool!"

"Okay, then go and lecture your poverty-stricken friends downstairs, if you think I'm a fool. Wake them up for a change! Tell them all about how rotten everything is!"

"You idiot!" Lundquist shouted. "I've been wasting my time with you!" Bell heard him thumping and banging as he got to his feet. He stamped around the loft, whacked his head somewhere and fell to cursing, took time out for a drink, and then cloddishly pissed in the far corner. Still, he didn't go downstairs. He was grunting and snuffing and padding back and forth, mad and offended, talking to himself, mostly in obscenities.

Bell felt a little ashamed. He guessed that the old man craved human contact, but that he knew only how to roar.

"You, ah, working on another book, Professor?" he inquired, placatingly.

Asinine question. Lundquist ignored it. Bell studied his

watch until he could piece out the time: three o'clock. He shuddered. Imagined himself slinging Lundquist over his shoulder and skating through the woods on his football feet.

"You think you've got troubles," Bell said, conversationally. "What about me?" The old man was silent. Was he still there? The wind had died; maybe Lundquist had, too. "Your wife is chasing you — but mine ran away from me!" Was he really alone? Couldn't see a damned thing. Might be talking to a ghost. "I married one of my students! That was a damned big mistake! She had no vitality! Why couldn't I have seen that?" He began crawling around, searching. "She wasn't a real woman. She was more like a book. But she didn't want to have me turn her pages! Where the hell are you, Professor Lundquist?" He heard snores from a corner. "Wake up, you old bastard," Bell shouted. "I listened to *you!*"

But Lundquist slept on. So Bell slept, too. And in the late morning, when he finally woke, the old man had gone below.

THAT AFTERNOON THEY put Bell to work splitting wood. The man named Lester took him through the trees to a clearing where sawed logs lumped under a crust of snow, handed him an ax and wedge, and left him.

The wedge was dull. Bell was weak. It wasn't healthy work for a convalescent. He sweated and he shivered. The air was thin, the sun feeble. Bell's grunts echoed for miles. The wood was like cardboard, but so were the ax, the wedge, his bony arms. He could run off, couldn't he? He'd pretended to be weaker than he was. He'd shambled out with Lester like a sick man, but Lester hadn't seemed to care one way or the other. Maybe they figured he'd never survive trying to find his way out. But he had no intention of leaving. Not now. Why, he couldn't quite understand, except that he had the sensation that he wasn't the real prisoner there.

At dusk he filled a burlap bag with chunks he'd split and dragged it back to the cabin. It took him four trips to bring it all in.

Lester and Fester were hunched down comfortably near the fire, having a chat.

"Read me a story, Lester."

"Now you know I cain't read."

Bell slumped against the wall, fagged out. Lundquist sat at his table, shuffling his papers.

"You cain't *read*?"

"No more'n you."

"Lester, you mean tell me growed man like you don't know how to *read*?"

"Cain't write neither."

"Lester, you sure a disadvantaged critter. You never had no chance, did you?"

"Reckon not."

"Lester, this sure shocks the shit outa me. How you 'spect to shinny up the social ladder less'n you can puzzle out a book?"

"Don't rightly know," said Lester.

Were they ragging Lundquist? The old man was simmering in his chair, papers rustling like angry whispers. Those two comedians were parroting him.

"Lester, you just a human cipher, ain't you? You ain't more'n a two-legged hound dog, seems to me." Fester, the sunshine singer, was long and lean and pale, with a ragged beard and yellowed teeth. Lester was dumpy; his skin had weathered to the color of spoiled apples. "Lester, you might be *president* now," Fester said. Lester sniggered. They both cocked sidewise glances at Lundquist, and Bell, looking on, caught the echo of what he'd heard earlier in a daze through the loft floorboards: it was a parody of Lundquist lecturing the Cowboy. "You made in the image of God," Fester was saying, "so how come they left you crawl like a pig in the mud 'thout no learnin'? Lester, seems like you got a mighty powerful complaint 'gainst folks that treat you so porely. Makes me tremble to think. With a grudge like yours, I vow you goin' to rise someday and kick up one hell of a rumpus somewheres — "

"*Shut up.*" That was Lundquist, stiff with rage.

" 'Scuse me, Cap?"

"*Shut up that jabber.*"

"Lester, you hear ol' Cap? You disturbin' him in his work. Ain't you got nothin' better to do than sit here a-yammerin' jest 'cause you can't read to yourself like a decent man would, nice 'n quiet? I tell you, Lester, I'm plumb shamed for you. You tell Cap you sorry."

"Lester's sorry, Cap."

They snickered just high enough to be heard. Bell stirred.

Lundquist glared at him, damning him for being a witness. He wouldn't stay longer, though. Fester was smirking under his ratty black beard, thinking up something else to say, and Lester was waiting for his cues with mouth agape.

Bell skipped supper. He took a hunk of bread up to the loft and lay there munching it. Below he could hear Fester tuning up. Not a happy situation. Bell didn't know what to make of it. Was it just the boredom of three men cramped together for too many weeks or months? Lundquist needed them. Did they need Lundquist?

THE OLD MAN came up again that night. The footsteps on the ladder reverberated through Bell's dreams, drumbeats heralding a demigod with glacial hair and blizzard beard — yet, waking, Bell sensed only the whiskey-rot wreck of a man held together by a ferocious despair.

"You there, Bell?"

"Where else?"

He'd invented the Lundquist he'd struggled with in the wilderness. That was the legend, this the reality. Yet both existed, somehow inseparable.

"Have a drink with me, damn you."

"Okay."

The bottle sloshed. Bell felt it thrust into his fingers. "Here's to you," he said, and drank. He wondered if he hadn't done Lundquist a terrible injury, blundering in as he had. His presence alone might be fatal, like that of the unclean stranger in a sacred grove. The old man — trapped, observed — was suffocating in a rage of pride.

"You married, Bell?"

"Sort of."

"Kids?"

"Nope."

"I've got maybe fifty or sixty."

"No fooling!"

"All bastards, every one. Some older than you are."

"Good God, how many of them do you support?"

"Support them?" Lundquist snorted. "Hell, I don't even *know* them. Bell, you really are a Boy Scout, aren't you? Listen, when I went out on the road, I lived by the moral code exactly as I found it."

"Guess you didn't improve it any."

"Why should I?"

"You'd be safe in Canada," Bell said suddenly.

"Who says I want to be safe?"

More posturing, Bell thought. He persisted: "I could get you out of here, maybe. Get you up there somehow."

"I've got no reason to trust you, Bell."

"You trust those guys downstairs? You think they wouldn't sell you out?"

"They might, they just might. How much did Nomad authorize you to offer them?"

"Oh, Christ," Bell mumbled. "It was just an idea. Forget

it." He was tired. His arms and back ached from the ax. The old man wanted something from him — what? "Go to Detroit, then. You've got friends up there."

"Who says they're friends?" Lundquist's voice was strangely gentle, though. "They don't want me. I can't help them."

"But you're helping the migrants?" Lundquist didn't reply. "That's supposed to be why you're here, I guess," Bell went on. "But if the program's a joke, then they don't need you, either."

"I didn't say it's a joke. It isn't a joke. It's violence masquerading as intellectual games. The people who pay for it are getting impatient. The violence is starting to show through."

"Your migrant friends aren't exactly Quakers themselves."

"We're all agents of violence!" Lundquist was becoming angry again. "What the hell do you think a social organism is, anyway? Nomad's right: the main object is to control the environment. That means violence."

"Frankly, I think you're overstating it."

"Sure you do! Because your precious skin has been sheltered and protected! You've never been up against the raw! You've just read about it, Professor Bell!"

"You're a professor, too!"

"By God, Bell, I *chose* to find out what it was like! I was damned if I was going to live my life as one of these old-maid professors hiding out in the libraries and letting farts when they're sure nobody is around to hear! A man can bow his head and submit and see nothing, or he can fight."

"Well, what does your fighting amount to? You take an ax

to a computer and you organize a few hillbillies to gum up interviews with dopey answers — "

"They want to finish me, Bell!"

"Oh, hell. The worst thing that could happen would be maybe you'd get placed under some temporary restraint."

"They'd find a way to take care of me for good. They don't know how to do much, but they know how to do that. Those people hate me, Bell — not because I'm violent, but because I force them to show that they're violent, too."

"So, what does that prove?"

"It's a violent society, Bell, and these are violent times. The only honest man is a violent man."

"Oh, crap," Bell said. "You're just a cantankerous old bastard with your guts in a turmoil. You see the world the way you want to see it, just like everybody else does."

"The hell I do! I see it the way it is!" Lundquist screeched this time. Bell thought he might light up there in the darkness. "I could see it a long time ago, too, damn it. The universities were breeding little maggots. They were going to take over. Now they've *taken* over! They hate what they study. You can smell it on them. You want to know what started Nomad? Nomad began when the study of man got infected by abstraction. Gangrened! Now it's all rotted. That makes the maggots breed all the faster. Listen, Bell. I didn't want to be a scholar. I wanted to *know*. The only way to know is to get down there and *be*. Not to plant your ass in some fat endowment — and I could have had those, I could have had the pick of any chair in the whole damned country!" He was puffing with fury. It made his voice sing higher. "If you're going to study living men, you've got to be a man yourself. You can't be afraid. You've got to go out there. Where it's raw."

"For sociology, maybe," Bell said.

"For manhood, damn you. Don't exempt yourself. You're in the humanities, too. Where's the human part of it? Being smothered to death. No wonder students riot. They know they're not wanted. The teachers have nothing to teach them anyway that isn't already in the books. *The teachers have nothing to teach them.* They aren't teachers, they're just clerks — "

"Hold it a minute," Bell said. "So what's a teacher, then? Don't answer that. It's not a question. Listen, did you know my grandfather?"

"A little."

"Well, he taught. You're right. He was a man. He wasn't afraid. He was a bastard in many ways, sure, but he had force. Not just that. He had pride. Don't interrupt me. He had a sense of himself. A sense of self-importance. Yes, he was arrogant, but he did teach. I mean, he commanded attention. He commanded it from everybody. From me, too."

"So you — "

"I wanted that for myself. You bet I did. I wanted that sense of personal power. Maybe not power, exactly. A feeling of strength. Of worth. And where'd it go? Don't butt in, old man. I'll tell you myself if I can. I've been trying to figure it out."

"They blinded you. Those — "

"I told you to shut up," Bell grumbled. "I didn't come all this way just to hear your damned opinions. Sit quiet for once and listen. What attracted me about my grandfather was something like this: I saw in him my own possibilities. Now, is that teaching? Damned right it is. It's part of it, maybe the most important part, because without it, what have you got? Not much. There's nothing to hold the rest of it together, I mean. Now, sure, I knew all the stuff about the teacher needing to be part poet and part prophet, and I supposed it must be true, but somehow it got lost in the daily shuffle — "

"The system forbids it."

"Forbids it. Oh, sure. Maybe it does. Now, it didn't matter that the subject was history. It could have been something else. Anything, almost. There has to be the poetry. By which I mean conviction — the kind of conviction that makes a man want to yell. And this can exist anywhere, can't it? Damned right it can. To make people sit up. To shake them. Worry the hell out of them, if need be. Well, my grandfather had a touch of it, you see, and maybe that's what got me up on my hind legs wanting to be something, Lundquist, but now it seems we're just a bunch of clerks, as you say. I don't need you to tell me that. But how come? That's the puzzler."

"You're isolated from life. Those aren't colleges, they're fortresses."

"You think you've got all the answers," Bell complained. "Well, I don't necessarily agree. Isolated, maybe, but there's something worse than that. Worse. Listen, I mentioned this matter of having conviction. Of having something to teach that isn't in the books, that's inside, that's personal. Where does a man get that? From himself, maybe. But from the outside, too. From what he sees and lives with and knows —

and what sort of conviction is there now? I'm talking about social conviction. What the hell is it that people want? I don't mean poor people, Lundquist, I mean the ones who send their kids into those nice clean classrooms. Well, they don't want anything, old man. They've got it all now. They've got as much as they think they need, anyhow. They've arrived. They've stopped moving. They're going nowhere. That's what the conviction is: finished. Stability, that's what's wanted. People have to be damned scared to want that, don't they? Those number games Franklin told me about. No wonder they seemed familiar. They're dedicated to stalemate. Everything gets frozen on the board. If anything starts to move, pinch its head off."

"Leave, then. You don't belong there."

"Leave? That's an easy thing to say. What about you, Lundquist? You never really left."

"I damned well did!"

"Hell, no, you didn't. You always went back. You climbed down always knowing you could climb up again. You have that out. The others don't."

"No, they don't. You're right." Lundquist spoke wearily, in a low voice. "I've known that all along. It's galled me. I've been cheating, even if I couldn't help it." He was silent for a few moments. Then he resumed: "Well, maybe that's what I've been working toward these last years, Bell. Cutting myself off for good. So I couldn't cheat. Never thought of it like that before."

"You can still get out."

"No, I can't. Not any more. I've done the job too well. Can't ever get out." He uttered something like a chuckle.

"I'm in for good now. Guess that's what I wanted, then. To be honest!"

"I could get you out."

"No, you couldn't, damn you!"

"Not if you don't want to."

"Why should I leave? It's my goddamned country, isn't it?" The wind whipped up outside, yelling in through the cracks. "They don't know what it's like. Neither do you, Bell. They don't want to, damn them. Maybe you do. But by God you won't ever know it the way I've known it. Those times have gone, boy."

"New times now," Bell said, but Lundquist wasn't stopping for him any more.

"Forty years and more!" The walls shook as the wind rushed. Dust blew about in the darkness. Bell shut his eyes, drew up his knees, and bowed his head against them. He heard Lundquist sneeze and curse. "More than forty years," the old man grumbled. "A damned lifetime — and I'm not finished yet, Bell. You hear me? I've been through it all a dozen times. I've seen every strip and stitch of it, by God. Black slums and red reservations, the deserts, the goddamned mountains, jails, whorehouses, hobo jungles, damn-all, you name it and I've seen it, I've done it, I've had my hands in it — and I could do it all again if I wanted!" The cabin stuttered in the wind. The trees outside were sawing. ". . . these pissants think they have me cornered now? Well, I don't give a shit! I've been worse off than this before!" The old man was rocking. He made the planks creak. "I spent time once in Mississippi state jail. Know that, Bell? Years ago. Years! Damned near died there, but by God I swore I'd come through . . ." His words ran together in Bell's drowsy mind, a rambling catalogue of sins and brawls. ". . . had a fight with a Cuban once — that was later, forget just when — he had jaws like a 'gator, bit my hand to the bone. Scar still there. That was in Galveston, I remember. When I was younger. Yes — when I was young!" Bell was dreaming it, maybe, dreaming the saga of a raw man prowling a raw land, stumping through forests, mountains, prairies, across deserts to the horizon's end, shaking down boulders and splintering trees — indestructible old nomad, ranging a whole continent in his greedy quest of life. Ah, he couldn't hear Lundquist any more. The old man was just mumbling, and the wind stayed high. Whatever truth was in the legend, now there was nothing left except unquiet memories and a bottle, a suspicious old tyrant glaring defiance from under his snowdrift mane.

"Maybe I'm finished, Bell."

Bell blinked awake. The voice was weak, almost whimpering. What, was the defiance gone, too?

"Maybe it's all used up, boy. It isn't the same any more. Can't even drink much. Tears my guts. They're closing me out." Lundquist gave a gusty sigh. "Bell, you there? Sometimes I don't blame the women. Treated them like dirt. Why shouldn't she come at me the same? And those bastards!" He laughed suddenly, high, a grandfather's cackle. "Maybe they've got a score to settle, too! Listen!" He thumped the flooring, as though in the room below had gathered tattered and resentful half-Lundquists of all ages. Crazy, thought Bell. "No room for me now, boy," the old voice whispered in the dark. "They can't let me run loose any more. Frontier's closed, Bell." His hand hit Bell's shoulder with a quick, hard grip. "I was raised badly, boy. Got the worst of the Protestant ethic. God commanded us to share the misery and pain of the weak — as if we could impart our strength to them!" He chuckled, but his grip stayed fierce. "Moral compulsions — but when I lost God, you see, then the compulsions remained, without the morality. To share misery for no purpose! That's nothing but self-indulgence. So maybe I'm no better than the others, Bell. We're all swindlers in our way. Just indulging in life. It becomes vicious finally. But they'll never find me!" He shouted that right in Bell's face. "Never find me! Never catch me!" He let go then and scrambled away, bottle bumping on the boards, and went swinging noisily down the ladder steps, laughing drunk or mad or maybe both, until he was below and his laughter merged with all the creak and bluster of that vagabond night.

Cowboy Jesus came next day. They heard him thrashing through the woods before he appeared to sight, a bulky figure whose face was wreathed in nostril steam. He still wore Bell's hat, with a scarf pulled down over his ears and tied under his chin. "They's lookin' for you, Shorty," he told Bell when he'd stumped into the cabin and crammed himself into Lundquist's chair before the fire, "but they ain't put out no reward, so I guess you ain't worth a goddamn. Don't that break yore heart, Shorty? Run yore ass to tatters 'n then find they ain't nobody give a nickel for you back?"

"Who's looking for me?"

The Cowboy ignored him. He told Lester to fix him some food and Fester to wake Lundquist, who lay snoring on a cot in a corner. No doubt who was in charge now. The hill-billies slunk around like hounds. Lundquist, still stuffed with sleep, sat up and massaged his face. "Here I am, ol' man," the Cowboy called over to him, roughly. "Didn't figure I'd be back so soon, did you?" Lundquist gazed blearily about. "We goin' to *settle* things this time," the Cowboy went on. "No more sittin' round the woods like hoot owls. I mean, they's goin' to be some *movement* now." He gave his massy head a shake and drummed one fist against his thigh. "Swear to God," he said. "You is the laziest bunch of four pure-bred white men I ever did see. Place stinks like a shithouse! Ain't nobody got the audacity to ever clean it up?" No one an-swered. Lester was crouched by the fire, frying bacon. Fes-ter picked his nose. "Well, leastways," the Cowboy grum-bled, nodding at Bell, "you might git that there swamp crane out to the woodpile. You don't 'spect this wore-out ol' darky to crack kindling for you, do you?"

"You heard him, son," Fester told Bell. "Git on out there."

So Bell went off to split logs again. The forest was blotchy with snow streaks. He saw rabbit turds and fox prints (Fester shot rabbits; foxes came scavenging for the bones). He swung the ax-head down on the wedge. *Whang-bang.* The impact stung his hands and broke a blister he'd gotten last time. But he felt stronger now. Maybe the Cowboy's coming had energized him. He kept swinging, splitting, chopping, making sparks fly from the steel, grunting like Pico's Piute weight lifter, Ruptured Moose. *Whangbang.* He paused, his breath steaming in the frosty mountain air. Sweat ran through his beard, where boils were flowering. His face must look like a strawberry patch.

Before noon he saw through the trees the two mountain men trudge off with empty sacks. Gone shopping again, north. He'd timed them on their last trip. Wherever they'd gone — a town, a crossroads store — it was no more than a dozen miles away. An easy ramble in the woods, but not if he had a captive Lundquist strapped and kicking on his back. The old man wouldn't go. Not with him.

Lundquist and the Cowboy were in conference. They paid Bell no attention as he hauled wood in, stacked it, and went back out for more. The sky was paved with marbled clouds. Bell was domed in, another wilderness creature making snow tracks. ". . . *gonna gitta goin'* . . ." The Cowboy's conspiratorial tone was like another man's shout. ". . . *cain't lay roun' no more* . . ." The field commander was seeking new strategy from HQ. Bell, sitting on the front steps, ripped a strip of burlap from his woodbag. Needed new socks. That topcoat lining was rotted through. Ought to complain to the store. ". . . *gotta git up there 'n join them city mothers* . . ." No, the Cowboy wasn't asking, he was telling. Lundquist seemed more cautious. His face was pouted by doubt, a defensive expression. Don't attack. When outnumbered, as at Bunker Hill, dig in: Don't shoot till you see the whites.

Bell finished a mighty woodstack. No applause. He didn't

wait to be told but climbed to the loft and lay there with his better ear pressed at a crack between planks.

He could hear the Cowboy pretty well. Lundquist was just a grumble. The squatters were pulling out soon. Heading south, Bell guessed. But the Cowboy was talking about going north. ". . . *hell, I go up there this minute, tell me where to go. I mean, these pea pickers here is mostly hopeless, but we got a few might walk on two legs like halfway men provided we got idea what to do . . .*"

Cowboy Jesus was pacing. Squinting down through the crack, Bell could see his own hat cut back and forth. Heavy-booted feet made the boards shake. ". . . *them city mothers, they been through it, they right in it now, you done tol' me . . .*" Couldn't see Lundquist. The old man wasn't talking. ". . . *don't want to waste no more time!*" The Cowboy was roaring now. "*Let's us 'n them hook up, man! Gittin' tired all this talk! Been trompin' my face forty years 'n now Jesus wants his turn!*"

Wild. It seemed that the Cowboy proposed to lead a rural platoon north to join the urban wars.

"*What's wrong, ol' man? Why you just set there? You tol' me lies maybe? You ain't the first white man ever lied to Jesus, then — 'n you wouldn't no more be the first Jesus cut a lyin' tongue from neither.*"

Bell scooted over to the ladder. The Cowboy sounded sincere. Lundquist might need help. ". . . *them mothers up there or ain't they? You tell me, ol' man!*" Bell hustled down on burlap feet. He squatted, half-hidden by his heap of wood. The two men, at the other end of the room, didn't notice him.

"I didn't tell you lies." That was Lundquist in the chair,

glowering. "I know people up there — some of them, if they're still around, but I'm not a goddamned directory. Most of what I know is out of date. Stand back, damn it. Your breath stinks."

The Cowboy turned and took two paces toward Bell and turned back again, working his fingers open and closed.

"You think there are *armies* up there?" Lundquist was contemptuous.

"You tol' me so!"

"No such damned thing. You got it mixed up! There are some men with guns — maybe more than a few, I don't know — but it's pitiful. They're in a jail, you damned fool! So are you! What the hell can you do when you're in jail?" The old man's voice was climbing now. "You can break out, maybe. If you've got somewhere to go. You can kill one of the guards before the rest of them kill you. You can set a fire, if you don't mind getting fried. But you can't take over the jail!"

"You yellow-mouth ol' sinner, you done tol' me about them people fightin' here 'n there, about them cells 'n such — "

"Not here! Not in this country! This country belongs to somebody else! They own it, they run it, it's *theirs*. You can't do it here! Get yourself killed if that's what you want. That's the only thing you can do. Just you once stick that big cabbage head of yours up and you'll get it blown off! And that's exactly what they want you to do. Cowboy, they've got you outmanned and outgunned and outbrained and you don't mean a damned thing to them except a toy to play with!"

"So you mean I'm s'posed to hide or crawl, that what you mean?"

"Get this through your head. You're screwed. Hide if you want. Crawl if you can. Die if you have to. But that won't change a thing. You're screwed! That's the answer, Cowboy. Like it or not. Screwed!" Lundquist was furious, sweating and stewing in his chair. "You want to go see a few men in Detroit? Chicago? New York? I'll give you a start, if you want. But remember this: that's what Nomad wants. They're waiting for that. They want you to start playing the game. That's all they need. You get in there and play. They need the practice. You'll make those computers hum, all right. And when they think they've learned all they can from you — even if they haven't learned a damned thing — then they'll cut you down, Cowboy, and the only thing left of you will be a couple of dots on a spool of tape in one of their machines — your monument, Cowboy. They need your contribution. Go on out and die, you damned fool. You'll be dying for Nomad whatever you do!"

Cowboy Jesus walked straight toward Bell. Didn't seem to see him, though. Wasn't looking. His ragged purple face was shining, his heavy chest billowing in and out. "Shee-it," he kept muttering. Bell snaked one hand onto a stovewood chunk, just in case. The Cowboy wheeled and tottered against the side of Lundquist's cot like a blind man, giving it a kick and the wall a punch.

"Then what you come here for, ol' man?" He spoke low. Bell could hardly hear. "I mean, what for you git us pore country trash all het up 'n riled then say ain't no use? This here game you say they play — well, what's *yore* game, ol' man?" He was weaving a little as he came nearer Lundquist. "You tell me that, massah. 'Splain this nigger why." He seemed to be shaking, but his arms hung stiff. Knife in the sleeve? Bell raised his stick, wondering, but Lundquist wasn't flinching, didn't even bat an eye with the Cowboy right over him. "I swan, ol' man, you surely couldn't do us no worse if you was still workin' for them fancy friends you had — 'n how the hell I s'posed to know you ain't? So what you come here for, then? This some special kinda interview, is it? You snuck down behin' the barn to waller with the hogs so's you can write it up real good for them Nomad folk?" The Cowboy yanked from a pocket not a knife but a tobacco plug and bit off a chew. "Maybe you just like messin' 'round with pore ignorant souls, show what you can do. That it, ol' man? You tol' me you done spent a lifetime a-rubbin' yore noble ass amongst various misfortunate unadvantaged fuckers. That make you feel good, massah? You come down like ol' Moses from the mountains lay down the laws 'n lead the pore childern of Israel 'n watch 'em bow down? But you ain't leadin' 'em nowhere. You tell 'em 'bout the Promised Land — but you just jokin', for they ain't no Promised Land, so what's it all come to? You just got them dumb migrant bastards a-freezin' in the woods so's you can spite yore friends? You playin' games with us so's you can play games with them or what?" He spat on the floor. Then he shouted, *"Speak up, ol' man!"*

Lundquist wasn't ruffled. What showed of his face between beard and mane looked sly, defiant, almost pleased. "I've told you the truth, that's all," he said in a truculent voice. "I didn't make it this way, and I can't do anything more about it than you can — except maybe I can destroy their goddamned pretensions, and show them what they really are. And show you, too, Cowboy. Maybe now you'll understand who's been riding you all your life."

"Hell, I didn't need you to tell me that, you ol' sinner. They done informed me down in Texas 'n elsewheres. Ridin' me! Ol' man, they been a-hoppin' on the Cowboy for years! It ain't no secret. Why, they's a damned crowd on my back. You up there, too, seems to me."

Lundquist made an angry gesture and began pawing through his papers.

"You just come down closer than most, that's all. You like to ride the same."

Lundquist was scribbling. "I'll give you what you want," he grumbled.

"Ol' man, you done educated me how come they a fire in my belly 'n now you best step aside so it don't fry you to a cinder. Yes, sir, you gimme what you got."

"Remember, even that face of yours is no passport. They won't trust you."

"Shit, with your ol' man stink still a-clingin' to me, they gonna smell something wrong till it wears off." The Cowboy studied the piece of paper Lundquist had handed him. "*De*troit? Well, hell. That's good. So how in sweet Jesus' name I s'posed to git up there? Ain't got a red cent." He folded the paper and tucked it away in an inside pocket. "Don't you fret 'bout the Cowboy, though. He'll find a way." He turned toward Bell. "That there long-legged monstrosity, maybe could sell him to a zoo somewheres." He noticed Bell's crestfallen look. "You surprised, Shorty? Think you could creep up on *this* ol' Injun unbeknownst?"

"Wasn't creeping," Bell mumbled.

There were sounds outside. The Cowboy swung around to the window for a look. "Mountain boys is back," he said.

He strode to the door and opened it. "Well, damn me if they ain't shot a deer besides!" Past him, Bell could see Lester and Fester dragging the carcass across the ground. The Cowboy went out to watch.

Bell hurried over to Lundquist. "Let's get out of here fast, Professor. Tonight, when they're asleep."

Lundquist stared at him.

"I'll come down about two o'clock. Maybe you can get hold of that rifle — it's the only gun they have, isn't it?"

"Go to hell."

"What? You don't mean to stay now?"

"Shut up. I don't need your help. I'll do as I please. Didn't I make that clear?" He slammed his hand down on the table. "When I reach the point where some young snot has to nursemaid me, I'll let you know. Do you think I'm ready to whine and crawl? You think I'm incapable of dealing with these cruddy louts?"

"I didn't mean anything of the sort!" Bell was astonished. The Cowboy's tirade hadn't moved the old man. Why had this? "I just — "

He broke off. Cowboy Jesus had reappeared in the doorway.

"You-all havin' a little set-to here?" He was grinning, his eyes shifting from Lundquist to Bell and back again. "Sometimes it seems best of friends never can agree, don't it?" He took a step toward Bell. "Shorty, I'm plumb amazed at you. You is the most pert critter, come a-bustin' into other folks' affairs. Ain't you got 'nough to occupy yore restless soul? Then I recommend you hie yore stilt-legged self out yonder 'n give them two rednecks a hand skinnin' off some steak!"

Tʜᴀᴛ ɴɪɢʜᴛ Bᴇʟʟ heard the loft ladder groan. But it wasn't Lundquist coming.

"Shorty? You 'wake there, Shorty?"

"Stay where you are." Bell sweat salt. His bowels bunched. This prince of poverty might have cat-sight and one long sharp claw.

"Shee-it, Shorty. You too jumpy, son." The Cowboy was speaking softly. "Ol' Jesus just wants to talk nice 'n easy, just us two. See? I'm settin' here quiet as a hen."

He struck a match. Bell wished he hadn't. That battle-field face grinned at him in sulfur light. Generations of outrage written there. The ultimate nomad.

"You ain't no fool, Shorty. I mean, you a fool but you ain't as dumb as some." The match was out, but the image still vibrated. "You found ol' Carl all by yore lonesome, didn't you? But they ain't goin' to pay 'less you bring him out, is they? 'N hell, you in no position to unloose yore own precious self now, is you?"

"Suppose not."

"We all seen that contract. Man, never heard so much money my whole life. Just for one ol' sinner! Why, make a man weep, to think you so close 'n yet so far."

"Maybe."

"Well, Shorty, I been thinkin'. Carl ain't doin' nobody no good out here. He liable to get hisself sick his age in the winter woods. Ain't no doctors, no proper vittles, no lovin' care. Ol' man should ought to retire."

"He doesn't think so."

"Swan to goodness, Shorty, but these ol' boys sometimes just ain't the best judge, once past their prime. Now s'pose he up 'n die? All gone to waste, seems to me."

"Maybe so."

"You know what I mean, Shorty? You 'n me together got a mighty powerful responsibility toward this lovable ol' feller. Now I cain't do it alone, see. I couldn't go up to them friends of his to 'splain the situation, could I? They'd never gimme a nickel for my trouble neither."

"Maybe not."

"You know it, Shorty! We got to hook up, you 'n me. You can't get outa here — 'n I can't get in there!"

"See your point," Bell muttered. So everybody wanted him to sell Lundquist. As if he owned the old man. "He's no more use to you, then," he added.

"Shorty, I'm right disappointed. You white men git things backways wrong sometimes. We just goin' to help ol' Carl, that's all."

"Sure," said Bell. Lundquist had run around lighting fires; now he'd be roasted in them. Maybe that's all the old man expected, though. Maybe in a way it was what he wanted.

"We split it half 'n half, Shorty. I wouldn't care for none of it, but I got to have me a little stake, see. I got plans."

Another match flared. Again, the Cowboy's face leaped alive in the darkness. Bell drew back. It wasn't the match that would scorch him, it was the fury, the force, the hatred. The passion. No wonder the Nomad people hid from this flame, no wonder they'd do anything to snuff it out. It was too hot for men to face who hadn't any fire of their own.

"Half 'n half, Shorty. You hear me?" Again the sudden light, the Cowboy's raging presence burning Bell.

"I hear you," Bell said. He tried to swallow. Couldn't. His throat was too dry. He might have wept, though. He felt his weakness rising, a sense of hopeless anger at himself that even as he recognized it began slyly to change, began turning against the Cowboy — yes, began informing him that it was the Cowboy who was the dangerous man. Ah, this was the Nomad weakness. He'd gotten it at last. But damned if he'd lie about it to himself. *He* was the dangerous man here. It was his emptiness that threatened.

". . . you 'n me light out in the mornin', see." The Cowboy was going on, talking fast. "Don't you say nothin' to Carl. I do the talkin'. Then, on the way out, we can figger out the whens 'n hows of it . . ."

Bell sat pondering, barely aware of what the Cowboy was saying. Something else was turning in his mind. A troublesome point. Like Franklin and the others, the Cowboy was assuming that betrayal would mean nothing to Bell, that's what it amounted to, because a man without conviction could not possibly possess a true moral sense — and he, Bell, was neither better nor worse than the millions of other Bells who'd been deprived by fate, by chance, by historical accident, who'd grown up crippled among cripples, not knowing what it was to walk straight. Dangerous men, these Bells. Killers, sure. The Cowboy knew what he was, even if he didn't.

"Hold it," he said finally. "Wait a minute." He was sweating. "Can't do that." Ah, but his voice was a whisper. He could barely hear himself — and where was the Cowboy now? "Hey, Cowboy." There was no response. "You here, Cowboy?"

But the Cowboy had slipped away. Remarkable how a man that big could move so quietly. Might not have gone down, though. Might be working around to jump him from behind.

"Cowboy — ?"

No, he was gone for sure. Bell crouched there, teeth clenched, breath hissing out. The Cowboy had taken his silence for assent, he guessed. He should have yelled. Too late. Still, he had the sensation that the Cowboy remained in the loft — a mocking nightmare figure plugged into the nothing dark — and feared that his terrific face might blaze in matchlight from the corners, face after face, now here, now there, as though all Lundquist's bastards were crammed into that single multicolored skin. And he was Lundquist's bastard in a way, that man. Lundquist had summoned him, had pulled him out of the mute mass of wanderers whose history lay drowned like Atlantis. But Lundquist had betrayed him, too, by arousing doomed hopes — had lifted him so that he might fall — and the old man knew that, surely, and so might be waiting to be betrayed in turn. Traitors, all traitors, all wanderers from broken tribes.

THE DAY WAS milder. Mud curdled the thin snow. In the night, foxes had leaped at the remains of the deer, hung from a branch; their nails had scoured the ground.

"Goin' to take Shorty out to the traps, see'f we got somethin' caught this time." The Cowboy was strutting around taking puffs on a corncob pipe. Fester had gone hunting with the rifle. Lester was cutting up deer meat for stew. "Maybe we bring back nice fat 'possum, Shorty." The Cowboy snickered and rubbed his belly. "We goin' to catch us somethin' for sure, though. This ol' sinner can like to taste it already!"

Lundquist remained monumentally still. His hair and beard showed matted and stained in the sunlight that came through the open door, near where he'd moved his chair.

"You got to be quick with them critters, though, Shorty. When they in a trap, they vicious. Man make a bad move, lose a finger chomped off. Got to brain 'em square, Shorty. I show you how."

Bell stood slumped, dull and dumb. He, too, felt trapped. Nothing he could do. Lundquist had no use for him. The seminar was finished, the professor had closed his book. Class dismissed. He caught just one quick glance from Lundquist, a look of what he took to be murderous contempt. Then the old man's eyes seemed to veil over. Limestone flesh, age-flaking. Old polar bear in hibernation. Small dreams of distant times.

"Sometimes they play dead, see. Then they git you when you up close. They right sly when they knows they ain't got no chance, Shorty, so you got to lay their head open. When you goin' to kill a wild thing, man, you got to swaller down yore big merciful heart 'n don't be satisfied till you got a mess o' brains on yore stick!"

Bell felt sickened. The Cowboy was pacing back and forth near the chair where the old man sat immobile.

"Oncest gotta ol' beaver been trapped so long he done forgot all 'bout it 'cept maybe his leg not too spry, 'n when he saw me come 'round the tree with my brainstick, oh man, did that ol' beaver scoot! Tried to, I mean. The trap, it fetch him smackass flat, 'n he sorta blink 'n waggle up 'n flap his tail, 'n I vow that was the most dumbgasted ol' beaver I ever did see! Couldn't hardly hit him for laughin'."

"Let's go," said Bell.

"You bet, Shorty. We off now." The Cowboy stood smirking at the two of them, his bull's head cocked. Bell tried to catch the old man's eye. Couldn't. Lundquist was studying something within himself that took his full attention.

"Sure do pity the critter that fall in *our* trap, Shorty." The Cowboy stuck his pipe in his pocket and grabbed a heavy, knot-studded stick from the corner by the door.

"Be back later," Bell said, and he meant it, really meant it, but he didn't look at Lundquist until he was outside, some steps away. Then he turned and saw him at an angle — one last glimpse? — and the old man seemed to have lost all depth, as if he were painted onto that patch of daylight in the dark cabin frame. Painted but fading, a memory already. One last step.

Gone.

THEY WALKED FOR hours through the gummy woods. It was the right direction: North, where the mountain men had gone before. Bell sought landmarks. He'd sworn to come back somehow — alone and on his own terms — but it would be hard to find the way again. Every tree looked like every other, each hump of hill seemed like the last.

Cowboy Jesus stumped stockily along beside him, making enough racket for ten men. He hummed and sang and whistled, club-thumped trees in passing, fell to swearing when he slipped in snow, told occasional jokes and stories, hawked and spat, passed wind and vented his nostrils. Still, Bell felt his watchfulness, and had no difficulty imagining how the Cowboy's quick hands could lay the club against his skull if the need arose.

"Never did sell a man before, Shorty. How 'bout you?" The Cowboy hadn't addressed him directly until then.

"Never did, either."

"Don't it give you some kinda strange feelin'?"

"Nope." Nerves twitched in Bell. Too late now to deny what the other man assumed he'd agreed to. Better just to say nothing and face whatever was coming — and something was coming, for sure.

"Mean to say, man could get in the *habit*. Like them ol' slave traders back in whenever." The woods were thickening. Their pace had slowed, but the Cowboy was panting. "Them fellers got to likin' it so much they'd a done it free just for the joy of it, you know?"

"I suppose."

The Cowboy had led them off the way. They were breasting thickets now, side by side. Going where it was deeper, darker.

"Mightn't you maybe have some of them slavers up yore family tree, Shorty?"

"No idea."

"Maybe runs in a man's blood, you reckon?"

"Don't know."

No doubt about it. The Cowboy was breathing hard, and Bell could see out of the corner of his eye that sweat was bobbing on his face.

" 'N them mothers who done the Injuns in, them what-you-call-'em piney-ears —"

"P-pioneers."

"That's it. Oh, they was sly ones, they was. When they seen a piece o' land they fancied, they up 'n took it 'thout payin' no mind to whose it was. Yes, sir, Shorty. Ol' Carl, he tol' me 'bout how them pioneers sold them Injuns black 'n blue 'n sideways. Like to chill my bones. 'N here I am, a-walkin' along with their kin-child who got all that ramfractious hist'ry roilin' in his innards 'n me thinkin' that with my own folks behin' me — hell, they *timid* critters, Shorty, 'cept for maybe a few pitiful white men who somehow got mixed in — well, the ol' Cowboy don't have much chance comin' out even when it comes to sellin' men with a fine practiced feller like you."

Bell blinked. Saw gnats where no gnats were. A sick sky puked sunlight through the snow-greased branches.

"Mean to say, Shorty, you done sprouted from mighty fearsome tradin' stock which been sellin' men regardless of creed nor color, as they say, 'n when you run outa blacks 'n reds, hell, you ain't about to balk just 'cause the next man's white — "

"Not me," Bell whispered. Man up ahead there. Someone waiting.

" — sell any damn thing, sell the buttons off yore grandma's shroud, I reckon. Sold ol' Carl today! Who y' gonna sell tomorrow?"

Fester was there. Yellowgrin. Had that rifle in his hands, port-arms across the chest.

"Don't mean to suggest you ain't to be trusted, Shorty." The Cowboy's voice was heavy in his throat. "But it do 'pear you got a record long as yore bony arm 'n black as the blackes' buck yore great-granddaddy slaved up outa Africa. . . ."

Bell's ears shut. Heard no more. He was trudging like a dying man already, just shambling to his grave with loose arms dangling, mouth agape — but he was damned if he'd die for historical guilt.

Fester's long head stretched longer. Splinterman with nicotine teeth. Three more steps, maybe. He guessed the Cowboy was dropping back a pace or two, giving that brainstick a preparatory whirl.

He waded right up to Fester with dull eyes and slack surrendering body.

Fester's grin didn't change. If the Cowboy were about to swing, Fester's face would show it. It didn't. He had time.

He drove his fist into the grin. Felt the jolt right up to his shoulder. Fester'd been leaning against a tree. Teeth and lips got smashed between fist and trunk.

And Bell ran.

Dodged, ducked, ran ostrich-style bent at the waist, head up and glaring for his way. He took bark off the trees as he caromed and left shreds of Bell instead.

Behind him, roars and howls. The Cowboy would have paused to snatch the rifle. Too many trees to sight a shot, though.

Bell had run cross-country at a high school meet once. The starter had fired a blank. No blanks here. Course different, too. He skittered, leaped, plunged, clawed spiky shrubs, hurdled toppled trees, ran highstepping in fear of the traps his faulty vision might not reveal in time — a whack of metal teeth and he'd have a few minutes' grace to gnaw his leg off at the ankle as foxes were said to do, then hop on, bloody singlefoot. His heart and lungs were flopping like sausages, his steam breath hot enough to melt his gums, eyes popping, laboring legs cold as stone, and he had to fight the traitor commands of body terror. Stop. Fall. Faint. Hide. Die.

He did stop once to listen, but heard only his singing veins, his cannonading heart. He ran on. North, north. Had to keep that afternoon sun on his left.

Legs were howling pain. Feet worse. He slowed to a trot, then to a jog, bending low sometimes to ease a side stitch. Up hills, down. Over streams. Through skinny woods, fat groves. Deer dwelt there. Ought to catch one, mount, gallop bareback. Or grab owls, five in each hand, and fly.

Run on. Oh, Christ, it was too much. He fell flat in that eternal wilderness and counted to one hundred until his own racket diminished and he could hear. Nothing. What, had the Cowboy been joking? Just wanted to scare him? Were they back there heehawing? No, hadn't been any joke. Cowboy had known he couldn't be trusted — right, too — and so had planned to take him off, finish him miles away, leave him for vultures, ants, foxes, first come first serve, a forest smorgasbord. At least he'd had a trial, albeit a quick one, summation of prosecution charges with no time left for defense except last-minute appeal via punch and scamper.

He went on. Sun to the left. Keep it there. Avoid the great circle route. Where was he? West Virginia, he guessed. Or Kentucky by now. Must hit a road sometime, somewhere. Maybe he'd run forward in space but backward in time, pelting through old years with every stride, a wrong-way treadmill into history, and might wind up in Pico's pre-Columbian fantasy with antic Indian sports stars. Fast-Foot Bell, cross-continent sprinter.

So, he'd left Lundquist. The old man would have figured that he and the Cowboy planned to turn him in. Unless it had been Lundquist's idea to have him brained. Doubtful, but possible. He couldn't be certain of that nor of much else. Was Lundquist host or hostage? Old fellow had gotten himself in a wedge, anyway, caught between power and poverty. Defiant bastard, though. Unquenchable and proud. A fountain of pride, in fact. Wouldn't ever be humbled. Stinking old brute with bad manners, but damned if he'd flinch. Tough as those old pioneers, those mountain men, the ones who conquered a continent by half-wrecking it. The Puritans, too. Hardy rascals. Hadn't whimpered. That kind of pride rarely met any more. Had Lundquist gone seeking it in others? Was that what bound him and the Cowboy, and why the Cowboy had been loyal to him finally?

Bell, too. Himself. Not unmarked by it. Yes, by God.

He'd run into the grinder and now was running out the other side, chopped and torn, but unashamed, and more than that. Something in his guts had yelled *survive*. If he was worth that, maybe he could be worth more. Bell, self-judged, had been reprieved. Okay, go ahead: live.

And maybe it was because of a shove from Lundquist. The old man might have loosed him, as he'd loosed the Cowboy, except that the Cowboy was heading somewhere, and Bell was running just to keep from falling down. Sure, running. But where? Lundquist's mark, it burned like damnation. But that old bastard had something. Made men jump. Put his brand on them. Scorched them, drew howls. Ruinous old coot, but had that majesty. Forced pride up in others. Old pride-hunter. Found some in Bell. Yes, some there!

Without warning, he came upon a road. He pushed through bushes and there it was, an asphalt river flowing through the woods. He followed it, jogging still, and became suddenly aware of his public self — what a ragtag wreck he must look. He kept jogging, staggering with fatigue and chuckling like a drunk, laughing outright when a car passed him and he saw how his appearance astonished even those backwoods souls.

He was running on burlap and blisters now. His shoes had died somewhere in the first mile. Topcoat was trailing shreds of lining like butt feathers. Rips and rents disclosed raw knees, haired thighs, knotty calves. He still wore his tie. It was stiff with dirt, sweat, grease, with juice of beans, with dried fear and old tears, and didn't just hang but sort of stuck out at an angle. Same tie, but different, too. Crazy. Bell was doing roadwork past seedy hillfarms and goofy musing cows, running with saucy tie erect!

He fell three times before he reached the crossroads store. Twice on ice, once on hilarity. When he appeared, chickens fled and dogs backed off.

In the store the old countryman behind the counter gaped. Three teeth. One cigarette, which fell.

Bell tried hard not to laugh. He bowed instead, saw ten swollen toes like eggs nesting in the burlap, and straightened up grinning like Peary back from the Pole. In the corner a pay phone. He tried his pocket. Car keys, yes. And an abstract symbol, thin disk representing labor frozen in convenient metallic form, his total capital at the moment: a dime.

"Where you been, good buddy?" the countryman asked, suspicious.

"In the woods," Bell said, lifting the receiver. "Running." He let the dime fall and dialed O. "Long distance," he added, addressing all within earshot: storekeeper, operator, self. Sure, he was a certified long-distance star now: he'd run for his life and won. Waiting for his collect call to Pico to go through, he felt his weary legs twitch and stammer beneath him. Running still, he guessed. Maybe they'd never let him stop.

PART IV

"We can't quite figure you out, Bell. We don't know what motivates you."

"What motivates you?"

"I'd be only too glad to tell you," the interrogator said, "if we had the time. I've got no reason to conceal my motives. None of us has. We're just trying to do our job."

"Listen," Bell said. "I'm going to have to go to the bathroom pretty soon." They'd had him penned up there for hours.

"What I've got to say won't take long. Let me put it to you frankly, Bell. We're pretty disappointed by your attitude. We've given you the opportunity to square yourself, but you've put on this slick performance, which hasn't fooled us, you know."

"Good for you."

"Don't get sarcastic." The interrogator, however, didn't speak harshly. Bell guessed they'd given up on him. He hadn't had anything to offer them; they'd finally figured that out. "We want to give you a word of advice," the voice went on. "You decided — Lord knows why — to involve yourself in the

Lundquist business. Maybe you imagine yourself as some sort of social rebel, I don't know."

"Don't imagine anything."

"Well, whatever you want to call it. In any case, you've been relying on our tolerance."

"What!"

"Yes, relying on our tolerance, Bell. You're a luxury article, to put it bluntly. As long as you do your work and stay out of mischief, fine. You can study anything you want to. Write books. That kind of thing. But when you start wandering about stirring people up just to relieve your own internal anxieties, then our tolerance may be strained beyond reasonable limits."

"Ech," Bell said.

"Stick to history, Bell. That's your field. Teach it, but don't try to make it."

"Got to go," Bell said. "My teeth are floating." It wasn't that bad, but he was ready to leave now.

"All right, all right. We won't keep you. We'll see that you get back to your car."

"Don't have a car. I came by bus."

"Well, then, to the nearest place where you can catch the bus again. To go back home."

Bell swung his legs off the cot and sat up. He was bushed. His head ached.

"Go back home," the interrogator repeated.

"I've been home."

"Listen, Bell. We advise you to return. You've got a decent place in society. You may have the half-baked notion that you're some kind of nomad — you were babbling about that a *couple of hours ago — but the only nomads in this country are honest nomads, real ones, and can't help being what they are, and as a matter of fact an increasing number of them are making a real contribution to society, by means of the project — "*

"Oh, crap," said Bell.

The interrogator lost his temper. "You'll learn, Bell! You'll learn! You're the kind of irresponsible who forces us to take action we don't want to take! But I warn you! Keep your nose clean — !"

"I want my glasses."

There was movement in the room. The interrogator was angrily withdrawing. Someone flung open the door. Sunlight burst in, blinding Bell. "Here are your glasses," *a voice said. Bell grabbed them and stumbled toward the door, toward the light.*

THERE WAS MUZAK in the lingerie shop. Fifty violins implored. Heavy St. Paul matrons wandered through scented air, fingering fabrics.

"Couldn't find him, after all," Bell said. "Guess I'd better bow out."

Rose Lundquist was smartly rigged out for a business day, a tough little tug of a woman, freshly painted, red hair sprayed stiff.

"Sorry you spent all that for nothing," Bell said. He was uncomfortable on several counts, one being his costume: a shabby suit, ill-fitting, bought at a secondhand store with money Pico'd wired him for clothes and bus fare.

"So you're quitting," she said.

"I gave it a try."

They were in the rear of the store, where she had a little desk. Bell wished he'd gone straight home. Why had he stopped off here? Maybe it was just the old closure complex. Leave no loose ends.

"You're not the quitting type," she said.

"Um."

"You wouldn't quit this soon."

Bell shifted uneasily on a fragile chair. In a mirror he glimpsed the results of his Appalachian holiday: face weathered to winter sunset hues, hands like lobster claws.

"Well," he said, "that's the way it is."

"I wonder."

"Hmm?"

"You're not a very good liar, Bell."

Bell considered this. She was right. He wasn't.

"You did find him," she said. She was irked. Her freckles were darkening.

"Listen," Bell said. He was a little surprised. How could she really tell? Must be guessing.

"You should have phoned me immediately!"

"I did."

"When?"

"Well, from Louisville. I changed buses there. You weren't home. That's why I decided to stop here on my way back."

"I meant you should have called from where *he* was."

"I had one hell of a time," he grumbled, unsure of what to say. She was giving him that sharp stare. They'd conversed in friendlier fashion last time. But what did he expect now, maiden blushes? Not from her. "I'd repay the money," he said, "except by God I feel I earned it. Besides, it was his, wasn't it?"

"Where is he?"

"I don't know."

"You did find him."

"I couldn't tell you where he is."

"I can smell him on you, Bell. Look at your damned face.

You came in grinning all over. You had to let me know somehow, I suppose. Fine. Congratulations. Now how about letting me in on your little secrets?"

Bell eyed his mirror image sidelong. Was it that obvious? Maybe she was right. He'd wanted someone else to know how bloody hard it had been. "How could I have phoned?" he complained, giving up. "He was stuck out in the woods, miles from anywhere."

"Where?"

"I'm not even sure which state. West Virginia, probably. I couldn't find it again. Anyhow, he'll be gone by now."

"That's incredible!"

"Truth."

"You had him and you let him get away."

"He had *me*. I had to run for my goddamned life!"

"Kindly don't shout here." She spoke in a vicious little voice. She was furious. She sensed he hadn't much to say and would tell her even less. "I'm delighted that you managed to survive, Bell, and now that you have, I'd appreciate your honoring our understanding. It's rather important to me."

"It seemed to be important to him, too."

"Meaning what?"

"He said you were already his legal wife."

"Ah." Her eyes widened, a glint of triumph, as if this confirmed what had been just her hunch: Bell had found him, all right. "Well, if he told you that, he was lying."

"Look," said Bell. Which to believe? Didn't matter. "I don't care about that. It's your problem, yours and his. I'm damned if I mess with it any more." Cole Porter melodies were drowning in Muzak treacle. His head ached. "You

wanted me to find him. Okay, I found him. He's alive and
well, as they say. But he isn't coming back, not for you, not for
Nomad. He's in there for good now. That's all I've got to tell
you."

"I refuse to accept that!" She managed to snarl while smiling. "We're going to get a map. You're going to show me the
precise lo — "

"Nix," Bell said. "I couldn't, even if I wanted to."

"You're lying."

"No, you were right before. I'm a lousy liar." He got up
and started toward the door. She came right after him. They
passed frilled nighties, kimonos, sheer pajamas. "He said you
wanted to help Nomad get him," he added. "Then they'd
do him in somehow."

"What? Ridiculous." She smiled at a customer. "And you
believed that? He's paranoid, you know. Maybe he ought to
be placed under treatment." She uttered a little social laugh,
but her fingers were hooked in Bell's bumpkin sleeve.

"He said Nomad would pay you for him."

"Absolute nonsense."

Black lace, net hose, bra pads. He was in a female armory.
These ladies were choosing weapons. Peekaboo panties. Hide
this, show that. Ammunition for the pubic wars. In a corner
a nude mannequin without nipples, futuristic symbol. So
long, Mom.

"Somebody's lying," he grumbled. "I don't care who.
Point is, I'm done."

"That old fiend brainwashed you," she said sweetly, keeping up appearances. They'd reached the door. "You'd believe
anything he said."

"Not so."

"You men stick together, don't you?"

"Stick, hell. It was like finding a rogue elephant. I damned near got killed in there."

"Even so, you're loyal to him." Her freckles were like pox now. "He goes blundering around the country making scenes and messes, and you admire that, don't you? You wish you could, too. You wish you had the guts." She was panting a little. "You don't think of the consequences. Or maybe you do. He never did."

"Sorry, but it's not my problem."

"You're involved! You promised me!"

"You weren't candid." He opened the door and stepped into November. The wind ran right through that cheap suit.

She stayed with him, still attached to his sleeve. "He systematically plundered and deprived me of everything a woman has the right to have."

Bell supposed she meant children, a home, a community position. Incredible. Surely she hadn't expected to tame that old bear. "You knew what he was, didn't you?" he said.

"Not then. How could I? I was too young when —" She paused. Resumed: "When we began living together." Too late. Now it was Bell's turn to gloat. She'd flubbed. They both knew it. Sure, there'd been a marriage. "He ought to be institutionalized!" She was really angry now. Her fingers were digging at his arm. "So he can't do any more harm!"

"I'm not his judge."

Mrs. Lundquist glanced back. The women inside the shop were watching through the window. She resurrected her smile. It was ragged. It showed teeth. "I thought he was a great man! I thought I'd have a creative role! I didn't realize he'd ruin everything with his deliberately offensive manners."

That made Bell marvel. Had she imagined herself presiding at faculty teas, guiding Lundquist grandly east to Yale?

"He got what he wanted," she shouted. "I didn't. He cheated me."

"That didn't give you the right to hunt him down."

"He's got to be brought to account!"

"Not by me." Bell jerked his arm free of her. "Those others, they'll never find him. They don't know what they're looking for."

"And I suppose you did."

"Yes, by God. That's right. I finally did." He started off.

"You're not out of it, Bell. You can't just walk away from it. They won't let you."

"Look," he said, over his shoulder. "I'm walking."

She actually trotted a few steps with him. "And you don't need to pride yourself in the sex department, either," she said, spitefully. "Let me inform you, Bell, you weren't so hot."

"You sure you remember which one I was?"

He bowed without breaking stride. When he reached the corner, he looked back. She wasn't there. He still felt her finger pressure on his arm, though.

He RODE THE bus all night, rolling northwest on another wintersea crest. It was slow going. There'd been new snow on the old. Giant highway plows chested the drifts aside for sand trucks with red-faced workmen on the tailgates, shoveling. Bell saw cottony towns, dim plains spread like foam, barns castellated in frost white, glassy orchards, the distant solitary gleams of lost farms.

He arrived after the late dawn, and ate breakfast at the bus depot, not far from the gym. Then he set off by foot for home, under an oatmeal sky.

It was 8:30 A.M. He paused when he reached the gate. The house had a startled look. All its windows stared: shades up, curtains pulled back. And the porch and walk were clean of snow. Not merely shoveled, but swept. Old Aaron never would have done that, not for a dozen returning sons. Who, then — Pico, Widow Watt, the fanatic Mrs. Finn, now rigid as a setter watching him from her house across the street?

He opened the gate — the fact that it was not merely swung shut but actually latched was another thunderous portent. Up the grainy steps. Couldn't even see snow in the cracks between the boards.

The doorknob was *polished*. He turned it with foreboding.

Inside, he cleared his throat and blinked a bit in the hallway gloom. Then they came popping out at him from different directions.

First, old Aaron. He skipped out of the living room uttering cries of welcome.

Then there appeared the thin pale figure of Norma drifting along the hall from the kitchen. A blue-jeaned ghost with handkerchief-bound hair, smoking a filter cigarette.

"Ham!" His father seized his elbows and began hauling at him. "Guess who's here!" He let Bell go and made a little dash at Norma, as though to grab her and thrust the two lovers together, but at this point there entered from the dining room a further surprise: Norma's mom, mop in hand, a winning smile on her good gray face.

"Professor Bell! You certainly gave us a scare being lost!"

Confusion. They all milled about in the hallway. Aaron was frantic with excitement. "Let's leave these two alone," he squeaked at Mrs. Hirlinger, but it was Norma who left, mumbling something about a hot pot on the stove, as Bell stood treelike in horror. "Listen, Ham, you ought to know — Mr. Hirlinger died," the old man announced in a stage whisper, tugging at Bell's suit jacket as if under the impression it was an overcoat to be removed.

"His Savior called," said pious Mom.

"And Grandpa left the house to me — "

"Poor Daddy's sufferings are over. He's in a Better Place — "

" — it's mine, Ham. I own it! You were gone when they read the will — "

"His will be done, which we accept below."

"I was liberally provided for, Ham! Father possessed valuable stocks and bonds!"

"He was nauseous to the very end."

Norma appeared, disappeared, came back again, was gone. She'd found what she wanted. A book to read while she stirred Mom's stew.

"I'm an independent man for the first time in my life, Ham!" Old Aaron let go of Bell's jacket. "See what I bought? A new suit!" He strutted back and forth. "Vest included! Got it the day they reported you lost." He caressed the fabric. "Only minor alterations required. I was going to phone Norma at once to tell her, but she called me first."

"It was the day her daddy was translated."

"So naturally I invited them —"

"A change of scene," said Mrs. Hirlinger, with wet eyes.

"We decided to worry together, Ham. The way a true family does." Old Aaron preened himself. "How do you like it?"

"Grief is binding. It makes our troubles seem small."

"Father remembered me handsomely!" Bell's father began nudging him down the hall. "You got a lump sum bequest," he said. "Two thousand five hundred. But he didn't leave a nickel to the University! They expected something. Now they're courting me, Ham. Me!" He had backed Bell into the dining room. It fairly smoked from Mom's scrubbing. "They're hinting at some suitable memorial to his name, which I'd pay for." He giggled. "Ham, I wouldn't endow a roll of toilet paper! Why should I? They've always looked askance at me, the black sheep, the high school graduate!"

Where was that familiar acid smell? Bell sniffed. Nowhere. Mom was stronger than old cat piss. She'd exorcised it. What next?

"Listen." Bell hauled his father back across the hall and

into the living room, passing Mom, who had refreshed the mop and was treading elsewhere. "Why'd they come here, Dad?"

"Why not, Ham? I invited them. I can do that now, you know," the old man said, defensively. "Actually," he added, with a sly look, "I think there's a little financial problem. Cancer costs a lot." He goggled up at Bell in sudden concern. "They say fat men rarely get it. Have you heard that, Ham?"

"You've got nothing to worry about now, Dad."

Bell made a quick exit before his father could grab him again. He went upstairs to his room. Norma's things were there. Spare blue jeans on a chair. He fished his extra glasses from his bureau drawer. Passing along the upper hall, he saw that Mom was occupying Grandpa's room, the TV in its old position facing the bed so that the dear lady could observe the "Late Show" in comfort.

He went down the back stairs, and cornered Norma in the kitchen.

"Norma, why'd you come back?"

She seemed puzzled. "Gee, Bell." He saw that she was reading Thackeray now. There was a spot of stew juice on *Vanity Fair*, page 240. "Well, when my mother called your father and he told her — "

"I thought you called him."

"Well, no. Actually she did. And when she said we ought to come at once, well." She made a slight gesture of despair. "Poor Momma, she's been through such a lot of trouble and worry, I certainly was anxious to help her through the read-justment period in any way I could."

"You mean I'll have to ask *her* why you're here?"

"Do you mind horribly we came?"

"It isn't that, Norma." He was pacing. He sensed Mom's presence. She was dusting nearby. He felt like shouting. Dust, dust. Didn't she know that man was dust? Oh, she knew, all right. "What do you *feel?*" he cried out.

Norma blinked. "Well, I don't know what you mean. I mean, we're getting over Daddy and until Professor Pico told us you'd called him we were just worried sick about you. And now." Her gaze didn't quite focus on him. She was looking through him, perplexed. "Well, there are some problems, I know. There certainly are."

"Life is a series of problems to be solved!"

"Um, that's so true, Bell."

Her languor was catching. He felt a jaw-breaking yawn rise up. He swallowed it; almost gagged. "But sometimes people solve them the wrong way!" He hadn't wanted Norma, he'd just tried to solve the Marriage Problem. He'd made a mistake by adding. Two zeroes made nothing.

"We really ought to discuss it," she said. She glanced down at her open book. "But I mean you're probably tired now."

She wanted to finish her chapter.

"Maybe, you know, later," she said. "When you're rested."

She preferred Thackeray's problems. Far more interesting.

"I have a terrible confession to make to you, Norma." He felt that if he failed to command her attention, his existence would be threatened. He'd become a floor stain. Mom would mop him up. "I have committed adultery!"

"Gee, Bell." Norma looked pained. She was embarrassed, too. She silently reproached him for having mentioned it. "Well, I'd prefer not to talk about that for the time being if you don't mind. I mean, this is not at all suitable in the kitchen and all." But she was relieved. Now she could pretend to be hurt and turn for solace to her novel.

Mom appeared in the hall doorway. Adultery. She'd overheard. She was grinning like Medusa. "You'll have time for a bath, Professor Bell, before we sit down to lunch." Oh, Bell was dirty. Better scrub him.

"Um," said Bell. Norma was reading, really reading. There. She turned a page.

"I scoured the tub this very morning."

"I believe you," Bell said. He raised one arm and sniffed the pit. Mom's gaze flew to heaven, where spotless Daddy harped.

"I know you must be tired," she said, forgiving that crude sniff.

"And dirty."

She didn't even like the word.

Bell moved, but toward the rear door. "Oh, say," he remarked, "what about your dog?"

"Wilbur? Poor Wilbur. He followed."

"Pardon?"

"Wilbur got sick and was making these little messes and the vet said so we decided it was the Lord's will and we had him gassed."

"Wow," he muttered. A bad omen. Take that shower, or else.

" 'Scuse me?"

"Nothing," Bell said, decisively. He glanced at Norma, the reader; at Mom, foe of dirt. "Be back later; got an errand."

He went out the alleyway and jogged the two blocks

to Pico's house, but Pico wasn't home. He was teaching a class, Bell's.

"Listen," Harriet Pico said, "you come in and tell me all about you and Norma. Oh, I do so hope." She was avid. Her mouth actually hung open, tongue like a cow's heart.

"Well, she came back."

"I know, I know!"

"I think she forgot a pair of gloves."

"What's that? Oh, you're joking. Come on. I'm dying to know. Tell Harriet!"

"Nothing to tell. That's the full story. Nothing."

"Bell, you are maddening! But I can see how happy you are. It's written all over your face."

"No kidding?" Bell was surprised. "Me?" He didn't feel happy. Didn't feel sad, though. He felt light of foot and nimble. Wanted to run. "Sorry, Harriet. I've got to beat it over to the building and report in to Professor Glass."

"Aw."

Running made Bell feel better. Winter was in the air, spring in his legs. Going somewhere, Bell? No matter. He felt he had to keep running. Wasn't out of the wilderness yet. The underbrush was thick, and there were traps everywhere.

In his office there were student papers on his desk, and a note in Pico's sloppy handwriting: *Welcome back you owe me $150 plus $6.70 expenses.*

Bell went down the hall to Professor Glass's office. He could hear the rumble of Pico's voice lecturing in a room below, a fifty-minute belch of history.

"Oh, young Bell." Professor Glass rose to greet him. "We've been expecting you."

"I'm back."

"Splendid." The old scholar gazed at him in inquiry.

"Yes, I found him. But he isn't coming back."

"Oh. Well, I'm relieved to hear that. Spare me the details, though. It's another fracas, I suppose."

"You might say that."

"For the past two weeks we've had repeated telephone calls from gentlemen apparently connected with the government, inquiring about Carl and you. I trust you aren't in any difficulty."

"Don't think so."

"Good. I hoped there wouldn't be any problems. It's always best to avoid them. Carl wasn't any good at that. He met everything head-on."

"He's a teacher."

Professor Glass seemed mildly surprised. "Why, yes, I suppose he is. A disturbing personality, but you're quite right. He does teach."

"And he has no place here."

"Absolutely not."

"This is a refuge."

"Exactly," Professor Glass agreed. "You did find Carl, didn't you! Yes, a university is a refuge. This one still is, anyway. We're quite safe here, young Bell."

"We have no contact with reality!"

"Of course not." Professor Glass smiled genially. "That's the whole point."

"I didn't look at it that way before," Bell complained. He searched his senior's parchment face for signs of mockery. Not there. "I mean, I used to think our function was to seek the t-t-truth and to impart it to young people and, through them, to the world."

Professor Glass chuckled.

"But now it seems as though our function is merely to amuse ourselves," Bell said.

"Oh, yes!"

"We don't teach at all!"

"You're right, we don't!" chortled the old history chairman.

"We're unfit to teach!"

"We couldn't be worse!"

"We operate a baby-sitting service for a society gone mad with power and violence!"

Professor Glass wiped his eyes. He was shaking with giggles. "Oh, do stop, Bell. I beg you. I shall laugh myself into an attack!" He leaned back limply in his chair. "Ah," he said at last. "That was almost too much!"

"You're agreeing with everything I've been saying," Bell objected, amused and also feeling a bit foolish.

"Yes, of course. Oh, except for that business about a power-mad society. Carl always saw things in such a gloomy Swedish way. I myself tend toward the view that society is so highly specialized and mechanized now that no career of any real importance is possible. Or, to put it another way, a truly modern man cannot possibly have a meaningful life in the old sense. Oh, you can still parachute into some backward region with your first-aid kit and be a kind of Schweitzer, but then you've left modern society, haven't you? And it's so *comfortable* here. We have our conveniences and our pleasures and instead of having real work to do — again, in the old sense — we are merely obliged to amuse ourselves, as you put it."

"To delude ourselves."

"Yes, yes. That's essential. We must convince ourselves

that we are of value!" And Professor Glass was seized again by hilarity. "Sorry!" he spluttered. "Can't help it!"

Neither could Bell. He laughed some, too. "But it isn't funny!" he protested.

"Yes it is!"

The old gentleman was a merry one, to be sure. Bell had always thought him just a fretful old bonehead. Yet Glass was Lundquist's last friend. This was the reason, apparently.

"Excuse me, Professor Glass. Why didn't you give me the benefit of your views before this?"

"How could I? You believed in yourself as a truth seeker and teacher. You were happier that way."

"I wasn't happier."

"You can say that now. And besides, it would be improper for a department head to go about undermining the morale of young professors. After all, you're the wave of the future!" More laughter.

"Oh, my God," Bell mumbled. It was funny and unfunny, too. "Shouldn't be this way!" he exclaimed, in a ringing voice.

"It needn't," said the chairman, struggling for solemnity. "I mean, you can construct another dream, if you like, Bell. But I very much doubt you can go back to the old one now."

"It's just a game."

"Game or dream, whatever you like." One last giggle. Old Glass smiled wearily. His skin was so pale that his features almost vanished against the albino wall. He was hardly more than a sketch of a man. "Don't make Carl's mistake, though. I implore you not to. He insisted on his own importance. To an unreasonable degree. A very old-fashioned fellow, Carl. Quite out of step with the times. He really should

have been an anthropologist. Then he could have settled down to live with some truly primitive people." The class buzzer sounded. The building vibrated from scraping chairs, shuffling feet. "Instead of the wretches he pursued all his life," Professor Glass added.

"But those people are important."

Professor Glass's lips formed an unspoken *why.*

"They are," Bell said. He felt agitated. Those shuffling feet, like yawns walking. The corridors were filling with them. "We may not be, but they are. They're struggling to live!"

Professor Glass merely shrugged.

"Men who live desperate lives are living. Aren't they? That's where the importance is. Isn't it?"

"Perhaps." Professor Glass drew back from Bell's intensity. It tired him. He thought longingly of early America. History congealed all passions. That's what made it so comfortable.

"Lundquist was searching for that," Bell went on. "He kept finding it. But never enough! There's never enough of that!"

Professor Glass nodded absently, as though in agreement.

"He was a real teacher, and a real teacher has to find real students — even if he has to hunt them down!"

Professor Glass mumbled his assent.

"Wait, though. He wasn't teaching them. They taught *him.* That's what he wanted! He was hungry to learn! So he fed on their importance!"

But Bell saw that Professor Glass was no longer interested. "Something like that, anyhow," he added, and got up to go, leaving the old historian peacefully in his chair.

It was lunchtime. Bell lurked in his office. At home was Mom's stew. *Clean* stew. He snatched up a student essay — "Andrew Jackson and Nullification" — and scanned it for neatness, found an agreeable number of typing strikeovers and erasure smudges, and graded it A. All those essays. Like autumn leaves. He raced through them. Some he graded by weight, some by smell. He was generous. All A's and B's.

His phone rang. He didn't answer. Nullification: he'd secede from lunch. Let Mom send out the troops.

Pico came in smelling like a meat market. "Bell, you bastard. There you are. Boy, am I glad to see you. You can give your own damn classes for a change."

They went to a café just off-campus. Pico ordered two hero sandwiches and a quart of beer. Bell asked for fried rabbit. "We're fresh out," said the waiter, used to academic wags. Bell settled for soup.

"Listen," Pico said. "What's all this hustling you're doing? Government work?"

"Yep."

"Can't divulge?"

"Nope."

Pico shoved half a hero into his mouth. Bell could hear the pickles juicing.

"What about Norma?" Pico asked. "Want to talk?"

"Her mother brought her here. It was her mother who came."

"I bleed for you. Me, I was lucky. Harriet's mother died in infancy. You know — second childhood." Pico nuzzled his beer foam. "On her last visit, she saw that the kids were starting to resemble me. She gave up then." He peered at Bell over rippling cheeks. "You look like the original country cousin, Bell. How do you feel?"

"Wild."

"Great. Listen, there's a faculty reception at five. In honor of some visiting nabobs. The point is, free cocktails. I'll pick you up. Home?"

"Office."

"You'd better change, though. That suit, it shines in the dark." Pico bit off another yard. "Oh, hell, probably won't matter. Not after the first round." He munched. "Morgan's wife is dieting. Gets tipsy fast. Empty stomach, full blouse. Quick feel in the cloakroom." He shifted facial flab into a leer. "Oh. By the way. I've got a little project going. A Fast-Foot *movie*." He gave Bell an exploratory glance. "A new dimension for the History. I figure we can borrow Morgan's camera for it. I've got a couple of script ideas knocked out already. All we need are some feathers for costumes, stuff like that." He drew salami rind from between his teeth. "I hear you can get an aged effect by shooting film through a silk stocking — like old newsreels, see? And then you speed up the projector." His tub face dimly glowed with creative visions. "Can't you see it? You could be Broken Crotch. Painted nut-brown. Feathered up. Running licketysplit. Hurdles falling like dominoes. How does it grab you?"

"Could be important."

"Yeah," agreed Pico. Then he squinted. "Yeah?" Was Bell poking fun? He decided not. "Well, maybe not important, but a real gas. I figured we could make a sound track. Old silent movie music. And maybe a love interest. Morgan's wife in a low-cut squaw outfit. High camera angle. Panoramas Pico's speciality." He licked his fingers one by one. "Say, you finished? Ready to go?"

"More than," Bell said.

They strolled back. It was all Bell could do to keep from breaking into another run. He was in a hurry. Another circle had almost closed.

When he entered his office, he found that Brant was waiting for him there.

"Hi, Dr. B. Long time, no see."

They shook hands. Bell sat down behind his desk. Brant looked fresh and neat; beardless, too.

"I brought your suitcase back, sir." There it was, in the corner. "And we took care of the car for you. The rental agency came out and got it. They'll send you the bill. You can turn the keys in to the local office, I guess."

Bell yawned.

"Well, Dr. B." Brant smiled and folded his arms in order to begin triceps exercises. "We understand you actually found him." Bell said nothing. Lundquist's wife would have telephoned them right away. "Naturally we'd like to get the full info straight from you," Brant went on. "I've got a little pocket recorder, sir. I mean, there's no danger I'd misquote you."

"Uh uh," Bell said.

"No?"

Bell shook his head.

"Gee, Dr. B.!"

"Don't say *gee*, Brant. That's a bad speech habit. Look. Wherever he might have been, he isn't any more."

"Dr. B., I am instructed to advise you — "

"Save it, champ. You couldn't find him anyhow. You don't have the training."

"Let us be the judge of that, sir."

"What I can't understand is why you're spending all this time and money on it. You, Reuss, Muller. God knows how many more. You've got to be kept busy, I guess." Bell thought of the federal buildings, crammed with files and records; of payrolls, stuffed with Brants; of computers, gobbling data. A desperate system, gaunt with hunger. True poverty there. "Why don't you just give up and study each other?" But they did, of course they did. That's what they were doing. They didn't know how to do anything else. No wonder they were so bored.

"We're doing serious work, sir," Brant said, reprovingly.

"No, you aren't." And it would be out of this boredom, Bell thought, that Reuss and Muller would zap the Cowboy. Then each other.

"Well, Dr. B., I didn't come here to argue."

"Swell." Bell got up.

Brant made one last appeal. "Come on, Dr. B. Give us a hand." He stood there, a blue-eyed bureaucratic youth. Unspeakably innocent. In ten years he'd be like Muller. It gave Bell the shakes just to look at him. "I mean, don't you want to change your attitude, sir? To cooperate?"

"Hell, no," Bell said. "Go away."

" 'Fraid you haven't seen the last of us, Dr. B."

"Out," said Bell, mildly.

Brant closed the door as he left. The phone began ringing again. Bell lifted his suitcase onto the desk, took out his manuscript — executive mechanisms, his own number game —

and gave himself a failing mark by ripping it in two and flunking it into the wastebasket. Then he set the ringing phone inside the suitcase, closed the lid on it, and stood moodily at the window staring out at the campus. Nothing much was out there. Just footprints in the snow, footprints by the hundreds, a stampede to nowhere.

The faculty reception was held in the lounge of the administration building. Bell entered yawning, his glasses askew. "Have a mart," said Pico. "Clean those cobwebs away." He nipped up two martinis from a tray and gave Bell one, then shuffled off to trade smutty stories with a pair of biochemists who always had some new ones.

The lounge was paneled in walnut. Dim portraits of ex-deans hung there. Bell backed up to one and sipped the mart. From his height, he saw a roomful of bobbing heads, quite a few of them bald, like zeroes.

One dome came his way. A heavy head, doleful eyes, a rueful expression. "Hello, Bell," said Dr. Grosch.

Bell stared down at him.

"Surprise," mumbled Dr. Grosch, uneasily. He gave Bell a tentative smile.

"Nomad," Bell said.

"No, no. Not any more. Not exactly." Dr. Grosch glanced about circumspectly. His drink, fizzing busily, seemed to be pure soda water. "I'm with a group of mathematicians and humanists, making a little tour of various colleges. Goodwill, mostly. We're, ah, doing a wee bit of recruiting, too. For various, um, programs."

"Nomad in the slums."

"Oh. That." Dr. Grosch took a reluctant swallow of his soda.

"You're going ahead."

"Well, yes. *They* are. I'm not with them now. Not in a literal sense, anyway."

"They don't need Lundquist, then."

"Ah, no. Perhaps they really never did."

"Then why have they kept after him?"

"They thought he could be of use, I suppose. And then — well, he was a loose end, and they detest loose ends."

"He was more than that," Bell said. "He wouldn't play their game. He played his own."

"Um," said Dr. Grosch, dubiously.

"He wouldn't let them control him the way they wanted to," Bell went on. "And if they couldn't handle him, how could they hope to handle all the others? So they had to get him off the board as fast as they could. He denied the validity of the game itself."

"Oh, no," interposed Dr. Grosch. "Hardly that. I mean, the game goes on, doesn't it? It's true that Carl's attitude emphasized certain troubling practical questions, but the theory, Bell, the theory is quite unscathed." He peered around the room nervously, and then plucked Bell by the sleeve. "Ah, somebody said you actually, um, found him." Bell made no reply. "I don't blame you for not trusting me, Bell," Dr. Grosch added, gloomily. "I really don't trust myself any more. I've lost all joy in life. I may end like Franklin. Poor fellow." He sighed. "Franklin began by objecting to his office, not because it was too small, but because it was too large. He insisted on something less spacious. They moved him to a smaller one and walled up the windows at his direction, but even that wasn't enough. A sad case. They should have known the symptoms. Fear of open areas. I forget which phobia it is. Anyway, apparently nothing but a closet would have satisfied him, and perhaps not that for long. The night they took him away, he was trying to climb inside one of the computers. He'd unscrewed the back and had gotten one leg in when the watchman came by."

Bell could think of nothing to say.

"Still, we must press on," continued Dr. Grosch, with an effort to achieve his former heartiness. "The new generation may do a better job." He glanced at Bell's face, seeking agreement. "Well," he muttered defensively, "at least they can try. Tell me honestly, Aaron Bell. What do you think of Nomad?"

"It's an attempt to search out human significance."

Dr. Grosch brightened.

"In order to destroy it," Bell added.

Dr. Grosch started in alarm. "Not so loud," he cautioned. "There are mathematicians everywhere." He mopped his forehead. "Do you really think that?"

"Sometimes. It seems to me — "

"Say no more!" Dr. Grosch clutched his arm. "I can tell

that a certain, um, mutual acquaintance has influenced your judgment!" He tried to lead Bell off to one side, as though Bell had given unexpected evidence of dementia. "We're all afflicted by doubts, you know. You are entitled to your views, naturally. Provided you express them with due regard for, um." They edged past one of Dr. Grosch's colleagues, at whom Dr. Grosch directed a glorious smile. "Decorum," he whispered up at Bell. "I can retire on full pension next July," he added, anxiously, "and I don't want any further stain on my record. You can appreciate that, can't you? I *need* to retire."

"They surely can't hold up your pension."

"God knows what they can do. It's all so mixed up. I mean, I wouldn't know where to begin if I was forced to file an appeal. Half the time I haven't been sure whether I've been working for public agencies or private ones — not that it makes any difference policy-wise. Or perhaps I shouldn't say that! To explicate: just because a private foundation is financed by public funds doesn't mean that its programs must be in line with public policy. Or does it?"

"Doesn't matter." Bell tried to soothe Dr. Grosch, who was in an agitated state. Instead of maneuvering Bell into a remote corner of the lounge, Dr. Grosch had inadvertently drawn him into the very center. They were wedged among tippling scholars, including Dr. Slough, chief resident mathematician, whose hand Dr. Grosch shook fervently.

"Give us your candid opinion, Slough," Dr. Grosch said. "Can human behavior be usefully studied by means of computer analysis?"

Dr. Slough smiled and stroked his grizzled beard.

"There's your answer, Bell!" Dr. Grosch seemed triumphant. "It's true that there's often a gap between theory and practice, but we're on the verge of exciting discoveries. On the verge! Right, Slough?"

Dr. Slough laughed agreeably.

"Intuition is all very well," Dr. Grosch continued expansively, "but it's damned sloppy. Look at the mess the world's in today!" His voice boomed. Several nearby guests turned his way. "Intuition is finished! Man's evolution goes on! We crawled out of the slime eons ago. How? By using our brains! If we'd depended on our hearts, we'd have stayed put!" Bell sought to calm him, in vain. "Man's highest function," declared Dr. Grosch, tapping his temple. " 'Theirs is not to reason why,' " he quoted. "But that's wrong! Theirs *is* to reason why!" Dr. Slough had drifted away. Someone else had taken his place, a youngish man with graying hair and a hard little smile.

It was Muller. As he spoke into Dr. Grosch's ear, he gave Bell a stony look.

Dr. Grosch listened broodingly to what Muller told him. "Yes yes yes," he muttered, nodding. Then he grabbed Bell's hand. "Seems there's a phone call for me." He smiled and gave Bell a wink, but his expression was piteous nonetheless. "When my wife died, I stopped caring," he whispered. He dropped Bell's hand, turned, and threaded his way out, closely followed by Muller. At the doorway, he paused to give Bell a farewell wave but couldn't see where he was and so made a generous good-bye gesture that took in the entire lounge, ex-deans and all. Then he departed, with an air of importance.

Bell wandered. Ladies' hats brushed his shoulders. The polished tonsures of academicians gleamed up at him. Here was Professor Glass, refreshed by sherry, pink polka dots on his powdery cheeks, and there was a matrix of humanists, locked in place by elbows and fixed grins. At the far end of the lounge, Pico could be seen assisting Mrs. Morgan toward the cloakroom. She needed help. Those marts had done their work.

Bell felt hemmed in and short of breath. Fresh air was wanted. He inhaled, caught a whiff of Lundquist, and jerked around in astonishment, expecting to see human zeroes scattering as the old man blew tempestuously in.

But he'd smelled himself. He'd bathed since Appalachia, but not enough.

Had that old man's stink still. He was armored with it. Would make people shrink and stand aside. Then move back, folks. Bell emerging. He made his way past the portraits, past old Glass, past molecular arrangements of humanists and inhumanists, past Pico and Mrs. Morgan in the cloakroom, and outside to see the million stars that shone down on Lundquist, too, wherever he might be.

Those little lights. They glittered from the human dust that rose. Old nomads had used them to guide their wanderings. They'd seen portents up there, too; celestial messages inscribed in the never ending patterns that slid across the universal roof, warnings emblazoned by great flaring novae, zodiacal decrees unfolded through the positioning of planets. Truth once had been a scroll of stars; men had gazed upward to read it. No longer. The dust that rose was blinding. Few looked up.

Bell did, walking home. Whipped off his glasses to see better. A winter sky, ice-chip stars casting cold fate. It made him shiver. Universe so vast, man so small. It took a brash nomad to eye those frosty specks. Bell, practicing, sauntered with his head tipped back, missed a curb rise, found an ice patch, and went skating impromptu into a telephone pole, embraced it, lost his footing completely and slid down, sprawling full-length almost beneath the window of the vigilant Mrs. Finn.

He got up, chastened. Mrs. Finn's eyes glowed catlike through the dark glass. *Bell drunk.* What joy. That repaid her for the funeral pot roast.

On his porch he paused to brush his trousers. Through the window he could see the little family group in the living room. Mom and old Aaron were both talking at once, and Norma on the couch was deeper into *Vanity Fair* than poor Franklin ever got with his computer. Bell, vibrating with chill, shook with thought as well. They were in, he was out. Were they fretting for his return? Not a bit. His father was enjoying a fresh audience. A man of property and substance now, he would be busy recasting his many roles. No more tears and tatters. The jester's cap was gone. The old fellow was all smiles and triumph. Bell would dampen him now. Likewise Norma. Her emotions were elsewhere engaged — in the novels she wept over, at the flicks where she was passion's toy. No *gee Bell* there. Norma committed two-dimensional adultery with Paul Newman, who smelled like popcorn. And why not? What harm? Let her.

He sneaked off the porch and around to the back. The door had always been unlocked, but that was pre-Mom. Now it was bolted. No help for it. Bell returned to the front and ankled in. Click, snap. From the hall, he saw their faces droop. Bell home, ugh. The problem child. He actually felt abashed. Amazing, how a little twist of fate could pinch.

But he wasn't hurting. He was just sorry. "Don't mind me," he apologized. In the living room looks were exchanged. He went upstairs.

"Your father would like to see you, Professor Bell." That was Mom, five minutes later. Bell gawked up from his bed, where he sat clipping toenails. Was old Aaron hiding behind her? "Mr. Bell is downstairs," Mom explained. Bell clipped, firing a horny crescent into the opposite wall. "Yup," he said. She smiled sweetly, sadly, and backed off.

Who was this mythic father-figure waiting below? Bell hurried into his socks to go down and see. It wouldn't be old Aaron. Maybe Mrs. H., having invented the character, would play it, too. By the time he got there, she'd have switched to vest and pants, and darkened her existing mustache.

"Listen, Ham. I guess you haven't really talked with Norma much yet."

"No, not yet."

His father was half old Aaron and half a new Mr. Bell. He paced with a board chairman's portentous tread, but also he threw quizzical glances at his son, checking audience reaction to the impersonation.

"Well, you understand the poor girl is still deeply affected."

Bell was confounded. Mom's message in Mom's own words! Old Aaron was her trumpet.

"She's like a flower," his father said.

"A bruised flower."

"Um, yes. Anyway, Ham, she needs rest."

"I'll sleep down here on the sofa," Bell announced, to shorten the negotiations.

His father blinked at him. Bell saw contrasting elements at war. The old comic troublemaker was struggling, but the new suit had it imprisoned. "Well, Ham, I certainly don't want to force you to surrender your, um, conjugal rights, but I do feel a certain responsibility for those who have sought shelter under my roof." That was Mr. Bell speaking. Immediately old Aaron giggled. "My roof!" he cried out, snapping his fingers. Then, guiltily, he looked past Bell to the door. Was Mom monitoring? "My roof," he repeated, but in a wondering voice. "You know, Ham, I used to hate this place! But now that it's mine — " He thrust back his shoulders and strode around the living room, frowning at chairs and lamps in a proprietary fashion. Did they please him? If not, out with them! "Oh, one thing more," declared Mr. Bell, hands locked behind his back, no easy trick in view of his girth. "Your, ah, contribution to the domestic budget won't be necessary in future." He addressed the curtains, threadbare from Mom's psychopathic vacuuming. "The income from my investments will be, harrumph, adequate."

"Fine, Dad." Bell meant the performance. "I'm glad to hear it," he added. His contribution had been everything except real estate taxes, which Grandpa had paid.

"I got a call from one of the University trustees today, Ham!" Old Aaron snickered. "I'm invited to the club for lunch Thursday! Don't worry, though. I'll lead them on! Let them fawn and crawl! Let them hope! I won't squander your future inheritance.

"Go ahead, Dad. Squander it. It's yours. You earned it."

"Did I? Well, perhaps I did. If Father had really wanted a memorial, he'd have written it into his will, wouldn't he?"

"Of course he would have. But he left it all to you. He trusted your judgment."

"Eh?" Old Aaron wheezed. "I hadn't thought of it that way, Ham. Maybe Father had faith in me, after all!" He adopted an expression of pious resolve. "I won't betray that trust, boy!"

"Listen," Bell said. "I've got to catch up on my work. I won't eat here. I'll grab a sandwich downtown on my way."

Mr. Bell nodded absently. He was studying his image reflected in the front window. Pomposity suited him. He wore it with style. "You'll always have a place at my table, Ham."

"Gee, thanks, Dad."

"As for Mother Hirlinger," Mr. Bell continued, pursuing unvoiced questions, "she's welcome, too, as long as she may wish. She's certainly making herself useful!" He was imitating Grandpa's imperious manner: clasped hands, head flung back, lips pursed. A fat little statue. The true memorial. "This place really sparkles now! That's what's needed! A firm hand!"

Bell withdrew, leaving the old actor in privacy to rehearse his lines. He could hear Mom in the back hall, grunting orgiastically. She'd found a cobweb, probably. No sign of Norma, though. She was hiding, between the lines.

Hanging on a hall peg was a coat at first glance strange but then remembered. It was Grandpa's black overcoat; it had an astrakhan collar. Mom had hauled it from a closet to be cleaned. Bell tried it on; a fine fit.

He wore it out into the northern night. It wasn't particularly heavy. Grandpa hadn't needed much besides his arteries in the old days. He'd demanded so much of life that it kept him warm when others froze. And maybe he, Bell, had something of that in him, too. It might not be the lingering breeze of Appalachia that made people shrink back, but that hot gust of pride.

He ate a sandwich at Roseman's, and walked an hour in the streets to air Grandpa's coat. When he returned, he found his toilet articles and a change of clothing for the morning nicely placed on a chair beside the sofa, which was made up for his repose. "Goodnight, all," Bell said to the furniture, and, still in the old man's coat, lay down comfortably on the floor to sleep backwoods style.

P̲ICO STOPPED BY in the morning to chauffeur him to the campus. "Just wanted to be sure you'd show up," he joked, but he meant it. Bell had a ten o'clock lecture on the post-Civil War period. Fifty freshmen would be waiting.

Bell breakfasted on toast. He didn't want his eggs; Pico ate them for him, plus three apples which happened to be there. While Bell shaved, Pico waded back to the kitchen to compliment the cook by sampling jam, cookies, yesterday's stew leftovers, and a can of beer. Upstairs, Norma slept with Thackeray. Bell's father had left early to be on hand at his broker's for opening stock-market quotations. "Oh, Professor Pico, you've got a stomach just like my departed," cried out flattered Mom. Pico left the kitchen, thoughtful.

"How'd you like the reception?" he asked Bell, in the car.

"Super."

"Yeah, well, Morgan's wife wears falsies," Pico reported. "No Fast-Foot roles for her." He parked in the faculty lot in buttery snow, churned by tire chains. "I want realism in my flicks," he grumbled, slamming his door. "Say, you've got your lecture notes, don't you?"

"Sure," Bell said. Pico, who never worried about anything, was concerned. He kept studying Bell on the sly as they went toward the history building. "We'll have a game of squash this afternoon," Pico said. They were walking among class-bound students. Galoshes, scarves, shaggy sweaters, ski caps. Bell in his astrakhan coat looked old-fashioned. "There's a girl in the front row with a real pair," Pico informed him. "Not only that, she takes notes with one of those giant pens. Red, mind you." Up the icy steps. The hall smelled of wet rubber. "When she's not writing, she sort of fingers it. But innocently!" They mounted the stairs to the second floor. "Put the end in her mouth once," Pico added. "Gave it a little nibble. No kidding." They reached Bell's office. "Luck, Bell," said Pico, as though Bell had never lectured before in his life.

Bell wondered. Did he look that strange? He didn't feel strange. He felt full of bounce, as he used to before a game, legs eager to drive for the basket.

His suitcase was still on his desk, the phone inside. Might

as well leave it there, he thought. He riffled his lecture files and pulled out a folder. *Reconstruction.* He'd given that one seven times; first as instructor, then as assistant, last year as associate. Seven notches, thirty-odd to go. When Glass retired, a full professorship would be up for grabs. Chairmanship, too. He'd get both. Then, if he fished his ripped manuscript out of the wastebasket, got it published, and wrote a few more, he might someday hop east or west. Higher stipends, more commodious chairs. Just needed to retrieve his wastepaper book and have it fixed.

He did. He pulled it out. Then, sitting on the edge of his desk, he took half-pages in his hands, crumpled them into balls, and practiced hooks.

Bzzz. Game over. Time for class. He fired a final shot, rimmed it, watched it topple in. A good omen. He picked up his folder of notes. *Reconstruction.* How could he possibly lecture on that? It hadn't started yet. So he left the folder on his desk in a litter of paper basketballs, and with nothing at all in his hands walked out into the hall and went downstairs.

The freshmen were edging into their seats as Professor Bell strode briskly in. He mounted the platform, and stood at the lectern, gently tapping his fingernails on it, before he realized that he still wore the overcoat. It wasn't hot in the room, but it wasn't cold, either. After a few minutes of lecturing, he'd be sweating. He removed the coat, therefore, and laid it on a chair.

Now he was ready. The class was, too. Caps had been pulled off, scarves unwound, notebooks opened, faces turned up to him like so many bowls to be filled. Bell moistened his lips. His hands had slid easily around the edges of the lectern, gripping it in a friendly fashion. It was oily to the touch. Pico's handshake.

He cleared his throat. He eyed the freshmen with a slight inquiring smile. Were they all set? Some of them, the eager ones, actually nodded back: *yes, yes, prof.* A few even commenced writing, heading their notes, inscribing the date. There was the front-row girl with the real pair. And a big red pen, no fooling.

Bell was really ready now. He pursed his lips, searching for the right opening phrase. That was important. It would set the tone of the whole lecture. Nothing particular came to his mind. Still, he was in no hurry. He decided he ought to cast up in his mind some visual images of the period in question. (Old newsreels: Lincoln shot, Booth in the burning barn, Cowboy Jesus ranging a ruined South, looking for old massah with a brainstick in hand.) He surveyed the class to see if there were any black students. Not a one, except a borderline tan case there near the back, maybe a meek scholarship student plucked from a slum and scrubbed hard.

Time to begin talking. Dammit, he was just standing at the lectern, not saying a word. He glanced at the clock above the door. Five minutes had passed. The class was past readiness and into impatience. Weren't they quiet enough to satisfy Professor Bell? They became quieter.

Fine. Everything was perfect. Bell cleared his throat in a businesslike fashion. He nodded, too. Firmly. *Okay, kids. Here we go.* The girl with the real pair got that red pen poised above her anxious lap.

Still, as he gazed down at his students, he couldn't help wondering. Were they capable of learning? Did they really want to? That was a puzzler, all right. If the answer was *no* — and he had to admit the evidence was pretty heavy on that side — then he had very little to say to them. Less than a little, in fact. Which was precisely what he was doing. But it was his job to lecture. He'd better get on with it!

Tick, tick. Listen to that clock. Those faces all looked like Brant's. They were getting worried on his behalf. *Gee, Dr. B. Don't just stand there. Give us the info, sir. We can handle it.* Bell cleared his throat a third time, backed off from the lectern, paced a few steps to and fro, and resumed his original position.

They were becoming perturbed. *Ten* minutes of silence. What was this, a Quaker meeting? Professor Bell might be waiting for inspiration. He was, he was. He was thinking hard, too. Teaching shouldn't be easy, should it? Hell, no. He heard snickers, shoes scraping, whispers, coughs. They couldn't stand it. They felt aggrieved and excited. This was avant-garde Eastern stuff! An antilecture!

Bell snapped them back to silence with drill-sergeant eyes. Dammit, they'd better obey him. He might not be offering them the conventional menu, but he was still in charge of the program, and by God he'd make that clear. If it came to cases, he could still whip any kid in the room, except maybe for that big fellow in the middle — halfback on the freshman eleven, wasn't he? — who was now sound asleep, snoring hardly at all, just as though Bell were actually lecturing.

He became amused. Well, he *was* lecturing. In a sense. If they weren't students and if he didn't know enough yet to teach, then this lecture of his was highly appropriate in form and content. His delivery, certainly, could not be improved. It was an honest effort! He was doing his best!

Fifteen minutes. The students looked hypnotized. They were staring at Bell in fascination, searching for signs of mental collapse, nervous jimjams, liquor, drugs, laryngitis, but saw nothing of the sort, for Bell was standing at the lectern in the most natural way, doing everything right (except lecturing). Sane as hell. That was the craziest part. They began examining one another. Were *they* the nutty ones? No, they weren't. Everything was just as it always was and should be (with that one little exception). Some leaned forward. Maybe the prof was mumbling today. *Little bit louder, please, Dr. B.*

Bell was listening, too. He heard his heart beat. He was aware of his respiration, thought about his nervous system, his blood, the arrangement of gray matter in his cranium. Caught up for a moment by the miracle of life, expressed in his body, he actually leaned forward, with a knowing smile, as though he'd summed up some historical subtlety with a clever turn of phrase. *Get that, kids? Write it down!* His heart was lecturing along his veins as his brain took notes. Theirs were, too. Didn't they know? Oh, hell. Probably not. They'd just come to splash in the heritage pool. *Twenty minutes.* Still, he thought, wasn't silence part of the heritage? It ought to be. He was creating a useful addition to the curriculum. An hour of silence in tribute to the empty pages of history. Empty faces, too. He gazed in disappointment from one to another, all vapid. There was nothing they could learn. He was teaching them that. Nothing!

At the half-hour point, a little fellow near the door scuttled out. Would that start a mass desertion? Bell willed the rest to stay. A few rose halfway in their seats, were caught by his searchlight stare, and sank back down again. *Listen,* he was silently shouting. *Listen to real nothing for a change.* The red-pen nymph was near tears. The urgency of Bell's nothing was shaking her. Next to her, a Norma-girl with pale straight features was watching Bell with troubled intensity, as though she might, just might, have some understanding of what he wasn't saying. Ah, but it frightened her, as it had frightened Norma. (Please, Bell. Don't. Let's just pretend.)

In the square of glass in the upper part of the door appeared a face like tropical sunrise. Pico. That little runner had called him down. What, Bell gone mute? An embarrassing situation. Pico was blushing for him in the hall. A white wisp of hair was visible there, too, property of Chairman Glass. Maybe the entire faculty had been summoned. This was a real event! The first nonlecture in University history! Might start a fad! Bell wasn't able to repress a grin. Pico caught it, but wasn't grinning back. (Christ, Bell. Play the game. Fun is fun, but.)

Forty minutes. He wanted to speak out. He really did. But not to these. No, not to these, not here, and it wasn't so much lecturing he wanted to do as questioning. But he knew of no one he much wanted to question except maybe that foul old character he'd left ruminating in the cabin doorway.

— Guess I'm getting nowhere, he remarked silently to an interior Lundquist.

— You're starting.

— Think so? Anyhow, I've torn it now. I mean, they're sore as hell out there.

— So what? They can't kill you.

— Guess not.

— Can't kill men already dead, you idiot. You're standing dead now. Better move before they bury you.

— Move, okay.

— But don't kid yourself, Bell. It won't make much difference.

— Made a difference to you, didn't it?

— That's my business! You're not the man I was! They never had me! They've always had you! You're screwed either way, Bell!

— Don't be so damned sure, old man. Don't be so damned sure!

Forty-five minutes. Bell's lips were moving. He clamped them tight. *See you later,* he told Lundquist. He felt a bit relieved now, though, and with a look at the clock, decided maybe he'd better give the students what they wanted. What was the subject? Post-something. Reconjabber. Didn't matter. Just open the old mouth and let fly. But how'd they know what he'd say? *He* didn't know. Might be better to continue as he was. He'd gone too far. He needed to finish. Closure on nothing!

Door was cracked a bit. Old Glass's papier-mâché face appeared, puzzled and alarmed. (See here, young Bell. True, I did say amuse yourself. Within the rules. If you don't like the pasta, don't eat it. But kindly refrain from throwing it on the floor.)

They were all waiting for the buzzer now. Bell was delighted. It was a memorable lecture. He'd given each of them something useful to carry away — a blank page in their notebooks to ponder, an unplugged spot in their minds where an idea might actually form. Or might it? Doubtful. Anyway, they didn't want it. They hadn't come for that. Look at them. Now they'd decided they'd been made fools of. That big clown Pico had made a bet with Bell. Something like that. Bell had guts, all right. But he'd cheated them. Now they'd have to read the textbook to find out what happened. When the buzzer sounded, they jumped up and grabbed scarves and caps, slammed notebooks shut, made a great racket with their boots and desks, and favored the happy professor with resentful looks over their shoulders as they scrammed out of there, fast.

Professor Glass entered. "Bell?" He saw at a glance that Bell was quite all right, as he'd feared.

Bell got into the astrakhan. His homely face was serene. He had a tremendous appetite, too. Was he ever hungry!

"Bell," said Professor Glass, despairingly.

Bell came down to him. Shook his hand. Then he went to a window and opened it wide. That icy winter air, magnificent! He filled himself with it.

"Bell," whispered old Glass.

Bell closed the window. He started out. He was in a real hurry now. Knew where he was going.

"Sorry," he said, as he left. "Got to run." And run he did, ran past gaping Pico in the hall and picked a quick way among the retreating students there. Then, outside, he sprinted across the campus snow, running loose and free.

I<small>T HADN'T BEEN</small> so hard as he'd thought. He'd avoided all explanations. They really hadn't wanted any. They were almost openly relieved. They'd heard about the lecture and decided that whatever might be stirring in him would do no good for them. His contribution wasn't needed any more, you bet. Not in that family. It was self-sufficient. *Gee, Bell. Well, if that's what you want. Take your time.*

Now he was far from there. Roaming. He walked with spirited steps in wet new snow, humming lightly, and watching for little signs that would show him the way through the wilderness. Lundquist wouldn't be there. He knew that. They'd have gone almost at once. Still, he'd sworn to come back, hadn't he? And it was a place to be, a thing to do, a point of departure. He didn't need to find the old man again. Once was enough. But he'd given his pledge, so here he was, climbing the same tree-clotted slopes, threading through those same wrinkled woods, a wanderer come full circle to start again from where he'd stopped once before.

Instinct guided him. He had a map on the soles of his feet, inscribed there when he'd run the other way. Objectively, he didn't know where the hell he was — but he sensed he was getting close. He quickened his pace. Clouds crossed the sun, sending their negatives rippling through the trees. Pale shadows on the white snow. He imagined he might come suddenly upon a scene frozen in memory:

whitened figures immobilized in attitudes of violence —
the Cowboy with stick forever raised, Bell himself eternally
confronting a grinning snowman holding a rifle of ice.

The melting sun slid cottony blobs down from the
branches; they softly smacked into the snow below, like
footsteps. Invisible men were leaping everywhere. Sometimes Bell got pelted with wet fistfuls. Playful ghosts; a cold
welcome.

When he glimpsed the cabin, for some reason he began
jogging toward it, noticing as he got closer that there were
fresh boot tracks all along the side, and that the roof was
bare of snow. It wasn't empty, then.

He stopped, some yards away. A man wearing a parka
stepped around the edge of the cabin. It was the military
anthropologist, looking pleased.

"You got him," Bell said. He couldn't believe it. Wasn't
possible.

Reuss just stood there, slightly smiling.

Bell kept coming. His heart was slamming around.
"You didn't get him," he said, but he didn't know.

"Come and see," said Reuss. He turned and went
around the cabin, Bell two paces at his heels, and marched
inside.

Bell followed. The room was dark. There'd been a fire,
but they'd let it die. The embers were bundled in smoke.

"Where?" Bell was blinking around. His eyes couldn't
adjust. He guessed there were four or five men in there. He
shouted, *"Lundquist."* He saw a grinning face nearby.
Those stupid bastards. Why couldn't they let the old man
alone? *"Lundquist."* He rushed forward, squinting, search-

ing, bumped into two or three of them, shoved them aside, got grabbed — "easy there, fella" — and then, in a rage, knocked one of them flat.

That's when they all jumped him.

"Do you know what treason is, Bell?"

"No," Bell said.

He was sitting on a wooden chair, facing a light.

"Treason is an act of betrayal. A traitor is one who knowingly endangers the safety of society. . . ."

Bell said, "I've never betrayed anybody."

"But you've been betrayed, Bell."

"You think so?"

"I'm convinced you have."

Bell began to chuckle.

"What's funny?" the interrogator asked.

Bell laughed outright. He couldn't help it. The other men stirred restlessly, evidently watching him. It had taken three of them to handle him.

"You're wrong." Bell controlled his laughter long enough to say that.

"Wrong about what?"

"Wrong ab-b-bout — " He had to stop for breath.

"Speak up, Bell."

"We've lost."

"What's that?"

"We've lost."

"Lost? Lost what?"

"We've lost our importance. We're unimportant men. Didn't you know that?"

Then he bowed his head to avoid the light, and offered no resistance to whatever it was they'd managed to do to him, letting it flood through his arms, legs, everywhere . . .

They moved him to a cot, but his senses were so bewildered by the drug that it seemed he was lying also on the floor and sometimes on the ceiling, too.

"Tell us how you found Lundquist, how you first found him, tell us, Bell, tell us. . . ."

"Inside," he whispered.

"What's that?"

"Inside of me. . . . There were two Lundquists, you understand."

"Two?"

"Yes, that's the answer. Two Lundquists — and the important one wasn't exactly a man, an individual man, but more like — well, the condition of being a man, you might say. . . ."

"Listen, do you know where Lundquist is now?"

"Um, think so."

"You do? Don't be hasty. Remember, you swore up and down earlier that you didn't."

"He's here."

"Here. What do you mean, here?"

"In this place right now. Can't you tell? He's in this room, in me, maybe in you, too —"

"You know that isn't what we mean!"

" — he's in Detroit, too. . . . And in these hills all around where he's been, he's still present, you see —"

"Bell, we're starting to have some doubts about you."

"Hmm?"

"You never did find Lundquist."

"I found him, all right."

"You think you did. But you didn't."

"I found him."

" . . . You can't face failure, can you, Bell?"

"Didn't fail!"

" . . . Stick to history, Bell. That's your field. Teach it, but don't try to make it."

"Got to go," Bell said.

"All right, all right. We won't keep you. We'll see that you get back to your car."

"Don't have a car. I came by bus."

"Well, then, to the nearest place where you can catch the bus again. To go back home."

Bell swung his legs off the cot and sat up. He was bushed. His head ached.

"Go back home," the interrogator repeated.

"I've been home."

"Listen, Bell. We advise you to return. You've got a decent place in society. . . ."

"Oh, crap," said Bell.

"You'll learn, Bell! You'll learn!"

Someone flung open the door. Sunlight burst in, blinding Bell. "Here are your glasses," a voice said. Bell grabbed them and stumbled toward the door, toward the light.

Bᴇʟʟ ᴡᴇɴᴛ ʀᴀɢɪɴɢ through the woods. Were they creeping in his wake to watch him go? He didn't give a damn; he wished just one would come scouting after him, one man he could wad up in his hands and throw away.

— They never found you, anyhow, he muttered, but there wasn't any echo this time, and he wondered whether Lundquist was lost to him now for good. Oh, it didn't matter. Whatever the old man had taught him was hammered into his bones. He wouldn't lose that.

Sometimes he ran at a jog, sometimes he walked. He kicked snowdrifts, threw pine cones. And he kept glancing back, but less frequently the farther he went.

Where was he going? Damnation, he had no idea. Looking for Lundquist, he'd mislaid himself.

He thought of his father, he thought of Norma; he thought of Pico, too, and old Glass and of his students, who'd been so full of nothing they hadn't room for any more, and it seemed to him that all this was Nomad, in a way. Sure, it wasn't just computers. Not just Muller and Brant, nor only Grosch and Franklin nor the ones higher up who had the big offices and the chauffeured limousines; no, not just those. *Amuse yourself, within the rules.* Nomad everywhere. The cry of human creatures, deprived. Poor devils.

Their fault, true. But his as well. He was one of Nomad's nomads as much as any, a lost soul wandering no-

where. Still, there might be a difference. *Amuse yourself.*
No, sir. Wasn't fun. Couldn't do that any more. Something in him had driven him through the wilderness to learn
things he'd known already but wouldn't acknowledge until
they'd been shaken up from his guts by that old man. Ah,
but which wilderness? The real one he'd damned near
frozen in, or the one where boredom killed the soul and
life was beer? And the old man might be Lundquist or the
memory of Grandfather Bell in his prime — or it might be
himself, yes, an intimation of a Bell-to-be. That thought
stopped him. Made him grin, even. And, marveling at it,
he moved forward again, his anger fading like his footsteps
in the melting snow.

He came to the asphalt road again. Which way to turn?
Well, he knew. Or at least he knew which way he wasn't
going. He'd been that way before.

H E DIDN'T TRAVEL by bus. When the weather was bright,
he walked. When it wasn't, he thumbed rides. Sometimes
he stopped in towns for a day or two to work at odd jobs —
washed dishes, dug graves, spread sand on streets — or split
kindling at farmhouses for his meals.

He was tramping, going nowhere on purpose. His every

step was a destination. It was gray winter — the birds had gone, leaves fallen, the grasses withered — and the land itself seemed weary. Bell wasn't, though. He walked with strong and regular strides, a tall figure topped by a hunting cap, a knapsack bunched at the back of his sporty old astrakhan coat.

The people he worked for usually asked him to stay longer. It wasn't that he had a knack for doing things — he didn't much, though he worked hard — but that he paid attention, that he really listened to them. It was as though he hoped that if he understood them, he might come to understand himself.

Of his own situation he spoke little. When he had something to say, he told it to himself. He'd rounded out several circles in his life, but he knew that closure was his habit. There'd be more circles to come. He swore he'd make the next one larger, that's all. He took to studying sunsets, to watching clouds and ridgelines. Faces, too, he saw more sharply. Ridges there, as well, and the glow and fade of light. Human geography, where old Whitman had tramped before him, drunk on people, and celebrating.

Had to stop sometime, didn't it? Couldn't stump on forever.

Go back home.

"Nope," he answered. He might sometime, but not now. It mattered less when or if he went back than what he went back as, and he wasn't ready to do more than guess at that yet. Home meant stop. If he wanted only that, he might as well hang himself on a wooden frame like the scarecrow there in that shriveled cornfield, a Christ of rags pointing at nothing with an empty sleeve.

Go home.

"The hell with that," he said. Wasn't grim, though. Didn't feel depressed. He was marching down that rutted back-country road as though he owned everything in sight. How come? He was a man without purpose, wasn't he? Ought to be gloomy, then. But he wasn't.

He'd survived, sure. Still, survival wasn't the same as purpose. Lundquist hadn't given a damn about survival. Nor had the Cowboy. Both might be dead by now — the old man rotted away in some lousy migrant camp, the Cowboy stretched on a city morgue slab. No survival for them, or if survival, then the survival of the reason for survival, of a sense of their own value so strong it burned them. Gave them a terrible happiness. Bell was hunting for that, too, wasn't he? But he'd been born wrong, he supposed. Wrong time, wrong color, too, maybe. The living history had passed him over. He'd never catch it. "Damnation," he said aloud. Why play a game he couldn't win?

Go home.

Uh uh. He wouldn't quit. He might, if what he was walking was just a treadmill. He might, except for the feeling that he was getting somewhere, not just away from the nowhere he'd left. His last lecture had been a nothing farewell to heritage, that was sure. But it might have been a hello to something else. To real teaching, maybe. He might actually learn enough to do that. Those blank pages of history — suppose he was able to fill in a few lines? He might, he might. But what mattered most was himself. That was the real subject. That's what Grandpa'd taught; Lundquist, too. And for him, it would be what counted: not to stand up there with his mouth open and other people's words falling out, but to teach because he was so damned passionately full of himself, to teach with such fury that the students would trample each other getting away from him, but leaving a few, a few — some young Bell or two — who'd rise up to meet him.

Might all be a mistake. He'd probably end up as a cranky old professor in a jerkwater college, or as a disappointed visionary in some seedy slum school. Maybe it would be just another dream, as Glass had said. But he'd have to try, wouldn't he? He'd started. He wasn't going to stop.

Go, that's what. Just go. Maybe not to find, only seek. He couldn't have the certainty of finding anything. Maybe he wouldn't want that certainty. But he could have, would have, did by God this moment have something better than that — his damned crazy human pride in seeking.

A road with no ending, but a road anyhow.

That was the Lundquist heresy, the preamble written short for men in too big a hurry to read much: *Life, liberty, and the pursuit.*

Not happiness. Who the hell had put happiness in there? A man can't pursue happiness. No more can a nation. If it's real happiness, then it overtakes a man in his full stride.

Not happiness.

The pursuit!